Montana Son

By

Alek Leslie

First Edition

Designed and edited by Theresa Leonard

Maps - Source: White, James. Manitoba and Northwest Territories [map].
1:950,400. [Ottawa]: Dept. of the Interior, 1900. University of Manitoba:
Elizabeth Dafoe Library: Map Collection
Whoop Up Trail courtesy of Galt Museum & Archives
Cover Art - ®Bigstock, ©Shutterstock,Inc.

Printed in the United States of America

Published simultaneously in Canada by
Rowe House Publishers

Leslie, Alek
Montana Son : a novel / Alek Leslie

ISBN-13: 978-0-9938600-2-7
ISBN-10: 0-9938-6002-8

Montana
Son

For those who smile in the face of adversity

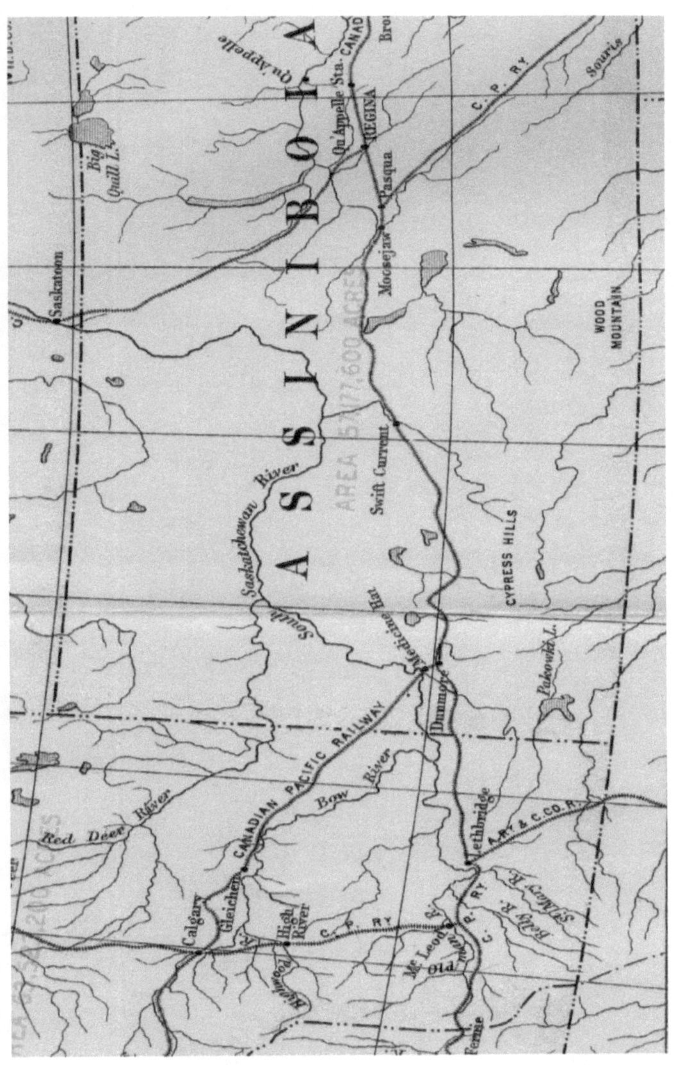

District of Alberta

Source Citation: White, James. Manitoba and Northwest Territories [map]. 1:950,400. [Ottawa]: Dept. of the Interior, 1900. University of Manitoba: Elizabeth Dafoe Library: Map Collection

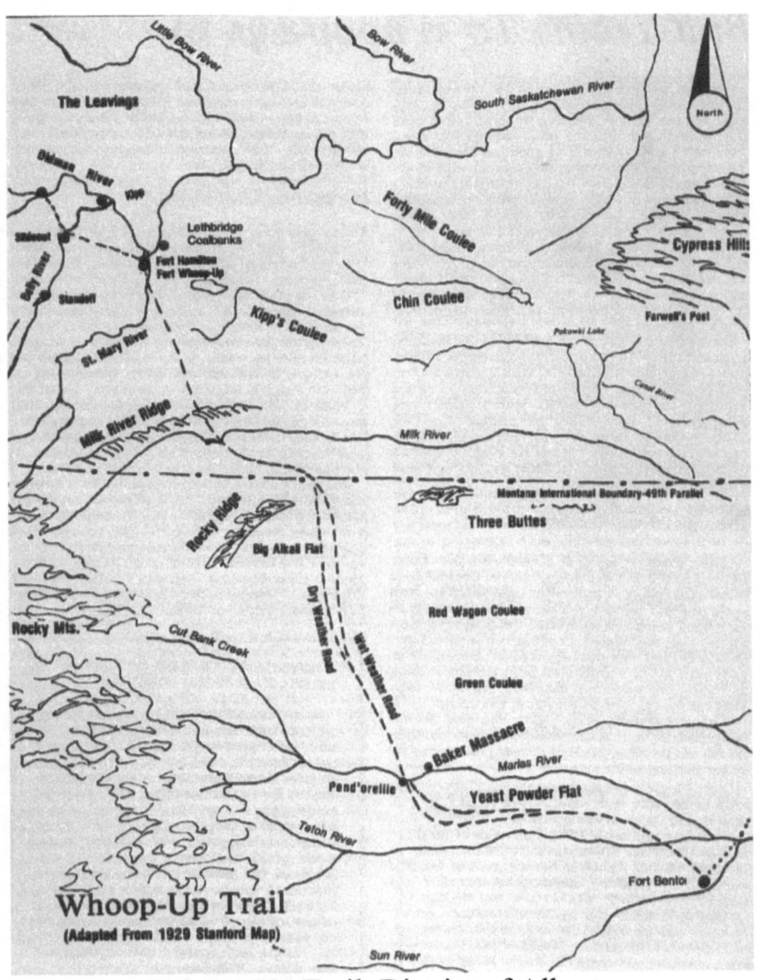

Whoop Up Trail, District of Alberta
Courtesy of Galt Museum & Archives

Part 4

A new country

Chapter 1

October 19th, 1882 – Blanketed by a grey sky, immersed in weariness and discomfort, the wind howled and the snow took flight from a sedentary earth as I entered the Dominion of Canada.

The terrain didn't change, though mounds of dirt about a mile apart were meant to indicate I was entering a different country.

Continuing along the Whoop-Up trail, an endless rolling prairie was cut through by coulees, that is until they appeared, so unusual; I blinked, figuring they were just a figment of a tired mind. Some were buttes, some pyramidal, layered in sand and stone of changing hues. Some were capped as if for protection from the elements, wind…sun. So fascinating was it that I just had to climb one steep slope and admire from a higher perspective. My fascination did not last long for the wind howled through the twisting canyons, summoning sand to swirl and sting; and the only things to tantalize my ravenous stomach were prickly cactus and bones of a strange creature long since gone from this world.

I stopped near Fort Macleod for a night and quickly learned that the lawmen of these parts were called 'North West Mounted Police'. When I passed a handful of officers on horseback, their strikingly unique scarlet jackets and white helmets commanded a second look, while their barracks needed only a passing glimpse. The abodes were rustic, appearing hastily constructed of log walls, planking, and sod roofs. Within the fenced fort were a few stores, a hospital, and a blacksmith.

My camp was made just beyond the Oldman River. The only light on this dark and cloudy night came from the dimly lit fort. Sleeping on the hard ground reminded me of my sores. Compassionate thoughts began flooding my mind for poor Jimmy as I writhed in pain, wondering if my last experience at Fort Macleod would be a trip to the hospital.

I awoke at dawn's first light, eager to continue my journey north. The jagged and snow-capped cliffs lined with ancient evergreens were fondly familiar; however, this land remained vastly wilderness. I passed three farms on my journey to Highwood River.

The flat terrain slowly gave way to rolling hills before arriving at Spitzee's Crossing, the warmth of October's sun already starting to fade.

I glanced at the main street. It took all of thirty seconds. The buildings were few: a blacksmith, a mercantile, and a school. I wasn't going to have any trouble holding onto my money here.

I dismounted Taffy, thankful there wasn't a soul in sight to witness me moan as my feet hit the hard Canadian soil. Stiffly, I walked to the mercantile with the two letters in my jacket pocket. If this desolate place had a postal service, it should be in this building. I could just mail my mother's promised letter and bolt right back to Montana.

With my hat tucked low, I entered and casually perused the store. The sun streamed an orange glow through two large windows over the meager supplies and food this small town store offered. I made a mental note that there was a piano in the corner.

As I limped over to the counter, I was very disappointed to see just one jar of candy, the minty green and white striped hard sticks not one of my favourites.

The short man behind the counter with a bushy black mustache asked if I needed any assistance.

"I might have a letter to mail. You offer postal service?"

"Sure do," he said. "Mail takes quite a trip, though. Goes through Fort Benton."

"You mean to say that my mail would go through Fort Benton and come back up to this country."

"That's correct. Mail goes through Fort Benton."

I frowned at the absurdity. It didn't rightly make sense, so I opted for my second choice. "I'm looking for someone, name's Thomas, Sean Thomas?" I asked nonchalantly while fixating depressed eyes on the lonely jar of sweets.

He gave me a blank stare, shaking his head.

I pulled out Sean's letter and added that he was staying at the Taylor ranch.

That extra bit of information swiftly changed his demeanor. "Well you must be the help he's been asking for?"

Leaning into the counter, my ears perked up for his next words.

"He's always asking for help on that farm. Too much work, not enough ambition, I say."

I took that opportunity to say, "I'm the hired help he's been looking for." Extending my hand, I introduced myself.

The clerk announced himself as Sam Tracey, proprietor of Tracey Mercantile and post master for Highwood River.

"Sean Thomas is two miles due west of here. The home has a barn and a windmill. You shouldn't miss it. Just head due west. Anything else I can do you for?"

I perused the food he had available and grabbed a couple carrots, apples, jerked beef, and a dozen of the candy sticks. As I paid, I asked if he had any whisky.

"No, we're a dry community," he informed.

"Well, it looks like you'd get a lot of moisture, what with the snowy mountains and river nearby."

"You misunderstand. We don't sell whisky here," he intoned slowly like I was dumb as a post.

Why?" I asked most inquisitively. "Is it against the law in this town?"

"No, not yet, and we ain't a town as yet, either. Heck, we ain't even a village. We just choose not to sell it in this, ah, in this community of Highwood River folk."

"Then what do you drink here, sweet tea?"

"No, we prefer hot tea."

I found it hard to believe Sean Thomas lived in a town of teetotalers.

I started to limp away when Sam Tracey chirped in, "We have a doctor, though. He may be able to help you."

I turned around. "Is it that apparent?"

"When you've had them, the signs are all too apparent," he grimaced. "We also have a bathhouse. It's two buildings over, on the left."

I guess it was apparent I needed that, too. After I tipped my hat and carried out the healthy food, my crunching began on one of the sticks. I needed to bite on something hard, and the help of a sugar rush would get me through my family reunion. I contemplated what I would say to my father and found no words came readily to mind. I was heading into territory that gave me such an awkward uneasiness, my horse stopped several times on the way.

"Walk Taffy," I spoke hesitantly, clucking my tongue.

As the farm came into view, I tucked my hat down low again, feeling oddly like I was heading to a funeral. No joy: just deep apprehension and sorrow. Though Sean Thomas spoke of regret and privation, I couldn't forget Momma's hardship and loss. It wouldn't be hard to hide my smile from him.

I stopped adjacent to the house and scanned the buildings and fields. The barn was along the far side of the house. To the left and south of it was a smaller building by a windmill, spinning slowly in the cool autumn breeze.

On the barn roof was a man, shingling and hammering.

I dismounted and led Taffy by the reins without my pain-relieving limp, lowering my hat to the point where I almost couldn't see. My heart was pounding so fast, I thought he might see it rumbling my shirt. I started sweating and my hands trembled.

Stopping a few yards from the barn, I said in a shaky voice, "Afternoon, sir!"

"What you want?" he shouted down, preoccupied with pulling out a nail.

"Sam Tracey informed me that you were looking for help around the farm?"

Sean glanced down. "Kind of help I need's a man's help, besides I'm doing just fine."

He seemed annoyed by my intrusion.

"I'm a hard worker and know a thing or two about working on a farm." I spoke with such little confidence, I wouldn't even hire me.

Sean hastily dropped his hammer, left the roof, and swaggered over. Looking down on me pointedly, he said, "Guess I wasn't clear enough, so I'll come a little closer when I say: don't need any help, like working on my own, and prefer to keep it that way. Understand me, kid?"

I swallowed, nodding, eyes on my boots. "Well, if its fine by you, I just get some water from your well for my horse and I. We've been traveling a while?"

"Well's over there," he said, glaring at the windmill. He climbed the ladder and resumed hammering in nails, paying me no mind.

"Thank you, sir," I mumbled, my cheeks feeling a deep shade of red.

Refilling my canteen, Taffy drank from the bucket, while I swore 'shuck' under my breath a couple times.

"What you think, Taffy? I just toss this letter to the ground and we head the heck out of here? I sure don't need to know this cranky, lazy looking, self-absorbed, albeit tall man."

Taffy shook her head, spraying water all over my coat. "I'll take that as a yes!"

I led my horse towards the house and just as I approached it, a young woman came out.

"What do you want here?" she asked flatly.

"Ma'am, I was just asking about a job around the farm. Looks like you could use some help?" I asked hesitantly, scratching the back of my neck.

"How old are you?"

"I'm…," hesitating, I announced, "eighteen." Which was technically correct: I was in my eighteenth year.

Anne studied me with intensity. "Would you be needing a place to stay?"

"I could work longer if I stayed on the property. I live…south a ways. Could sleep in the barn. Don't mind being with the horses."

The slender woman with blonde hair loosely pinned away from a pretty face eyed me scrupulously.

"Fine, you can sleep in that building, there," she pointed. "Can't pay much, but I can supply meals. Come with me. I'll show you the guest house. It's certainly better than the barn."

I followed her to what I figured was just a place for storage.

"By the way, I'm Anne Taylor and this is my farm," she said, glaring at Sean. "That there hunched over the barn roof is Sean Thomas."

Her eyes returned to me. "And you are?"

"Patrick Sullivan," I replied, wiping the dampness from my hand on my chaps before offering it.

Anne accepted it with a light smile while her blue eyes sparkled over freckled and rosy cheeks.

"Well, Patrick, this is our guest house. You've got a fireplace in the corner, a small table and chairs, a desk, and a warm bed."

I was impressed. I could cook my own meals, had my privacy, and a comfy bed instead of a bale of hay. "This will be fine Mrs. Taylor, thank you."

"Call me, Anne. Everybody else does. Let me show you the barn. Why don't you take your personals off the horse. Just put them on the porch."

All the while, Sean's eyes were blaring at Anne like she was giving away his house.

Anne's eyes blared right back as she waited for me to remove my saddle bags.

I followed her to the barn which was just built, the scent of freshly cut spruce filling my nose. It was small, had six stalls, and room for tools and bales of hay.

"Have you had any snow in these parts?" I asked.

"No, not yet. We get a lot of shelter from those mountains," she replied, peering west. "Unless snow's blowing from the east. Then we're covered up to our heads."

She turned, flashing those pretty blue eyes my way, again. "Looks like you've found some winter, though."

"Yes, Ma'am…Anne," I said, suddenly very curious about the face my eyes hadn't seen in weeks.

Her feet made hollow steps into the barn.

"You can use either one of the end stalls. Let me introduce you to Sean," she muttered rather unpleasantly.

"Sean!" she hollered, waiting patiently while glancing at her stubby fingernails. "This is Patrick. He's going to help you build a fence, finish the barn roof, patch the roof of the house, and whatever else needs fixing and cleaning around here."

She stomped off with Sean quickly at her heals.

They obviously needed to be alone, so I went to inspect Taffy's stall and found a shovel to remove the old straw. This farm seemed to need a lot of work, so I felt I could be useful.

Grabbing Anne's arm, Sean swung her around.

"What are you doing?" he asked gruffly.

"I'm getting my place fixed up before winter comes. My hands are worked to the bone and you still need help. He's willing, able, cheap, and....and," glaring at the barn, "that's all!" Yanking her arm away, she stomped to the house and slammed the door.

Sean stood stock-still. His livid hands could wring Anne's neck but this was her property so he had to be careful how he treated here. He stormed back to the roof.

I felt his disgruntled eyes on me as I cleaned the stall. His fierce hammering shook the walls as I looked up and asked politely, "Do you want some help?"

"Go find something else to do!" he glowered.

I walked away, leaving Taffy with the other horses at the front of the barn. Inside the bunkhouse, I tossed my stuff on the bed, questioning whether I should really unpack. Maybe I didn't want to know this man.

Oh, come on Patrick, I silently coaxed myself. Came here to do something, and couldn't lose my nerve in the first hour. Besides, I couldn't sit in that saddle another hour.

There was a knock on the door. It was Anne with an enquiring look on her face, wondering if I would patch the leaky roof of the house, conceding that Sean was in no mood for company. I agreed, though I was none to pleased I'd have to take that ladder from the barn.

She must have read my mind for she marched right over, saying I would be borrowing the ladder and for Sean to call over when he needed it.

"What….Anne!" he snapped.

She told me to grab that ladder and I did for I never argue with a lady, especially one as pretty as Anne.

I climbed the roof of the house to find some rotting shingles and a number of spots where they were completely missing. I eyed Sean. Then I eyed the small square slats at the foot of the barn door. I would also need a hammer and some of those nails.

He must have read my mind for there was a hammer and nails resting beside the wooden shingles. I didn't have to ask for anything which was a relief.

As soon as I repaired one part, I found another spot to patch. I ended up fixing a quarter of the roof. Luckily, there were enough supplies for my job.

"Hey, kid, you want to bring over the ladder so I can get down?" Sean hollered arrogantly.

"I'll be right over," I hollered back.

Still needing to replace a few shingles, I waited patiently 'till I could have the ladder back. I squinted at the bright, round sun disappearing behind the wall of mountains.

"Better get ready for supper," he said. "Anne likes her men punctual."

"I've still got a few spots to patch, so I'll kindly pass on supper, tonight." I also wanted to say that I smelled, hadn't bathed in days. But man to man I didn't.

"Your choice. Put the tools and nails in the barn when you're finished," he muttered, walking away.

Glancing at the half covered barn, I figured that it should have taken a day to complete, surmising that Sean was not a fast worker but sure had a fast mouth. I hoped it wouldn't rain all over the tools, nails, and horses.

Sean washed up and walked into the kitchen.

Anne peered from the stove. "Where's Patrick?"

"He's declined your supper invitation. Wanted to finish the roof of the house, tonight."

"My, my, that young man's got some work ethic," she spoke with a hint of sarcasm.

"What exactly is that supposed to mean?"

Unblinking, she glared, "Patrick has some work ethic, period."

They listened as the hammering stopped and footsteps started, followed by more hammering.

"Will you let him help you finish the barn, tomorrow?" she asked eagerly.

"Anne, I prefer doing it alone, quietly….work faster, concentrate better."

"The two of you can work even faster, and you won't have to concentrate so hard. Besides, the way this weather's going, we could have a snowfall, anytime."

They sat down to supper amid the ambience of pounding and more pounding.

The crimson sun had vanished, leaving soft pink and orange hues lingering above the mountain tops.

"Shuck," I said, hammering my thumb in haste to finish before darkness prevailed. I could be having a nice hot supper that smelled so good, but I won't be eating it. Instead, I'll just hammer my fingers to the roof. Smart Patrick, real smart.

"Do you think I should call him down from there?" Anne spoke with kindness.

"No, Anne. You wouldn't want to mess with that work ethic. Pass the carrots, please."

"You take a good look at Patrick?"

"No, I seem to recall ignoring him, and then my girl invites him to stay in my man cave. By the way, when I'm snoring so loudly you kick me out of the house, where am I supposed to go?"

"Well, you have two choices. You can sleep with Patrick or you can sleep in the barn," she smiled sweetly.

The bang, bang, bang, started again, then stopped.

Sean gazed at Anne with puzzled eyes. "Why would I want to take a good look at the kid? What are you implying?"

She hesitated. "He's the right age, and there's… there's something about him if you look beyond the chafed skin and lips."

"How old is he?"

"Eighteen."

"Well, math's not my strong suit. Would that be the right age?"

"If he was born in 1865, he would be seventeen."

Sean thought about Anne's words but immediately shook them off. Deep down, he knew his son was dead.

"I don't think he's my son. He's a Patrick Sullivan. Besides he's not tall enough to be my son," he said matter-of-factly.

I finally finished the roof and dragged my tired and sore body back to the bunkhouse after all of the tools and ladder had been put away under the half-covered barn.

Once inside my abode, I glanced at the small mirror hanging above my bedside table, noting how my face looked as irritated as my posterior felt. I shoved the mirror in the desk drawer and grabbed my journal.

Lying on my stomach atop the lumpy bed, I gnawed on a carrot while writing a letter to Ma. I felt she should know that I was in the Dominion of Canada, just south of a town called Calgary. In the morning, I would mail the letter and go to the bathhouse.

****

I slept most of the night, stirring once while darkness still flooded my room, coaxing me back to slumber again.

I awoke, glanced at my watch, and sat up too quickly, nearly vaulting off the bed. It was already ten o'clock.

Peaking out the window, I found Sean already on the barn roof. I was cussing up a storm flinging on my clothes. My shirt was half tucked in to my suspendered pants, one boot on, one boot off, as I staggered out the door. I hopped until I shoved my foot in, scurrying to the barn.

"Sorry I slept in," I spoke ruefully. "Wish someone would invent an alarming noise to wake me up," my voice muttered in a lame attempt to be funny.

"They call that a rooster," Sean answered. "And that can be arranged, if necessary. Climb up. You can help me finish this roof."

The sun stung my eyes. I tapped my head and dashed to and from the bunkhouse like a man on fire.

"Never leave home without your hat, huh?"

I looked at Sean flatly. "No."

He passed me a hammer and said I might want to put in a nail before noon. I made up for lost time. Every now and then, he would glance my way. If he figured me for a talker, he was wrong. I had proven to myself I could be silent for months if necessary.

"Where you from, kid?"

"I'm from just south of here."

"Would that be north or south of the border?" Sean asked, eyeing me intently.

"I'm from Montana," I replied, striking in a nail.

"What part?"

"I was raised on a ranch just north of Helena."

"Helena," he muttered slowly. "What are you doing all the way up here?"

"I was traveling and wanted to see what the world north of me looked like, but started to run out of money until that lovely lady over there offered me a job," I spoke appreciatively while peering the direction of the house.

"You're going to be working here a while to see the rest of this country the way that lovely lady over there is gonna pay you," Sean mocked.

"Well, when the work is done and I get paid whatever it is, I plan on going west. Aim to see the Pacific Ocean. The only traveling I've ever done is through my books. I aim to change that."

"You learned most of what you know from books?"

"Actually, most of what I do, I learned from my pa," I said admirably. "He taught me what was necessary to survive alone and amongst people," I paused, "I'm very grateful to him."

"Then why aren't you with him now?"

"He died about six months ago. Thought it time I got out on my own for a while…see the world around me."

"Well you haven't gone very far, kid."

"I know. Guess I should have planned it better. Though sometimes its life's surprises that gives the most rewards," I declared, descending the ladder to get more shingles.

I felt Sean's eyes on me as I grabbed a handful of the wooden squares.

We worked the rest of the morning in silence.

Anne came out with two dinner pails filled with ham sandwiches and apples. However she didn't linger, wanting the job done by end of day.

"Mind if I bring my horse out?" I asked after gobbling a sandwich.

Sean shook his head.

"Taffy!" I called and whistled.

"What did you call your horse?" Sean asked, showing me his ear.

"Taffy, like the candy."

He appeared amused.

"I was nine when I named her," I blurted out, even though I didn't have to justify anything with him. "What do you call your horse?"

"Horse…just horse. Actually I don't call him because he won't come anyway."

"Well, I can name your horse and train him to come if you like. I could also train him to come with a whistle like this." I contorted my lips, sucking in air. "I whistle for her when I'm in the company of rugged, pig-headed cowboys who don't know better than to make fun of a man and his horse. Let me take a gander at your horse. I'm sure I could come up with a proper name."

"It's the first horse on the left, kid."

I brought the horse out and stepped back. He was a chestnut with two white socks. Grabbing a handful of oats, I moved a few yards away, holding out my hand.

The horse slowly sauntered over, head hanging low and lazy.

"How old's this…this is a Morgan." I stated.

"That's right," Sean answered. "What's your horse?" he asked with a curious hand along Taffy's striped back.

"My horse is half mustang, half thoroughbred."

"Is that so," he said with some incredulity.

"It's what happens when a thoroughbred stud finds a pasture full of wild mares," I said matter-of-factly.

Sean's fascination wore off quickly. "My horse is not that old," he said defiantly.

I inspected the horse's teeth and stroked him from head to haunches.

"Are we gonna get back to work or just play with the horse?" he snapped.

"Well this gelding, which I assume you know is a horse without its male parts is, as you said, not that old," I lied, for the horse was simply put, as old as dirt. "He's just out of shape, so I'd call him 'Slowpoke'. If you like, though, I could train him to come with a whistle," I offered with hope that the horse still had his sense of hearing.

Sean turned with a spiteful glare. "Kid, we don't have time for this. I won't have my manly parts if we don't finish this roof!"

As we climbed the ladder, I felt I might have been a little insensitive about his horse, so I decided to tell a joke. It also made me feel less nervous around the man.

"What's the best type of story to tell a runaway horse?"

"I don't know, Patrick."

"A tale of WHOA. Get it, WHOA."

Sean wasn't laughing, so I gave my mouth a rest.

We worked in silence for the rest of the afternoon.

I turned down supper again, desperate to scrub my grimy skin clean.

Heading into the small main street, I found that bathhouse run by friendly Chinese immigrants. My dirty strewn clothes were eagerly scooped up and carried away by a small, smiling man. I was about to refuse when a glimmer of hope emerged that they might come back clean. The china man returned and tried to take my not so dirty clothes folded neatly on a nearby chair until I clasped them to my naked state.

"Over my dead body!" I blurted out, uselessly.

He smiled and waited, and would keep on waiting until the turn of this century and still wouldn't get my last set of clothes. I wagged my dripping head from side to side until he nodded, raising one finger.

When he returned, he offered the strangest looking soup that I learned to like while the steam wafted from my tub of water. As the last few drops of broth trickled from the bowl to my mouth, I figured I'd let my skin wrinkle and peel off before I was forced out of this place.

After the bath, I went to the mercantile and picked up potatoes and an armful of apples and carrots. All of this healthy food was creating more open space between my waist and pants. Thank God for suspenders or they'd be around my ankles.

I asked Sam Tracey if I could play his piano.

He seemed quite pleased that it was going to be used.

Wiping the loose dust from unpolished keys, I played simple tunes.

I called over to Sam in a polite tone, "You still dry?"

All he had was tea. He carted it over in a china cup. How splendid was that?

I said silently, *Yes Patrick, my horse is Taffy, I play the piano, and drink my tea in a china cup with my pinky in the air. I'm one mean, shucking person.*

I didn't care. I was alone and loving it with the exception of Sam Tracey, who was very pleased with my playing. He told me I could come and shake the dust off the keys anytime. I told him to make part of his store into a restaurant and he had a deal.

Chapter 2

I woke up late on Saturday morning. Not as late as the previous day, but late nonetheless. Sean was sitting on the front porch drawing out plans for a fence.

"Anne's got breakfast inside waiting for you," he said with eyes never leaving the drawing.

I walked by and casually perused his sketch.

Upon opening the front door of the small house, I walked into a cozy kitchen warm from a fire that blazed in the hearth. Behind the kitchen were two rooms.

Turning from the dry sink, Anne smiled, "Morning Patrick, or at least I think it's still morning."

She was such a fine-looking woman. And she also seemed too young for Sean. "I'm sorry," I smiled shyly.

Anne stared like she was examining every crack in my dried face. I didn't care for that kind of attention, looking away.

"Sit down. Your breakfast is getting cold. Looks like you've missed a few meals."

When I finished my plate of food, she scrapped more eggs and bacon onto it, saying it would make me a faster worker. I didn't refuse, not knowing when I'd eat again. She gave me toast, sliced apple, and I ate it all. That seemed to satisfy her, so she shooed me off, requesting I look at the plans for the fence.

As I headed out the door, she stuffed a jar into my hand and told me that Sunday supper was a must to attend, clean and prompt for six o'clock. Sunday was also my day off but only until six o'clock, she stressed again.

I thanked her and walked out to Sean, who was still making sketches.

I peaked over his shoulder but not before glancing at the jar of lubricating jelly.

Sean pressed the paper into his chest and looked up. "Can I help you with something?"

"Might I make a suggestion? I lived on a ranch and know a thing or two about fences."

"Well, I might be the luckiest fellow in Highwood River. I have a handy man who's an expert in fence building right here on the property! Is there anything you're not good at kid!" he snapped.

I began walking away. "Sorry, just trying to help. I'll go feed the horses."

"My kid would have more backbone," Sean mumbled. "Hey, come on back!"

I tipped my hat so low, Sean couldn't see my unhappy eyes.

"Take a look at my sketch."

As I glimpsed it, I could feel his heavy glare on me.

"You have two choices for fencing," I said. "A split-rail fence which requires no nails but more wooden rails for balancing, or a standard three or four rail fence nailed to posts.

"Well, if you had to do this fence all by yourself, which fence would you choose?"

"Does it have to be completed by a certain time?"

"Before winter's first snowfall or I move into the bunkhouse with you."

"Well then, I'd suggest a four rail fence. It requires a lot less wood. Do you still have nails?"

"I can provide you with nails."

"I still suggest making the fenced area bigger and cordoning off a small section for a corral over here."

"Why would I want a corral? I don't plan on breaking horses."

"A corral is good idea for other reasons. Say you've got a new horse and he doesn't get along with the other ones. You could corral him and slowly introduce him to the others. Maybe your mare will have a foal, if you even have a mare, and they could be separated from the other horses. It's just a nice thing to have. It will take more time to build but then you have it done."

"Why would I want such a big fenced yard? I only have three horses."

"Well, they say a man is measured by the size of his pasture, and I just figured that pasture is way too small for a man like you. You need a bigger pasture, a bigger fence to cover that bigger pasture. Besides, you've got good grazing fields. You could add cows, too."

Sean nodded in agreement. "We best start building this thing since it's gonna take longer."

"Where are we getting the wood from?"

Sean pointed to the forest behind the house.

"Let's get started," I spoke keenly.

"I got a real life Davy Crockett living on my property," Sean said under his breath, shaking his head. He took an ax and cross-cut saw out to the grove of evergreens.

"I'm glad this forest is filled with spruce and not cottonwood," I exclaimed.

"Why's that?"

"Cottonwood trees harden when they dry, making them impossible to work with. Spruce is much easier to work with and the wood doesn't rot so quickly."

I was so knowledgeable and eager to show Sean what to do, he seemed happy to let me do the laborious work. He watched me grind the teeth of the saw into the thick trunks, and watched as I removed the limbs and dragged the tree to the barn. I showed him how far away the posts should be, how deep, and how high. Then he watched me cut a trunk into six foot pieces before splitting them into three or four rails dependant on the thickness of the trunk.

After I dragged and cut several trees, Sean finally pitched in as I wiped copious amounts of sweat from my forehead. My brows were as wet as sponges. I hoped he saw that I laboured hard and for the most part, silently.

While we worked, he tried to persuade me to have supper with Anne and him, his brash smile indicating some ulterior motive. I feigned exhaustion, saying I'd be clean and on time for Sunday supper.

****

I woke to a cool and crisp cloudless Sunday and decided to venture east along the Highwood River. Quickly dressing, I grabbed an apple and bolted out the door.

Sean was on his porch sipping coffee. When I peered over, I blinked a clear view of a devious smile until his lips started flapping.

"Anne has breakfast ready! Best not keep her waiting!"

Changing my steps for the house, I gave him a brief nod. "Morning," I said cheerfully.

"Afternoon," he smiled.

Anne had another big breakfast on the table which I wolfed down at great speed. I was anxious to get moving so I said very little.

"Where you off to today?" she asked.

"I thought I'd travel east a ways," I replied, sipping the last of my coffee. "Explore some of this wild country."

"Most people want to explore the mountains," she said plainly. "Let me make you something for your journey. Wouldn't want you to go hungry."

I was very appreciative.

She reiterated that supper was promptly at six o'clock.

Riding away from the house at a swift gallop, I was happy to be alone for a while. It was already mid-morning by the time I arrived at the tiny commercial district and was soon accosted by Mr. Chan, owner of the bathhouse.

I reminded him that I just had a bath a day ago, but he was insistent, his agile little body clutching at my clothes, pulling me closer and closer to a giant steel tub.

A little girl came over and translated her father's rambling words. "He would like you to have a bath and wash those filthy clothes."

"I can't smell that bad, can I?" My face looked on in deep denial.

Approaching, she sniffed rather palpably, exclaiming, "No, not as bad as Sean!"

I chuckled. "Listen, I'll have a bath when I return. What's your name?"

"Lilly," she replied, turning and translating my words to her father.

Mr. Chan nodded happily, taking Lilly's hand and whisking her away.

I rushed over to the mercantile and got delayed again when I met Sam Tracey's assistant, Rudy Smith. The tall and lanky fellow with curly black hair shook my hand vigorously as he stood beside Sam, making him appear four feet tall.

"You need an assistant to run this store?" I asked quite tersely. I had never seen more than two people in this store at one time.

"Well, Patrick, sometimes I have inventory and deliveries to sort out, and I like to take several breaks to rest my weary feet."

I nodded politely while inching towards the door with my procured apples and candy sticks.

As I journeyed east, I passed ancient wooded groves of Pine and Spruce. A flock of noisy geese filled the cloudy sky in their 'v' pattern as I passed a small farm.

The ten or so cows were meandering freely along the unfenced pasture, and beyond the shadow of a covered porch, sat an old man smoking a pipe and petting his hound dog. He didn't see me until his dog started barking.

I vanished into a thickly wooded forest for several hours. There would be no farms dotting my path on this day. Once along the bank of the Highwood River, I was alone amongst a rim of cottonwood trees.

That is, until three Indians appeared on ponies. Time stood still as my careful eyes roamed over their calm stances, hands contentedly holding the reins.

Dressed in fringed deerskin, their solemn eyes took in my horse and uneasy face with little emotion. I was about to speak in Lakota when I realized it might not be such a good idea. I didn't know what Indian tribes lived in these parts and if they weren't Sioux, they would most likely be foe of the Sioux.

Speaking in Lakota might invoke a different type of sentiment than the inoffensive one I was getting now. As long as the arrows stayed strung on their backs, the arrows would stay strung on mine.

When they finally turned, I resumed breathing, and once alone, galloped my way out of sight.

Thanks to Taffy's fast pace, I returned in plenty of time to have that bath and get changed. I wore my newly laundered clothes the china man had washed.

In my bunkhouse, I pulled out the mirror and tousled back unruly hair to see that my skin was healing. I rubbed a smooth hand along my scant beard that looked much more like a midnight shadow. Despising it intensely, I threatened to scratch it away, though it made me look older; and that's what I desperately needed.

Tossing the mirror back in the drawer, I reached for my hat but decided against it, ambling out the door.

Sean was on the porch with a fellow who looked part Indian. They were having a drink, and I doubted they were sipping tea.

"Patrick, I'd like you to meet Joseph. Joseph, I'd like you to meet Patrick," Sean said pleasantly enough.

I shook Joseph's hand and took in the man's calm and friendly manner. He was the only Indian I'd ever met with short black hair. While his skin was russet like Strong Bull's, he had fine facial features. His eyes were dark but sincere as he greeted me warmly.

"Nice to meet you, Patrick," he smiled. "Sean's been telling me what a help you've been to Anne. This place is coming along nicely," Joseph voiced laudably.

I almost blurted out that I was a lifeline to Sean. Instead, I curtly nodded, my insolent glare wasted as he eyed an empty glass.

"Shall we go inside?" Sean suggested. "Wouldn't want to keep the lady waiting."

Anne had the dishes of food nicely spread on her checkered tablecloth. She had cooked a pot roast of venison with potatoes, carrots, pickled green beans, mashed turnip, and fresh bread sliced thick with butter.

"Anne, this looks delicious," Joseph complimented.

"Wow, I'm wishing I hadn't passed up all those suppers," I said pleasantly.

"Well, we don't always eat like this. Most nights it's just soup or stew, but Sunday supper has always been special to me," Anne smiled. "Please sit." She cleared her throat, "Ahem."

"I guess that's my not so obvious hint to say grace," Sean said, winking at Anne.

She held out her hands and we followed her lead.

"Lord, we are truly thankful for this bountiful meal and for our guests, Joseph and Patrick. May they eat well and….enjoy it. Amen and thanks again for goodness sake, amen."

We started to pass the food around, and I didn't take one bite before the questioning began.

"So Patrick, Sean tells me you're from Montana?" Joseph questioned in a soft-spoken voice.

"Yes, from a place north of Helena," I replied quickly.

"Gold town Helena?"

"Yes, it's a big town. Has a theatre, several rest-aurants, and hotels. I think one could find everything he needs in Helena. I didn't spend a lot of time there, though. I probably spent more time in Fort Benton."

I hoped what I said would suffice, my attention solely on my supper plate as I kept telling myself to eat slowly, chew each bite.

"Fort Benton. Isn't that where the steamboats come in?" Joseph inquired again.

"Yup," Sean spoke definitively. "Headquarters for the United States Cavalry. That can be a wild place despite the military presence. A lot of men and very few women if you know what I mean."

I glanced at Sean, trying to hide my knowledge about him and the women of Fort Benton.

"I didn't see that particular part of the town," I lied, forcing my mind to memories of the candy counter across from the brothel. "My pa sold horses to the Cavalry. Wild mustangs wrangled and broke by him, by me, and a handful of ranch hands," I said proudly.

"Breaking horses can be back breaking work," Joseph asserted.

I agreed, saying I had the scars to prove it.

"Where would you get these wild horses?" Sean asked, reaching for the salt.

The venison was a bit tough so I had to finish grinding my teeth at it before answering. "We would go into the High Plains, specifically Big Horn area."

I thought of Pa and felt a twinge of sadness.

"You don't mean Battle at Little Big Horn? Custer's last stand with Sitting Bull?" Sean asked with disbelief, still dousing his food in salt.

I nodded with an acknowledging smile on my face.

"Yep, same place. My pa was there just before the battle took place. Said he saw Indian camps spread three miles along Little Big Horn River....claimed there must have been more than a thousand tipis scattered along the water's edge."

"What did he do?" Joseph asked.

"Got the heck out of there! He was returning home when the battle took place. Couldn't believe that so many Indians had banded together and wondered why they didn't do that more often to defend their lands. If so, maybe Sitting Bull wouldn't be hiding in this country somewhere," I said bluntly, forking a mouthful of mashed turnip into my mouth.

"I believe Sitting Bull and his tribe have returned to the United States, however other tribes are still here," Joseph divulged. "They are camped in the Fort Walsh area just east of Medicine Hat."

"May I ask your tribe?"

"My mother was Sioux, Dakota Sioux."

I kept prying eyes on Joseph, willing him to share more of his heritage.

"My father was Scottish, a Trader. They both died several years ago," he spoke softly.

"Joseph is his Christian name," Sean said matter-of-factly.

I remarked silently, *you don't say*. And nodded safely, *I'd never have figured that out.*

"That's correct. My father, Andrew Borden, was a Christian, and Joseph is my Christian name."

Sean piped in, "He's known as Joseph, Healing Balm around these parts, though. He has a balm for what ails you. Have arthritis? Well, he has a balm for that. Have a burn? He has a balm for that, too, and they work. He has healed a lot of people."

"I use a lot herbs…..leaves and roots in my medicine. This type of healing has been a part of our way of life for a long time."

"Do you understand the Lakota language?" I asked keenly.

"The Lakota and Dakota speak the Sioux language; however, there are differences, but they are minor."

"Iyúškinyan wancínyankelo," I said, hoping to pronounce it correctly.

"It means nice to meet you," Joseph informed Sean and Anne.

"Well, hold on now....not only do I have Davey Crockett at my table, but it appears he may be part Indian, as well," Sean stated. "Tell me, do you have an Indian name, too?" He leaned into the table, chin propped on his knuckled hand.

"Actually, I do," I confessed but wished I hadn't.

"Please, do tell?"

"Hope I'm saying this correctly....Waanatan Makha." I skipped adding Tȟaópi to it.

Joseph nodded, quite perplexed.

"Well, what's it mean?" Sean asked.

I hesitated a moment before answering, "Earth Charger. It means Earth Charger."

"How did you earn that name?" Anne asked.

"I was digging in the dirt a little overzealously, I guess; and that's what I was named."

"You digging a hole to China?" Sean joked.

I looked at Joseph apprehensively. "I was digging a grave....graves. Many of the tribe were sick. My pa thought it might have been dysentery. There were casualties, so I offered to dig some graves." My voice went soft as I spoke the word 'graves'.

Eager to change the subject, I asked, "Are most of the Indians in this territory Sioux?"

"Why do you ask that?" Sean probed heavily. "You run into any lately?"

Despite his confrontational demeanor, Joseph replied, "In answer to your question, Patrick, yes, but Nakoda Sioux. They live on the Morley reserve east of Calgary. In this country, they are called the Stoneys. But you don't have to travel far to find other tribes like the Blackfoot, Cree, Metis."

"How do you two know each other?"

Sean glanced at Joseph. "I almost shot him."

I choked on water, figuring there goes Sean with his gun again.

"Patrick?" Anne cried with worry.

I squeaked out an, "I'm fine. Go on."

"Well, I decided to go hunting," Sean began. "I'd been here a month and wanted to pull my own weight, and provide food for my lovely Anne, who was just a friend at the time because we weren't…"

"We get the point, continue," she said flatly.

"I'm positioned fifty yards from a buck and aim with my Spencer rifle, ready to take a clear shot, when a tree branch snaps. The buck runs off, and the bullet I fire heads directly across to Joseph. "

Sean laughed at the recollection. "It you hadn't made so much noise, your life wouldn't have been in such jeopardy."

"I never snapped a branch," Joseph spoke calmly. "That noise came from your end of the forest."

I liked Joseph. He had a mild disposition.

"Well, I've heard it been said that a miss is as good as a mile," I chirped in.

"That's right, Patrick," Sean smiled coolly at me. "I've heard that saying, too."

Joseph eyed his friend. "I take him hunting with me so I know I'll be safe. Keep him beside me at all times. Never know when that mile is closer than you think."

We all had a chuckle with that comment.

"You hunt, Patrick?" Joseph asked.

"Patrick does everything. Of course he hunts," Sean voiced with sarcasm.

I glared at Sean, never knowing how to react to his demeanor; however, he still didn't know who I was, so I took it as a compliment from an old, envious fool.

"I hunt when I'm hungry. Take only what I need when I need it and use a bow and arrow. I guess when it comes to hunting I'm more like Sitting Bull than Davey Crockett." I shook my head at the thought.

After finishing my supper, I said, "Imapi yelo. That means I'm full, Sean."

"I hope not, Patrick. I have apple cobbler fresh out of the oven," Anne enticed.

Sean gave me an odd stare. Maybe he wanted my piece, too. Regardless, I managed to stuff in one piece.

The men were going to have another drink on the porch.

I declined, having had enough with the questioning and talking, I retreated to my bunkhouse, waving good-bye.

"Patrick seems like a nice, young man. He's helping you out immensely," Joseph remarked.

"Yep, he's what Anne calls our Saint," he murmured while pouring whisky into two glasses. "No chance that Saint's related to me."

"Pardon?" Joseph asked with furrowed brows.

"Anne calls Patrick a Saint," he sneered. "You know what, Joseph? I think we're gonna see what our Saint is like when's he's woken up at the break of dawn. Drink up. We've got to go on the hunt for a rooster."

"You mess with that Saint too much, you'll be finishing the fence by yourself," Joseph warned, swirling the amber in his glass before draining it empty.

Chapter 3

The next morning, I woke to the sound of….of what I thought was a rooster. Glancing at my pocket watch, I discovered it was barely six o'clock in the morning. I stomped to my front door, and there he was….a big bold rooster in a little cage on my front porch. I was so mad I could spit hot water, calling him a pain in the shucking ass before slamming the door.

A few hours later, I peered up from a spruce rail, nail nestled between my lips, to find him poking his fat head out of the warm house.

"Patrick," he called over. "Breakfast's ready!"

I snatched that nail and whacked its head, but my fury didn't abate. Even when I was scooping up mouthfuls of oatmeal, I cast icy glares his way.

Sean couldn't resist, though. "It's nice to see you up so early this morning." He smirked at Anne, who was rubbing her head.

"Well, I'll have you know I was up before that screechy thing let out a sound. Actually, I think I woke it up," I lied matter-of-factly.

"Oh, I'm sure you did. I'm sure you did," Sean replied with pleasure on his smug face.

"Now, if you'll excuse me, I have work to do," I spoke crisply, squeaking my chair across the floor. "We all know how fast I work around her, right Anne? Have to set a good example for the ones who lag behind."

I directed that comment towards Sean, though it probably flew over his inflated head.

"Patrick, would you mind going to the mercantile for me?" Anne asked politely. "There's a package waiting for me, but I have a painful headache. You see, I'm a light sleeper and something loud and obnoxious woke me too early this morning."

I glowered at Sean, figuring he really shouldn't do that considering this was her property. If I was her, I would have kicked his....

"Well, Patrick," Anne pleaded.

"Sure, I'll go to the mercantile," I said kindly.

"Anne, I'll go," Sean offered kindly, as well.

"No, you're going to do these dishes while I lie down," she commanded, while I quickly escaped out the front door.

As I made my way to the mercantile, the only sounds to be heard came from a flock of crows in a willow tree. The population of this community must have been in the single digits for I rarely saw anyone other than a handful of merchants, or Sean and Anne.

As I walked out of the mercantile with Anne's package and a handful of peppermint sticks, I saw Lilly sitting on the boardwalk, hunched over with a somber face.

I sat down beside her and offered a stick.

She glumly took the sweet and thanked me with little enthusiasm.

"Shouldn't you be going into that school over there?" I asked as the bell rang.

She nodded miserably.

"What's the matter? Don't like learning?"

"The boys call me names," she replied solemnly.

I nodded sympathetically. "Sticks and stones may break my bones, but names will never hurt me. Well whoever said that's never been called a bad name over and over, because it hurts. It might not leave a physical mark, but it sure does leave a memorable one."

Lilly agreed and smiled at me like I was her thoughtful, big brother.

"Well, Lilly, you may just have to stand up to those ignorant boys. You're a smart girl and smart girls can teach ignorant boys anything. It just takes patience."

As I mounted my horse, I watched Lilly stomp over to the school as two young men were coming from a southerly direction. To my shock, they were just boys my size heading to class. Hovering over her, their mouths spilled unkind words. She tried to speak but was rudely interrupted by noisy, intimidating voices.

I grabbed my whip and marched over to the stumpy one called 'Hadley' who was doing the loudest insulting.

"What are you calling my sister?" I roared.

"Your sister?" Hadley whined.

"She's my sister!" I spat out, getting right in his face.

"I wuz just telling Lizzy she missed a school day on account of another Chinese holiday," he muttered.

"Her name is Lilly. Why don't you try saying it, Handmedown!"

"My name is Hadley, and I don't have to say anything! You can't make me!"

My eyes raged at him. "Ever have a whip coil around your legs? Cut right through your clothing....almost chip at the bone, Hatfield?"

He nervously peered as it snaked from my tight grasp. "No, and my name's Hadley."

"Well, Hadley, this is Lilly, and it does feel good to hear your name said correctly, doesn't it? So let her hear it or you'll hear from my whip," I demanded.

Hadley cowered while his brother fled to the schoolhouse.

"Lilly," he whispered.

"Pardon?" I asked rudely.

"Lilly!" Hadley shouted.

"What's going on out here?" the teacher asked.

"Oh, Hadley's just learning Lilly's name. I think he gets it and shouldn't make that mistake again, or I'll be forced to use some gentle persuasion," I smiled scornfully at the quivering young man-boy before walking to Taffy, who never strayed despite that she wasn't tied to a post.

Sean was chopping down a tree when I sauntered into the forest. I was gracious enough to help him carry it to the front of the barn despite that he looked quite capable of doing it himself.

"I have a question that is of a philosophical nature?" I asked.

Sean glanced my way. "Will it take long?"

"If a tree falls in the forest, does it make a sound?"

"I heard this tree fall down, so yes. You feeling poorly?"

He tapped my head.

"No, I mean if a tree falls in the forest, does it still make a sound even if we aren't here to hear it?"

"If I went into that house right there and shut the door, would I still hear a Patrick making all this noise with his mouth? My answer is no. I wouldn't hear the tree. I wouldn't hear Patrick. I'd be at peace, right now, sipping my whisky, hearing nothing. Am I making myself clear?"

"Oh, you're as clear as…." I stopped myself from saying Willowtree creek, "your Highwood River over there."

Our conversations during the fence build were difficult. I learned more about Sean during those Sunday night suppers than I did any day working on that fence.

****

On a temperate and cloudless November day, I was tempted into journeying to Calgary. Light snow was dusting the ground. I was thankful to the shucking rooster I called 'Screeches' for my early morning start.

As the sun was still climbing the sky, I mounted Taffy and moved away from Spitzee Crossing.

The Rocky Mountain ridge was my guide as I traveled north. Crossing the shallow river, I wondered what kind of fish could be caught. I would have to ask Sean when he was in a good mood if there ever was a time he was in a good mood. As Taffy splashed along, I pondered whether we would, one day, be standing together pulling trout the length of my arm out of the clear waters.

However, I knew it would never be like it was with Pa. It could never be like that again, and it saddened me.

My gaze turned to the sharp-toothed crags, untouchable and majestic. It brought familiarity and comfort to me even though I was so far from home.

The winter sun, though bright, shed little warmth on my skin, so I continued a fast pace along the vast emptiness.

When a large ranch came into view, memories of my own Montana ranch passed through my mind as I watched lazy cows searching for the last of the pasture's green grasses. I imagined my Pa, just a silhouette against a brilliant orange sun with strong hands on the rope as a mustang bucked and whirled. I remembered how quickly he could settle a horse with his touch, how he could settle me so easily, and I missed him.

My thoughts were interrupted by a grim-faced man galloping my direction.

I asked if his cattle were for sale.

He told me to come back when the owner was around.

I couldn't help but ask if they broke horses.

"If you're interested, come back in the spring when we do a local round-up," he hollered. "We could always use an extra hand or two."

I nodded appreciatively and continued north.

When I approached the town, a smile lit up my face. Nestled in a valley, businesses were scattered along the Bow and Elbow rivers. But the most interesting part about Calgary was construction of a railroad. A passage-way went through the thousand mile wall of mountains, and Calgary got the distinction of being the closest post to that opening called 'Kicking-Horse Pass'. Wagons, with their canvas covers stretched over heavy loads of supplies, would continue to use the pass, creaking westward until the railroad was completed.

My cowboy boots clomped along the boardwalk until I entered a mercantile called Hudson's Bay Company. I opened the door and a bell jingled, echoing into the open spaces of the store, and there were lots of open spaces. In the centre of the stark room, a rack held a few tweed jackets. The long counter displayed a handful of plaid shirts, while a lone pair of black laced boots adorned the pine-planked floor.

"May I help you?" A young male clerk asked too eagerly.

"Do you have any food?" I asked.

"Not currently. Our shipment doesn't come in for another week or two."

"Oh," I said surprised, unintentionally blurting out, "a man could starve waiting for that to happen."

He scrupulously eyed me up and down. "Say, I think this finely sewed jacket would fit you just fine."

Patting the sleeve, dust particles frantically swirled around the sun-soaked room.

"If you want food, you have to go to the I.G Baker store," he advised. "That's where I go." His face soured. "American run, American goods, but cheapest you'll find in Calgary."

I nodded, very familiar with the store also located in Fort Benton, and decided not to tell him I was American.

His face became forlorn. "How am I supposed to sell what I don't have?"

I figured that was a rhetorical question, looked about the empty room, and offered, "Why don't you sell the bell?"

There was an awkward pause.

"Good day," I said, turning for the door. Upon hearing him sigh, I felt so badly for the poor clerk, I almost bought something out of pity. "When I need a jacket," speaking optimistically, "I'll know where to come."

He returned my smile and warmly told me to have a nice day.

I made my way to the I.G. Baker and Co. Store, and was not dissatisfied. This mercantile had everything. I felt right at home moving around the crammed store that offered food, dry goods, saddles and harnesses, as well as hardware and farm tools. But most importantly, it offered a selection of candy that I was never going to see at Sam Tracey's small store.

A little boy was salivating at the various jars so closely his breath was misting up the glass.

I asked for a bag, glancing at the child. "If you could choose anything, what would you pick?"

The boy turned saddened eyes on me. "I've never had candy, but if I could, I'd try all of it."

I took the lids off and scooped big handfuls of each kind while he watched in awe.

"What's your name?" I asked.

"Jordan Cuthbert, sir."

I felt old.

"My name's Patrick Sullivan. Let me see if today's the day you can have candy. Where's your mother?" I asked, scanning the store.

He pointed to a woman with two children clinging to her knees and three others hovering nearby.

Mrs. Cuthbert peered my way, calling out, "Sir, don't get too close to my boy. He's sick!"

"That's fine, ma'am. Mind if I give the boy some candy? It'd be my pleasure."

Mrs. Cuthbert shook her head at Jordan, who was nodding in a beseeching way.

"Please, ma'am. Everybody should try it at least once in their lifetime," I smiled boyishly.

"If you insist, and thank you kindly."

I handed Jordan the bag, told him to share with his siblings, and offered some good advice to go with the candy. "Always clean your teeth with baking soda and water afterwards, and if you have chokecherries, pop one of those and one of these sweets in your mouth at the same time; and they'll make a taste explosion you'll never forget."

Jordan's eyes lit up with my wise advice, though I doubted he knew what a chokecherry was.

I proceeded to fill another bag for myself when Jordan sneezed my direction. I hastily removed the bandana from my neck because there was some kind of explosion all over his face that he needed to wipe up.

"You can keep that bandana, too."

As I reached for my half-filled bag, Mrs. Cuthbert approached.

"I want to thank you again for your generosity and kindness," she said warmly.

I smiled and turned to Jordan, who was grinning from ear to ear with my bag completely filled.

After Mrs. Cuthbert and her brood of children left, I paid for the candy and gave the clerk money to settle the poor woman's account. The female clerk seemed very surprised by my generosity, clutching and shaking my hand erratically.

My face turned crimson, trying to pull it away; but she just wouldn't let go until I yanked it out of her tight grasp.

"Come back anytime, you generous and fine looking man," she purred sweetly.

As I walked into the noon-day sun, I passed Whitman's Saloon and opted for a drink or two before returning to the dry community of Highwood River.

There was a tableful of men, two of them Mounties in an animated conversation, with hands on glasses and gloves on the table.

I ambled to the bar and couldn't help but listen as their voices filled the saloon.

"Ever have any incidents with them Indians?" a plain clothed man asked.

"No, not really," the Mountie, William Walden replied. "Well, just the once. It was just a sound like a whizz. And then another, and another. I looked down at my arm and there were the arrows. Fraction of an inch more," he said, "and I'd have died."

"And you're telling me that these savages are not dangerous!" Lyle spoke with disbelief. "Hell, I sleep with a rifle next to my bed."

"Now, now, Lyle," the Mountie replied with an inflection similar to my pa's. "I don't think they intended it. Maybe they were hunting for birds."

"Come now. You were hit three times," another named Tom said with indignation.

"They weren't poisoned arrows. They didn't come screaming at me. In fact, I never did see them."

I peered at the middle-aged Mountie, who showed no enmity to the Indians for his near-death experience.

"We've got a tough job bringing law to this land. These Indians have never had laws and now we're telling them what they can and can't do."

"How much you get paid to do this job?" Tom asked.

"Fifty cents a day, all weathers."

"And Indian attacks," Lyle spoke crudely.

"I believe Indians are as good as any white man!"

Lyle leaned into the table, eyes blazing, "Then you haven't travelled far enough!"

"Yes, I have. I used to trail herds of cattle from Texas to the Plains."

"You're not from here, though," Tom said.

"No, I'm from England. Most of us who joined the police are either, English, Scottish or Irish. Alec, here, is Scottish."

Alec, the second Mountie, spoke for the first time in a strong foreign lilt, "We're here to settle this land by enforcing the law set out in the British North America Act. And it would make our job easier if you put your guns away."

"And what if I don't," Lyle warned.

"The Law stretches to every man in this Dominion of Canada, white or Indian, and every man shall be treated the same under this law," Alec informed.

"Best you get back to your police patrols," Lyle said with eyes on William. "Wouldn't want it to get too dark and you just happen to get taken for food, again."

"Let us worry about the Indians and maybe you'll live a long life," William advised with authority.

My whisky finished, I felt it time to exit the establishment. As I was leaving, my eyes brushed over the Mounties again. They seemed nothing like our Cavalrymen who were bent on forcing every tribe onto reservations far from their ancestral homes. But I had much to learn about the life on an Indian in the Dominion of Canada. I just hoped these Mounties didn't have Highwood River in their sights. They'd have a hell of time taking a gun away from Sean Thomas.

While I rode south, I moved into the ramblings of the mountains and found a flock of wild turkeys. I brought one home, plunged it in boiling water, plucked its feathers, lopped off the head, cleaned it with salt, and proudly brought it to Anne. We had it along with boiled potatoes, creamed carrots, cabbage and fried onions, pickled beets, and cornbread.

I said grace this time. "Heavenly father, bless this food that we are about to eat, and take in your care the people seated at this table, for all the gifts that you bestow upon us, we give thanks, forever humble and in your servitude, Amen."

Sean shook a groan out of his head.

Anne practically squeezed the life out of his hand.

"Well, Anne, everything looks delightful as usual," Joseph said, pleased.

"Where'd you find this turkey, Patrick?" Anne asked in appreciation.

"Oh, just north a ways in a densely forested area not far from the mountains."

"Did you use an arrow?" Joseph asked.

"Only thing I use. Never did get used to firing a gun."

"Oh, I'd be lost without my gun," Sean said matter-of-factly. "It can be the only thing protecting you from an early grave."

"It can also be the one thing to put you in an early grave if you're not that good with it," I replied plainly.

"Well, I've never had that problem," he said brimming with confidence. "Guess that's where my talent comes in. I've always been good with a gun."

"Maybe not so much with a rifle, but good with a pistol, right Sean," Joseph aimed at correcting the distinction.

"Just be happy my aim was off that day, Joseph."

"How many men have you shot, if I may be so bold?" I inquired nervously.

"Well, I don't like to brag."

"Doesn't sound like you at all," Joseph said shrewdly.

Anne's head wagged frantically while she chewed food politely.

Sean ignored everyone, but me. "I say somewhere in the vicinity of five, maybe six…I've killed six men," he boasted. "How about you? Ever shoot anyone?"

"I've never shot a man…..frankly guns," I stuttered, peering at my plate. "The sound they make…I don't like the blast that they make. Just rely on my bow and arrow," I said, trying to keep it together.

Sean leaned in with both elbows perched on the table. "That's all fine and well, but when it comes to a skirmish between gun and bow and arrow, the gun will always win," he said unequivocally.

My head shook, eyeing the last bit of food on my plate. "Not necessarily. Take a single shot rifle. You miss and three arrows could be into you while you're reloading. Indians had rifles, but they didn't always have ammunition, so their most relied upon weapons were bows and arrows, knives, hatchets….."

Formulating my next words, I recollected my conversations with Pa about the Lakota Indians and the battles that they fought in. "It's the repeater rifle or the Gatling gun," I paused. "Gives the prospect of shooting off multiple rounds like some kind of impenetrable wall of firing that decimates and kills everything in its path…men, women, children. It can do the most damage with the least amount of personal feeling attached."

I peered up and all eyes were on me, so I figured shutting up for the rest of the meal was a good idea.

"Well, I'll take you shooting one day. You bring your bow and arrow, and we'll see who's fastest," Sean suggested in a kind of dare.

"Can we stop talking about killing and guns for the rest of this meal?" Anne pleaded.

Joseph agreed. "Enough people have been slaughtered with that weapon on both sides and we don't have to talk about it again. Besides, Patrick, in this country, the only ones wielding guns are the North West Mounted Police. They so much as see a raised pistol and it's confiscated. Use one and you'll get hauled off to jail," Joseph warned with eyes on Sean.

At that point, I was focusing on finishing my meal and going for an evening walk alone. The talk about guns got me thinking about Momma and how I wished I'd never picked one up.

"I know we promised not to talk about guns….."

"And we aren't" Anne snapped.

"But we have to get in one more hunting trip so we can have meat throughout the winter," Sean urged.

"Why don't we go next Sunday?" Joseph offered. "Patrick, you're more than welcome to come."

Sean's eyes were already set on me, mouth poised to speak. "You know, I have a question, a philosophical one. Patrick likes philosophical questions. What's more important, honesty or truthfulness?" he asked, perusing everyone at the table.

"If you're honest, your truthful, am I not correct?" Joseph answered with a quizzical face.

Sean glared my way again, but I didn't really feel like talking about honesty or truthfulness, so I didn't.

"Well, in my line of work neither are most important. For me, patience is most important because if I don't have that when taming a horse, I could be injured or worse, and do irreparable damage in winning the horse's respect and obedience."

"I didn't ask about what you felt was most important," he pointed. "What's more important, honesty or truthfulness?"

Sean's demeanor indicated that he was ready to strangle the answer right out of my throat. It felt oddly like I was being tested.

"I would think they mean the same thing, however I guess sometimes you can be honest and not necessarily truthful….."

"Like how?"

"I had this situation in Helena once where this strange, old woman came up to me and grabbed my face, saying,

'Nathaniel, Nathaniel, I thought I'd never see you again. You're a strong and healthy man now, aren't you?' I looked at the young man accompanying this crazy, old woman and he proceeded to tell her that I was not Nathaniel. She ignored him, saying sadly, 'Please tell me you're healthy and happy, and I will live out the rest of my days in comfort.' I looked into her gloomy eyes and said I was healthy and happy. She smiled, said thank you, and walked away. Well I was healthy and happy even though I wasn't really Nathaniel."

Sean couldn't pass up the opportunity to ask, "You ever had any other name?"

Confused, I said, "Sorry?"

"Let's see, you've been Nathaniel, Earth Crusher, Patrick….I just wondered if you went by another name," Sean taunted.

"My name's Patrick Sullivan and this person before you living and breathing is Patrick Sullivan," I spoke defiantly even though I felt deeply hurt. My sorrow filled eyes shifted to an empty plate.

Sean sat back in his chair with a look of regret. 'I've changed my name before…to Filbert Cunningham," he admitted in an effort to lighten the mood, and Anne's sudden kick to his leg gave him more incentive.

"It was my pseudonym when I was in a poker game. I did very well with that name. I also used that name when I was running whisky from Fort Benton to Fort Whoop-Up. Nothing wrong with having another name! Nothing wrong at all!" Then, he put in quickly, "Can we have that pie now, Anne?"

"Filbert Cunningham," Joseph chuckled. "Couldn't come up with anything better than Filbert Cunningham?"

"I wanted to pick a name that far resembled my shady character."

"Well that would have done it, Filbert."

Joseph chuckled again, and I eked out a grin.

After dessert, I helped Anne with the dishes, as I did almost every Sunday. Then I excused myself so I could have that quiet and peaceful walk.

After Joseph had departed, and Anne and Sean were in bed, she lashed out at him. "Why do you treat Patrick so rudely?"

"I don't think I do that."

"He's your son and you mock him. You treat him coldly….test him every time you open your mouth. No wonder he doesn't want to admit he's your son. Heck, I wouldn't want to be your son," Anne said vehemently.

"I'm just tired of playing this game. Want him to come out and say it, and we get on with our lives."

"Maybe this is the kind of relationship Patrick wants. He's all grown up, and maybe he just wants a friend who happens to be his father. It probably won't get any different than this," Anne paused, "ever wonder what happened to his mother? Why he was taken in by strangers? It may not be what you want to hear, and it might be pretty painful for him."

"I want to know what happened to Mandy. That's why he has to reveal his true self."

"Don't put him in a corner. Let him come to you when he's ready. You push too hard and you may lose him forever, and that won't go over well with me. The barn just might become your permanent dwelling."

There would be no tender kisses or lovemaking, tonight. She turned away, giving the coldest shoulder. Sean thought he could catch a chill off of it.

With hands behind his head, staring into darkness, Sean's mind turned to a day months ago in Fort Benton, to that saloon with the drunk who staggered in barely able to sit on a bar stool. Sullivan was his name, was it not? Sean tried to remember the conversation, tried to remember the face; but his memories were too faded and cloudy.

His thoughts turned to Patrick. Shouldn't he be feeling something by now if it was his kin? All this time, he's been searching for a nine year old boy. This young man building a fence, eating at his supper table, going off this direction, that direction, was all grown up and already had a father. Why the hell would he need another one?

Chapter 4

Over the next week, the weather turned colder. Frost was covering the ground and the morning's sun slept in much longer than I did. Apart from a lingering tiredness I undeniably blamed on Screeches, the days moved relatively quietly.

Sean hammered in his fingers a couple times, cussing just like my grandpa did. Momma obviously didn't teach him the most ultimate swear word. I used it once when I cracked my nail in two.

"Shuck!"

Sean called over, "What did you say?"

"Pardon?" I mumbled, swollen thumb in my mouth.

"What did you just say?"

"Who, me?"

"No, the man behind you!" he bellowed with a scowl.

I turned around, wondering who the 'shuck' he was talking about.

"Oh for pity's sake, forget it!" he grumbled.

Lord, the man was so confusing at times. I blamed the start of a nasty headache on his confounding attitude.

By Sunday, I felt lousy. Throughout that night, I tossed around in a feverish state that gave way to teeth chattering chills. I didn't have the energy to keep the fire going through the night, so by morning my breath was frosty white, my cheeks numb.

The only thing luring me out of bed was the hunting expedition with Sean and Joseph. I dressed quickly in my warmest woolen clothes and walked over to the well.

The fresh, icy water on my face shocked and revived a weary state. I was feeding the horses when Sean's voice echoed across the barren field.

"Patrick, breakfast time! Then, we've got to get a move on!"

Breakfasts with Sean and Anne were now a daily routine for me.

I entered the warm kitchen as Anne was putting a plate full of crispy bacon on the table.

"Morning, Patrick," she intoned cheerfully.

"Morning," I said, yawning.

"You look tired. Not sleep well?"

"Not the best night's sleep, but not the worst either," I smiled weakly.

"Patrick, when will that fence ever be finished?"

I slid two eggs onto my plate, shrugging. "We're moving as fast as we can. It's been slow breaking up hard ground for the posts. I also made it more onerous, adding a corral."

Sean entered and announced that Joseph had arrived. I hastily made my eggs and bacon 'to go', stuffing them between two thick slices of toasted bread before heading out to the men.

Anne glimpsed the plate of bacon and bit into a crisp, greasy piece before scurrying to put the remaining pieces between thick toasts, and adding them to the rest of the food she prepared.

With packaged sandwiches in hand, she stepped out of the house and tightened her shawl around trembling shoulders. She didn't linger in the chilly air.

Sean was given the food, a quick peck on the cheek, and a quicker wave good bye. Back under the shelter of the covered porch, she smiled, watching father and son ride out together.

"Where's the best place to go hunting in this area?" I asked curiously as our horses moved northwest.

"Depends on what you're hunting for," Sean said. "We're on the hunt for deer so I will take you where deer are plentiful."

We must have travelled a good forty-five minutes before we were tying the horses to trees and removing our essentials. I grabbed my bow and quiver of arrows while Sean and Joseph grabbed rifles from their scabbards.

As we proceeded into the densely forested area on this damp and chilly morning, every bone in my body ached. A sunless sky, pale against the evergreen trees, did little to galvanize my tracking capabilities; so I followed Joseph, assuming Sean was following me.

When Joseph raised his hand, I stopped. He motioned for me to crouch low, and we gingerly made soft steps east of a tall pine.

We were perched on our haunches as two deer came into sight by a stream no less than seventy yards from us.

"Where's Sean?" Joseph whispered.

Popping up, I peered around until Joseph pushed me back down.

"He'll shoot your head off," he warned. "Stay down."

"I don't look like deer."

"Neither did I."

Joseph positioned his rifle at the buck with a clear shot.

Suddenly a branch snapped and the deer scattered.

"Not again," he groaned. "Where did it come from?"

"I think it came from the far right side," I believed, standing up until Joseph pulled me down.

"Sean?" he called.

"Joseph?" Sean answered.

"Where are you?"

"I'm beside this tall pine. Where are you?"

"I'm beside this tall pine."

"Oh, well, that clears it all up! We're beside two pines in a pine filled forest," Sean muttered sarcastically. "Is Patrick with you?"

"Yes, I'm here," I said irritably.

Joseph whispered, "Well, now that we've thoroughly scared all the deer away, let's make it safe to find Sean." He hollered out, "Put your rifle down and we'll come to you!"

"Do we have to?" I whined. "I was so enjoying this time away from him. Couldn't we just let him sit there a spell behind his own pine tree? Clearly he makes too much noise to be hunting anything."

"Well I could have a drink," Joseph said, grabbing his canteen and offering it to me.

I declined, not wanting Joseph sick with what I had.

"We could attempt to lose him for a while," he grinned. "I'd just prefer he was unarmed."

"Just imagine…Anne I'm home and we're having gutted Patrick for supper, tonight," I laughed.

"That's not funny," Joseph cringed before chuckling heartily.

Sean appeared, though he wasn't laughing.

"I see you picked up your rifle, Sean," Joseph spoke with humour. "Should we be worried? Tell me you don't see any deer before you."

I clutched at my wool cap to conceal a wide-mouthed grinnish laugh.

"It's not funny!" he griped. "We here to hunt or have a laugh at Sean party!"

"We're here to hunt," Joseph spoke in seriousness. "Just don't like it when you take off. It threatens our peace. Makes us feel….hunted." He slowly rose. "Come on, Patrick. Time to get to work."

I felt I had composed myself enough to put my hat back on a chilled head. I decided to stay behind Sean so we wouldn't have any more interruptions.

We walked deeper into the wooded forest, and the dampness I'd been feeling changed to a warmer than usual feeling in my body. My cheeks felt flushed.

Following a trail of scrapes, I hoped the deer weren't too far away, and this time they weren't. A buck stood forty yards from us, and Joseph waved me ahead. I bent my knees over a mossy stump, feeling like Strong Bull was encouraging me.

My tip freshly sharpened, I slid my fingers along the shaft, flexed the string, and took a deep breath to steady myself. I had perfect trajectory and perfect aim as the arrow found its way to the buck's torso, followed by another. I didn't have any energy to chase after it, so I waited for the buck to fall to the ground.

Joseph patted me on the back before his eyes searched for Sean.

I placed my hand on the warm animal, but its heart had already stopped beating. "Thank you for sacrificing yourself for me," I said, believing its spirit remained a few minutes after death.

Joseph reappeared and said that Sean had gone off to find more deer. He pulled out the arrows and inspected the bloodied iron tips.

"They were given to me by a Shoshone named Strong Bull, a good friend."

"However, it's a Sioux arrow, Patrick: the length, the wood, and these markings along the shaft," he said, fingering them with high regard. "Let's get to work on cleaning this animal."

Of all things we do in the wilderness, this one was by far the grossest. From removing the feces, organs, and entrails, this job was bloody messy and a lot of work. The organs just steamed out. That's when I started coughing, which didn't make the churning of my stomach relax any more.

As Joseph was bagging the heart and liver, he glanced my way. "You want me to finish this?"

"No, I'll be fine. Just need a drink." I reached for my canteen and chugged back half of its contents.

By the time Sean returned, we had the animal completely gutted. Joseph also made a deep cut and took the windpipe out.

"I've killed one gentleman, just a quarter mile from here," Sean boasted.

Joseph and I shot him an outlandish stare, while sweat streamed down our faces and blood dripped from our hands.

"You killed one gentleman?" I asked, coughing.

"No, I shot a buck just up yonder," Sean retorted tartly.

Joseph eyed me. "You stay here. Make sure he's completely cleaned out. I'll help Sean with his kill. We'll meet back here."

I nodded, content not to be gutting another animal or having to walk up yonder to find it.

After the buck was cleaned out, I put a thick branch between his ribs and flipped him over to dry and cool off.

Then I washed the tools, along with my hands, in the icy stream. Clutching a towel, I attempted to dry them, though the dampness in the air kept them cold and moist.

Another sip of water from my canteen did little to soothe the scratchy sore throat I had suffered from all day.

There were no signs of Sean or Joseph, so I leaned against a fallen tree and closed my eyes.

I didn't hear the grey wolf until he was just yards away. He was growling like I'd stolen his supper. I silently reached for my bow and arrow, knowing my precision had to be bang on.

The wolf pounced, my arrow pierced, two times lucky on this day, as he whimpered and fell to the ground. I didn't want to wait a third time to test my fate, so I paced our hunting grounds, my eye on the lookout for more predators.

It took Joseph and Sean an hour to get back, dragging the buck. They glimpsed the dead wolf before passing worried eyes over me.

"You hurt, Patrick?" Sean asked.

"No, I'm fine," I said wearily, my face noticeably pale. "Just a little shaken. It's probably 'cause of hunger."

Sean nodded. "Let's eat before we have more unwanted visitors."

We rushed through our food, eager to get back to the house and preserve the meat.

After we dragged and lifted the heavy carcasses onto the empty wagon, I was visibly worn-out. Even the brisk coolness of the rapid pace home did little to revive me.

There was still much work to be done with these deer when we got back to the homestead. Preparing one animal to be skinned and cut into strips, roasts, and chops was plenty of work; and we had two to contend with.

Some of the meat would be packed in ice and put in barrels, while the rest would be pickled in brine. Joseph wanted to make pemmican, so the meat would have to be dried as well. Anne was given ample fresh kill for a fine venison roast. She also fried the liver with onions.

By suppertime, I struggled to stay awake amid a feverish state and a pounding headache. Anne went through so much work to cook the roast, potatoes, fall vegetables, and pound cake for dessert, I felt I had to stay. It was all quite delicious, but my appetite had disappeared like my energy.

"Patrick, you feeling poorly?" Anne fretted with eyes on my flushed appearance.

"I'm just tired. Long day, long bloody day," I said weakly, while my arm propped up a heavy head, and my fork picked at food, until a cough came on.

"You're welcome to leave the table if you're not hungry," Sean suggested.

"Thank you. I believe that time had come," I said, grabbing my dirty dishes.

"Leave your plate. I'll take care of it," Anne smiled.

"You've probably caught a chill," Joseph diagnosed. "I'll bring over some of my special tea, tomorrow. It'll fade away in no time. Just make sure to get plenty of rest and liquids."

"With this slave driver," I uttered, pointing to Sean. "That's highly unlikely."

****

The temperature plummeted during the night. I was too tired to keep the fire going, and by morning, the water in my glass had completely frozen.

The frigid room was an instant motivator to get myself dressed quickly. Buttoning up my long coat, I sauntered over to Screeches, half expecting him to be as rigid and cold as a block of ice.

He wasn't. He was proudly walking through the pasture, palpably unaffected by the deep freeze. How unfortunate.

I saw the fence, only halfway completed, and felt a twinge of guilt. It was my big mouth that made it such a big shucking job, so I better get my shucking hands moving regardless of the temperature. I was not in a good shucking mood this morning.

When I came back from the forest, dragging a limbless tree, I was called in for breakfast, but waved it off.

Sean appeared minutes later. "If it gets any colder, we call it quits for the day."

I didn't notice that he gave me a lingering look, and didn't realize that he paid attention to how hard I worked.

By mid afternoon, I was coughing, but pushed on.

It wasn't until the sun had disappeared behind the mountains that I retreated to my cold, little bunkhouse.

A roaring fire soon warmed the place and eased the chills that lifted every hair on my body. There was a knock on the door while I was kneeling and tending more wood to it.

"Come in."

Sean walked in carrying food. "Brought you some soup and biscuits."

"Thank you," I said, approaching the table.

"If you need anything else, just let me know."

He passed the desk and picked up Dickens 'Great Expectations'. "Have you read this book?"
I glanced over, sniffling, "Haven't had time, yet."
Sean nodded. "Night, Patrick."
"Night. Thank you."

****

As the hours of the days ticked away, extremely cold weather persisted. Dull grey sky lingered and offering nothing to enliven my gloomy mood. The cough persisted, so I was quite pleased that Sean and I worked in silence. With no desire to talk, I was taken by total surprise when he asked to hear a joke.

I halted the teeth of my saw, my mouth agape, trying to think of one.

"You don't seem too impressed with my horse jokes, so I'll tell an Irish joke." I took the deepest breath my lungs would allow of bitter wintry air. "Two Irish lads had been out living in sin with their lady friends." I put a deep emphasis on the word 'sin', hoping the word would sink in to his arrogant, fat head.

"One felt guilty and decided he should go to church and confess. He went to the Priest and said 'Father I've sinned. I've committed fornication with a lady. Please forgive me.' The Priest said 'Tell me who the lady was.' The lad said he couldn't do that, and the Father said he couldn't forgive him unless he did. 'Was it Shannon O'Malley?' asked the Priest.' The lad replied 'No.' The venerable man asked 'Maggie Kelly?' Again 'No' was the response. 'Was it the red-headed wench, Rosie O'Donnell?' The lad said 'No.'

I coughed and unwittingly spit out mucus. "Where was I, oh…'Well then' said the father 'you'll not be forgiven.' When the lad met his friend outside, he asked if he had been forgiven. He said 'No, but I picked up three good prospects'!"

Sean laughed, and that was the first time I saw his full grinned laugh.

I picked up the tree and pulled it, coughing.

Sean snatched it away and recommended I see the Doctor.

I said I'd take it into consideration, though I felt I just needed a rest, shuffling to my bunkhouse. I forced myself to light up one of those thin cigarettes. Whatever leaves Strong Bull lined the paper with did the trick.

Taking in deep puffs, the hacking subsided while I flipped through my journal to find two blank pages remaining. It was obvious I ripped out too many for morning squatting rituals while in the Plains, the torn edges still wedged in the spine.

Sean rapped at the door and asked if I wanted to go to the mercantile to pick up supplies. I felt some foolish sense of obligation, but also felt confident the lingering effects of the smoke would keep the cough at bay.

"I'll just saddle Taffy."

"No need. I have the horses hitched to the wagon and ready to go." He eyed the lit cigarette. "Better put that thing out before you leave."

I nodded, pondering whether to bring it, but extinguished it, shoving it back into the drawer.

I climbed onto the seat and was the closest I'd ever been to him. Despite my woolen hat and mitts, the cold bit right through the woven fabrics.

We remained relatively quiet amid the swirling wind and light snowfall that dusted our coats.

"So…..ah, how many people live in this area?" I asked, my breath puffing out in small clouds.

"Let's see."

Sean seemed to be making a mental calculation.

"Twenty-four, now that Mrs. Rowe has had her second child. Oh, and I can't forget you. That makes twenty-five people."

"Wow! I think small is too big a word to describe this place," I spoke frankly.

Sean laughed unexpectedly.

I laughed, too, and that was my fatal downfall. The cough returned with a vengeance, and of course after every cough came the wheezing, which became more pronounced as the cough persisted.

By the time we arrived at the main street, Sean had me walking along a covered porch of a white building and into a stranger's home.

"Patrick, I'd like you to meet Doc. Andrews."

Doctor Andrews was washing his hands when he turned and looked curiously at me.

"Hello," I said hoarsely as the cough subsided.

"I'll be back real soon," Sean spoke speedily and exited, slamming the door.

"What can I do for you, Patrick?"

I took too long to answer.

"How long have you had that cough?"

Looking at the stout, middle-aged man with round spectacles, I said carefully, "Oh, about a week. I see you're really busy," I said, spinning around, "so I'll just…"

"I'm not busy. My last patient was two days ago. Please come and have a seat," he said, padding his examination table.

I hesitantly removed my outerwear and draped it over the table.

He asked me to take off my sweater and unbutton my shirt even though I gave him a good medical diagnosis and didn't feel I needed any further examination.

He listened to my chest with his cold metal tools and felt my forehead.

I glanced out the window. "You have a nice view of that…that…."

The Doctor turned. "That hill. Could you just be silent a moment and take a deep breath?"

I unhappily nodded. He didn't need any stethoscope to hear the wheezing, though. It seemed to permeate the quiet room.

"I just want to listen to your back," he said, walking around the table.

"Shuck," I said under my breath, however doctors rarely commented on my scars. I assumed it was because they couldn't do anything about them anymore.

He pulled up my shirt, and a moment's silence filled the doctor's quarters. "Can you breath deeply again and try to give me a little cough. I don't have any patients waiting so take your time," he spoke gently.

I coughed, and it became uncontrollable.

He patted my back and returned to face me rather solemnly. "You have a cough all right, and you're wheezing. You ever do that before?"

What was the point in lying? "Yep."

"Well then, you know how important it is to take it easy over the next week and stay warm."

He handed me a cough syrup with laudanum.

"Come back in a week or sooner if things get worse."

I peered up from buttoning my shirt, nodding.

"By the way," he continued.

I waited.

"Do you have anything else to take if your asthma gets worse?"

"Yep," I said, staring blankly out that window, again.

"Good. Get Anne to make you soup, and you'll be better in no time."

I grabbed the cough syrup and offered money.

He refused, advising he'd see me again soon.

I muttered, "Not if I have anything to say about it."

As I was fleeing his porch, he yelled, "Tell Sean, doctor's orders are that he do the heavy lifting!"

While I was swigging the cough syrup, Sean was found sitting atop the wagon waiting patiently.

"Where are the supplies?" I asked.

"Delayed due to the storm. I'll return tomorrow," he said casually. "What did Doc say?"

"Nothing a little sleep and this cough syrup can't cure."

"Good 'cause I have a fence to be built and prefer not to do it alone."

As I climbed onto the seat, I wondered whether Sean was just lazy and needed the extra help, or whether he liked having my around. I didn't read too much into his words….was too worried about getting home still capable of breathing normally.

That night, I may have taken more than the prescribed dosage of the syrup, for I had the weirdest dream. I was cooking a pile of snakes, and they kept slithering up the sides of the pot. At least the cough didn't bother me, anymore.

Chapter 5

In the following days, the thermometer had a respite from temperatures in the negative digits. Even though the pale sun was too distant to emit any real warmth, it did cheer up my tired and gloomy disposition.

I felt stronger despite that the cough lingered. Screeches continued to wake me; however, he was now free to roam anywhere he pleased. I wondered why he didn't just wander to the house.

One morning, I tossed him on the house porch; but Anne and Sean were already awake, their voices louder than usual. I knocked, but nobody answered. After a few moments, I slowly peaked in to witness them shouting at each other.

I was ready to retreat when Anne motioned to sit down, my breakfast already on the table. I assumed Sean had gotten up on the wrong side of the bed. Well, it seemed that Sean wasn't in the bed. He'd been forced to sleep in the barn after Anne kicked him out on account of his snoring, which I found out got worse after he drank.

"Maybe I'd be in a better mood if I didn't have to sleep on a hard bale of hay!" he griped bitterly.

"So I should suffer a sleepless night?" Anne snapped. "Your snoring sounded like a fretful pig. I almost used my rifle to put me out of my misery!"

"My pistol would have had better aim at such close range!"

I didn't care for that comment towards Anne.

"You're not making any sense," I hissed at Sean.

They stared at me with great surprise.

"I mean, what do you think…..is our most important sense?" I was scrambling for something to divert their attention away from me and each other.

"Right now," Sean replied, "you're not making any sense!"

He glared at Anne, fork pointed, when I interrupted, "Most important sense? You know, sight, sound, taste, touch or smell, which is it?"

"I'd say it's sight!" he bellowed scathingly. "Without it, I wouldn't know where to point my fork, would I?"

Anne took more time to answer. "Most important sense. That's a tough one."

As she pondered the question, I gobbled my oatmeal with overloaded spoonfuls. Grandpa would have been impressed by my fast and focused pace. I didn't even chew.

"My father lost his sense of taste once," she spoke reminiscently. "Said it was the worst thing he'd ever experienced. Of course, that was prior to getting tuberculosis, which turned out to be the last thing he'd ever experience. Anyway, he didn't feel like eating because everything had no taste to it."

Sean turned away, mumbling that he didn't have to imagine it…that half the stuff she cooked had very little taste to it.

Anne didn't appear to have heard him, focusing on me. "What do you think, Patrick?"

My eyes peered up, oatmeal finished, fruit finished, toast finished. "I would love to stay and discuss this topic but I've got a fence to finish building." And with those words, I abruptly left the two of them to finish their breakfast. At least I left them in a passive state. Sean's fork no longer ready and aimed at Anne's torso.

"See you out there, Sean," I said, putting my bowl in the dry sink and scurrying out the door.

The rest of the day remained relatively peaceful. The only sounds to be heard were the rasping of saws and hammering in nails throughout the sedentary pasture.

When the fair sun began to fade, I was bushed and still uncomfortably short of breath, despite not having to use it in polite conversation.

As Sean was putting the tools away, he mentioned we were invited to supper at Doc's. I wearily declined, opting to stay home and rest.

He offered to bring more of Anne's soup before leaving the farm.

After their departure, I went to the barn. A strong, northerly wind was blowing across the fields, sending the temperature plummeting again, so I blanketed Taffy. I touched her velvety soft nose with raw fingers and offered a handful of oats when an elderly man appeared.

"Sean Thomas!" he called out.

"No, I'm Patrick Sullivan," I said, walking toward him, extending my hand.

"I'm Jim Phillips. Live about five miles east of here. I seemed to have lost some of my cattle and Sean helps me retrieve them from time to time. My eyesight's failed these past few years."

I studied the elderly man, who truly looked older than Sean's horse, and offered my help.

He smiled appreciatively as I saddled and bridled Taffy.

"Boy, you sure do look like Sean Thomas," he said, as we rode along.

I smiled and couldn't resist. "Am I as friendly as Sean Thomas?"

"Anybody help a neighbour out is friendly in my books. Now, my cows have bells on them, and they could be scattered a mile from the property."

I thought it was just like being home, looking for Mrs. Talbot's lost herd except I didn't remember it ever being this frigidly gusty.

We passed Doc's house, and I regretted not accepting the invitation to supper.

Anne and Sean were enjoying a nice roasted beef supper, seated across from Doctor Andrews and his wife, Louisa.

"I say, Sean, you have a strong, nice mannered young man working the property," Doc spoke heartily.

"He's a hard worker, too!" Sean exclaimed. "Puts me to shame, I dare say."

His words softened Anne's heart.

"I hope he's not been working too hard," the doctor said. "I told him to take it easy over the next few days. He was wheezing when he came to me, and that can be a sign of trouble if not well taken care of."

"I didn't know that," Sean's voice denoted concern. "He never mentioned it to me. I'll be sure to…ah…to make sure Patrick gets plenty of rest."

"Is he still coughing?"

"Yes, he is."

"Then have him come to me, tomorrow. People with his particular malady are more susceptible to bronchitis and pneumonia when they're sick."

Recognizing the paternal angst in Sean's face, Anne's growing love for him was marred by the worry over Patrick's condition.

I was still searching for Jim's cows when the moon disappeared behind a veil of clouds, shrouding me in darkness. As I brought in another cow, I prayed that was the last of the lost herd.

"Mr. Phillips, are there any more out there?" I asked as my heavy breath formed white clouds.

"I believe there's one more missing but don't bother. It's getting too cold....too dark."

"I'll look by the river," I foolishly offered while rubbing my hands back to vigour.

I was always good at retrieving stray cows, never giving up until they were all found. It was like finding a needle in a haystack and I was good at finding them needles. I wasn't so good at listening to my lungs struggling for air. Moving toward the river, I found the crazy bovine idling by the water's edge away from his warm barn. After forcing stiff fingers to lasso the cow, I proceeded back to the Phillips farm.

Jim was very appreciative, offering warmth in his cabin.

"I think I best get home, Mr. Phillips. May I ask how old you are?" My teeth chattered and bones shook.

"I'm eighty-six years old and call me, Jim," he smiled sprightly.

I felt his senior as an uncontrollable hacking fit hit hard.

He took me by the shoulders despite his dotage and strongly guided me to the log cabin.

"You've got quite a cough."

"Comes and goes," I said hoarsely. "Could I have a cup of coffee?"

He spared little time in bringing me a mug of the steaming, black liquid. Moving to the hearth, he stoked the burning logs.

As the coughing subsided, I asked him how long he'd lived here.

"I've been here thirty years. Came after my wife died," he informed. "There was nothing here but some Indians scattered here and there. My vision started failing a few years ago, making it hard to search out my cows, hence the bells."

"Would you ever consider parting with a few of those cows? Be fewer to round up?"

"I could be convinced, especially if it were for such good neighbours like you."

"I was thinking…we fence in your pasture, and you give us a few cows," I bartered boldly.

"I think that could be arranged, Patrick. You're more than welcome to stay the night."

"Thank you kindly, but I think I should get home. Appreciate the coffee," I smiled warmly

"Take this scarf," he offered, pulling it from a hook off the wall.

"Thank you. Night, Jim."

Spurring Taffy into a gallop, she brought me to the Taylor farm in little time, where Sean stood under flickering light on my porch.

"Where've you been?" he snapped truculently.

I pulled the scarf from my face. "Phillips ranch, wrangling cows. Why?"

"Just think it's a bad night for you to be out…."

"Thank you for your concern," I interrupted churlishly. "Good night!"

I walked guardedly to the barn, avoiding his glare. He didn't have the right to lash out, me being a hired hand and all.

With mechanical hands, Taffy was unsaddled and unbridled. Then I made slow and heavy steps to an empty porch, despite that I expected a pouncing from the dark abyss onto my weary shoulders. However, all Sean left behind was a roaring fire that warmed my small room. I watched unblinkingly as the flames danced and crackled.

There was nothing left in me to remove my clothes. Popping the cork of the medicine bottle, I chugged back an ample dose and lay atop the bed. I prayed for restful sleep and was so blessed that it came so willingly. Even the soft mumbles of distant voices weren't going to keep me awake.

When Sean slammed the door of the house, Anne peered over her glasses with concern. "Is Patrick not home yet?"

Sean paced the small kitchen with hands on his hips.

"No, he's home!" he growled. "Damn fool's home! You know, he doesn't have an ounce of common sense in his brain! No, not a bit!"

Anne returned to her knitting.

"What are you doing? Why are you knitting so late?"

Eyes squinting, she didn't peer up, desperate to pull her needle through the small loop in such dim light.

"It helps to ease the worry when I do something," she paused. "I'm making a soft hat for Patrick to put under his wool one. He's been scratching his forehead red."

Sean grunted out a "Hmm" while reaching for a glass and bottle of whisky. "This is what eases my worry. Maybe if I have some of this I won't be so interested in stomping over to that cabin and clobbering some since into the kid!"

"Your son, Sean," she reminded softly. "Your son. And the only thing you're going to get from that bottle is a nasty headache. Why don't you talk to him? Tell him...."

"Tell him what, Anne? He doesn't need someone like me in his life! I have nothing to give him!" he roared, driving a whisky shot down his parched throat. "No home, no money, and no fatherly advice, except to say that he's crazy for risking his life for someone else's cows!"

"Why don't you tell him you're his father, you care for him, and don't want to see him...you don't want to see him get sick?"

"I don't feel like his father. I'm not his father!" he cried vehemently with hands gripping the table. Snatching the bottle, he spun around, blasting, "Going to the barn! I'll save you the trouble of kicking me out of bed!"

Anne tossed her knitting and glasses aside, scrounged for the warmest blankets, and made quick tracks to the barn, eager to stop the man she loved from turning into a frozen cadaver.

****

The sun peaked through the curtains of the bunkhouse, and for the first time in many mornings, I could see everything in the room. Glancing at my watch, I was surprised to find it past ten o'clock. As I raced to the barn, Sean motioned me in for breakfast.

"Sorry I slept in."

He politely held the door open as I brought in a chilly gust of air.

"Morning, Patrick," Anne said while placing fried potatoes and ham on the table.

I peeled off my coat and sat across from Sean.

"I didn't hear Screeches, this morning. Hope he's fine," I lied.

"He probably froze to death," Sean alleged heartlessly, while stabbing at a piece of pork. "Or maybe, just maybe, he was smart enough to take shelter in the barn and stay inside like any other wise being would do!"

I hastily devoured my breakfast, eager to be away from his livid glare.

Anne scrapped more potatoes and ham on my plate.

"Anne, I have to get to work on that fence."

"Not today," Sean replied curtly.

"Why not?" I asked curiously.

"It's the lady's farm. It's the lady's decision," he said, nodding to Anne.

"It's too cold outside, Patrick," she said matter-of-factly.

"Then I'll just go to the mercantile. I have a…"

"Patrick, you see that bare wall in the room behind you? I would like you to build two shelves to house my books that have been sitting in a box for a year now. You'll find planks of wood in the barn."

"Fine. I'll get started right after breakfast."

Anne smiled, seeming happy I'd be indoors.

I would make and mount two neatly cut bookshelves and also be tasked with placing her sizable assortment of books along the shelves.

"Anne!" I called while perusing the collection.

She walked over and sat on the edge of the bed.

"Would you like me to add these to the shelves?" I inquired, cupping three carved wooden horses in my hand.

Anne took one and traced the tip of her slender finger along its smoothed edges. "I've never seen these before. Must be Sean's. I wonder why he'd carve these toys."

I shrugged my shoulders, offering, "Something to do during a grueling, interminable winter. Could I take two of these books?"

"Why don't you take them and read them in your room for the rest of the day," she recommended kindly.

"You're making me feel like an eight year old child," I smiled.

"Then stop acting like one and take care of yourself. I've had too many in my family die from pneumonia to stand around and watch it happen again," she spoke crisply. "Be back here by six o'clock for supper."

I nodded to her motherly gaze.

****

Weeks went by, and the winter season slowly faded into spring. Work on the fence came to an end at a perfect time for the fields to be ploughed and prepared for planting. The cough and persistent wheezing finally subsided thanks to Joseph's tea, Anne's constant pressure to stay indoors, and those Chinooks that thawed us from the deep freeze.

I read most of the books on Anne's shelf and was heading to the house for Sunday supper with two of them in hand.

Everyone was already seated at the table when I entered the warm kitchen.

"Evening, Patrick," Joseph said with a smile.

"Evening everyone," I replied, tucking the books with the others.

"Patrick's read every book on that shelf," Sean informed with raised eyebrows.

"Well, not every book," I said honestly. "I didn't read 'Scarlett Letter'."

"Why not?"

"I wasn't interested in that story. It's seems kind of depressing. I'm much more interested in adventure stories like Moby Dick, 20,000 Leagues Under the Sea, Tom Sawyer or," I mumbled, "Through the Looking Glass."

Sean was puzzled. "I know nothing about that book."

"I like it because it has imagery and odd poetry."

"It's a popular children's book," Anne exclaimed. "I like it because it has portmanteaus."

A huge smile lit up my face. "You know about portmanteaus?"

"Of course I do."

She informed Joseph and Sean that it was when two words were put together to make a new word. "Let me think up one, now." Taking a moment, she blurted out, "Frable."

"Spexcellent," I replied.

Sean watched as Anne and I took turns mouthing out these outlandish words, leaving him in utter confusion. The final straw was when she affectionately touched my hand, holding her gaze on me a little too long.

"Knock it off!" Sean cried loudly.

We quickly turned with faces of bafflement.

"I think somebody's flurious," Joseph said with glee.

That brought laughter from everybody but Sean.

"I knew a man who brought his dog into the saloon," he spat out wildly. "Well one day this man got drunk and angry, and kicked his dog halfway across the room. Everybody in the bar laughed or carried on, but I couldn't do it, so I shot that man. Had to do it! Couldn't stand seeing a defenseless creature being hurt so wickedly!"

"I don't understand," Anne uttered in confusion.

"I guess I'm just not a lighthearted person. I've had a lot to deal with!" he spoke grumpily.

I snatched the bowl of potatoes, scooping copious amounts onto my plate in a nervous reaction.

"You hungry, Patrick?" Joseph asked.

"Guess so. I'm planning on breaking mustangs north of here, tomorrow," I said anxiously. "Just want to fill my stomach. It'll probably be a long day."

I stared at my plate; however, the silent tension remained in the room, so heavy it could physically be cut with a knife.

"I have a joke," I mumbled hesitantly. "Unless someone else has one."

"Let's hear it," Joseph voiced with optimism.

"A cowboy goes into a bar, has a beer, walks outside and finds his horse has been stolen. He walks back into the bar, firing his gun through the ceiling." Taking a mouthful of potatoes, I hastily swallowed. "He calls out to everyone asking who stole his horse. No one answers. He says he's gonna have one more beer, and if his horse ain't outside by the time he's finished, he's gonna do what he dun in Virginia City. He drinks another beer, walks outside and his horse is back. So he gets on it and is ready to ride out of town when the bartender walks out and asks, 'what happened in Virginia City?' The cowboy turns and says 'he had to bloody walk home'."

I got a soft chuckle from Joseph, but Anne and Sean looked like somebody had just died.

Sean spoke ominously through a grimacing face, "Why Virginia City, Patrick?"

My cheeks went scarlet, the silent tension returned almost stifling me, and to make matters worse, I still had a mound of mashed potatoes on my plate to wolf down.

Joseph thankfully broke the silence, but not before his head wagged from me to Sean, followed by a peculiar grin like he'd just discovered the magic herb to cure all that ails, despite that it was under his nose the entire time. "I've heard that joke before, and it was Virginia City."

"Oh, you heard that joke amongst your Indian friends," Sean sneered scornfully.

"I have other white friends," Joseph retorted heatedly, "though, they're not quite as colourful as you!"

I was shoveling potatoes in my mouth by the forkfuls so much they got painfully lodged in my throat. They were either going to come back up or be pushed down by gravity, so I forced a glass full of water down my gullet. Thankfully all eyes were downcast as I winced in great pain. Reaching for the gravy, I coated the rest of the dried potatoes and stuffed them in a mouth desperate to leave this Sunday night's table.

I avoided Sean for the rest of the meal, though I couldn't avoid him when he knocked on my door later that evening.

"Come in," I said, still atop the bed.

"Patrick," he began while closing the door. "You plan on being armed tomorrow?"

Stopping the whetstone against the sharpened tip, I answered him, "Thought I'd bring back a rabbit or turkey for supper."

"Why are the feathers white on that arrow and black on the rest?"

I held up the arrow. "This tip's been tainted. Figured if I met up with a grizzly bear, I might need a little something extra; however, it's doubtful I have enough poison to do any real damage. Just wouldn't lick it," I said simply.

Sean nodded in agreement. "Listen, I overreacted at supper and wanted to apologize."

I nodded, shrugging my shoulders. "It's just silly talk about silly words and jokes."

"Well, maybe you can teach me more about them tomorrow when we go north. I'd like to see you break horses."

Raising eyebrows, I couldn't hide my gladdened demeanor. "I'll see you in the morning, then."

"Night, Patrick."

After Sean departed, the whetstone resumed its duty while I thought about how angry he would be if he ever found out about my past. I shook my head, believing it best to let sleeping dogs lie and go to my grave with that information kept to myself.

Chapter 6

When Sean and I arrived at Springridge Ranch, we were approached by Dexter Franklin, who seemed to be my age despite a prominent limp. He gingerly walked us to the corral where Clarence Dooley and the lead ranch hand, Samuel Bickford, were carrying on a heated conversation.

"Dexter, go with Clarence and get the black stud," Samuel commanded.

Dexter glimpsed his short and wiry friend turning away with cheeks still red from Samuel's scolding tone.

"Go on now!" Samuel bellowed. "Don't make me ring your ears, too!"

I couldn't deny how uneasy the two men appeared as they walked behind the barn.

When they returned, I could see why. This mustang was already rearing and stomping heavy hooves as he was forced into the corral.

"Welcome to Springridge Ranch," Samuel said, attempting to break my attention from the fretting horse. The white haired man had a confident, cocky smile when he firmly shook my hand. "That there on the right of the horse is Clarence, and you've already met Dexter."

"This is Sean Thomas, he's …he's a friend," I said.

Sean nodded with his usual grimness; however, he soon was distracted when the mustang fitfully rammed the fence.

"So, you think you can break this stud 'cause we get horses like this all the time?" Samuel jeered.

"Can you give me a few minutes?"

Samuel shrugged his shoulders. "If that's what you need, however I'm not standing here all day."

I climbed the six foot fence and leaned my arms onto the rail. Observing the high-spirited horse, frisky was too tame a word to describe him.

"What are you thinking, Patrick?" Sean asked as he joined me.

With eyes planted on the horse, I said, "He's angry."

"How can you tell?" he asked with a hint of sarcasm.

"Well, when he stops charging, you can see his ears pinned right back. The tail's also whipping frantically from side to side. His whinnying is aggressive, coming out sounding like grunting noises. And if you look closely enough, you can see rage in his eyes."

"You ever break an angry horse."

"I'd prefer not to. My pa said some horses just cannot be broken and this might be one of them. Either way, it'll take more than a day to break this stud."

"Well, Mr. Sullivan, your five minutes are up! What I'll it be?" Samuel bellowed.

I climbed down and took my lariat in hand.

"You don't have to do this, Patrick," Sean exhorted. "Just walk away."

I thought it peculiar advice considering it was coming from his mouth and continued marching to the corral.

As soon as that pugnacious stud saw me, his head, held wildly high, was masked in fury: nostrils flared, lips tightened, teeth exposed. As I inched closer, he reared, his front hooves driving up dirt as he whinnied. I waited until he was loping before my loop whirled in the air; however, he remained too erratic, too unpredictable.

He collided with the wooden rails again, one finally splitting, dangling loosely. He didn't want to be in the corral and neither did I.

"Son, you want us to put him on the ground for you?" Samuel spat out.

I attempted to swing my rope a few times but the mustang was too out of control.

Samuel scoffed, "Where I come from, my rope actually reaches the horse's neck!"

I blasted a frown Samuel's way until Sean yelped, "Look out!"

The crazy mustang came thundering at me. I jumped by the skin of my teeth, landing on the unforgiving ground. Never have I moved out of a horse's way so fast and continued to move right out of the corral.

"Clarence, Dexter, get in there and show Montana boy how it's done!" Samuel waved them in with a tenacious arm.

I was embarrassed. If I had a tail it would have been between my legs. I had never seen such a loathsome, mean-spirited mustang.

"Patrick, let's get out of here!" Sean demanded.

The black horse was chased into a corner. Clarence's lariat slithered across the ground, snagging forelegs and sending swells of dust to envelop his fallen ebony torso. Dexter deftly tied the rope to a hind leg.

I was grudgingly shaking dirt from my chaps when the stud was standing and being saddled by Clarence. The horse was hobbled, head forced in, unable to move; but once he was free, Clarence would be tossed around like a rag doll.

"You should stick around Montana boy! Find out what's it's really like to break horses!" Samuel hissed.

"Let's go, Patrick," Sean repeated.

I hesitantly followed but couldn't resist a last glance.

Clarence mounted the black stud, and the ropes were untied.

Almost immediately, the horse started bucking and jolting. The thin man was being corkscrewed and twirled so much I thought he'd be broken in two. That horse kicked, and kicked again; however, Clarence bravely hung on. It must have been a rough ten seconds before he was dusted by one of the stud's double kicks.

"Get up, Clarence!" Dexter hollered.

A sick feeling overwhelmed me when horse hooves cruelly pounced on Clarence's back.

Instinctively, I ran into the corral and cracked my whip repeatedly against the hard ground. The horse folded up and bolted into the wooden fence, snapping more rails before thunderously stomping the ground again.

"Clarence!" I called, stirring him to move.

I could hear Sean cursing at Samuel to get in the corral to fight off his horse, then Samuel telling Sean to drop dead.

Sean rushed to his horse and took the rifle from its scabbard. If anybody was going to drop dead, it would be Samuel Bickford.

Dexter wobbled into the corral and wobbled right back out, slamming the gate just before the black mustang lunged at him.

The stud was tearing all over the corral while I wrestled with Clarence's inert body, squinting through surging brown clouds. By the time I was ready to make for the gate, it was too late. That black wrath charged at us, I covered Clarence, and a single shot rang out.

Everything went quiet.

When I looked up, the horse was dead and Sean was lowering his gun. Dexter opened the gate and told me to go quickly.

Samuel charged at Sean, screaming about having to pay for the dead horse.

Sean roared at Samuel, calling him a coward.

Samuel tried to reply, but not before the end of Sean's rifle whacked him in the head.

I speedily ran over. "Sean, let's skedaddle."

"Is it time to go now, Patrick!" he snapped.

"Yes, it's time," I said while Samuel shook his head, trying to get vertical.

As we walked briskly to our horses, I looked appreciatively at Sean through gritty eyes.

"I'll never question your skill with a gun again. You were dead on."

As our horses trotted away from the corral, he asked, "How many ranches you lived on?"

"One," I answered plainly, spitting out dirt that crunched between my teeth.

"Well, I guess not everybody breaks horses like they do on your one particular ranch. Remember that!" he said wryly.

I nodded.

We rode home in silence most of the way. At one point I though we should hunt something for supper, asking, "Do you think we should…"

"Nope," he cut in rather crisply.

I figured I could go meatless this Monday.

****

Sean sauntered into the kitchen to find Anne kneading dough on the kitchen table. Strong arms hugged her tightly as his lips kissed the soft nape of her neck.

"You keep doing that and we won't have pie tonight," she warned softly.

"I'd gladly give up pie for something sweeter," he coaxed with a deep velvety voice. "Are we alone? I haven't seen the kid for a while."

Anne turned with floured hands. "He's gone rabbit hunting. Said he'd be back this afternoon," she smiled provocatively. "Let me wipe my hands so I can work you all over."

"I can live with the flour," he asserted, scooping her up.

She was laughing at his impetuousness when he tossed her on the bed.

He fervently pulled suspenders away as his lips tasted the sweetness of hers.

She placed floured hands into his thinning hair until her dress was effortlessly hoisted over slim shoulders.

Yanking his shirt and pants off too heatedly, buttons popped off and would have to be mended.

Breathless, he hesitated at the sight of her white skin against the soft cotton undergarments. His fingers did a sensual dance journeying from corseted breasts, to soft stomach, to lean legs.

Anne arched her back at the arousal of his touch, so uninhibited for a man so aloof at times, and yet so gentle for a man so violent at times, that she shuddered.

But she knew the heart of this man. And she knew she would forever be safe and warm in his arms, when he wasn't cuddling with a loaded bottle of whisky.

With bodies soon entwined, their lovemaking was full of tender caresses.

Laying in each others arms, Sean was twisting a finger around a curl of her long golden hair when he remarked, "You know, Anne....I will miss that pie."

Anne lightly smacked him with her hand, long since de-floured.

While the pie was baking in the oven, Sean entered the kitchen with a look of concern. "How long does it take to hunt a few rabbits? Joseph will be here soon."

"He said he was going to the mercantile afterwards. Maybe he got held up with Sam Tracey." She looked up from chopping onions. "You may want to wipe your hair. It's clumpy and white in parts," she bashfully admitted with a hint of amusement.

"I swear Anne, I'm gonna put a cow bell around his neck one of these days," he exclaimed, walking out the door.

It was already mid-afternoon when I arrived with four black tailed jackrabbits and proceeded directly to Mr. Chan. He gladly took two, grinning and pushing me toward his steel tub again. For a small Chinese man, he was very strong and nimble.

"Not today, Mr. Chan. Don't have time but will return tomorrow," I spoke slowly, but he was still working the coat off of my shoulders.

Lilly appeared in the nick of time.

"My father says thank you for the rabbits and wants to see you clean, soon," Lilly translated with a smile.

"Your welcome, Mr. Chan. You will see me tomorrow," I said, waving goodbye.

I ran into the mercantile and hastily placed my letter on the counter.

"Good day, Patrick! Any candy for you?" Sam asked with raised brows. "I now have taffy."

"Another time, Sam. I've been putting on the pounds now that Ms. Anne sees it necessary to feed me three meals a day, not that I mind."

As I turned to leave, he clasped my arm with ominous eyes. "Pass on a message to Sean for me?"

"Yes," I replied warily.

"A man was asking for him. Could be a lawman. I didn't like his tone so I sent him another direction."

"What did he look like?"

"He had a knife scar under his left eye and was limping quite heavily."

A shiver ran down my spine. "Which way'd you send him?"

"Southeast to Lethbridge," he divulged. "Said that was where all the outlaws evade capture. I hope he'll head that way and just give up, go home."

I nodded, my head filled with uneasiness as I ambled to the covered porch.

While mounting Taffy, I toiled with whether to go back to the farm. By notifying Sean, I figured he'd likely go after O'Flaherty and either get shot or shoot him. Neither scenario sat well with me, so I thought it a good idea to ensure O'Flaherty was gone for good. Lilly waved my direction, however I was too focused on how to handle this lawman if we were to meet face to face.

Mr. Phillip's farm came into view and I headed up his passageway. The brown and white patched hound dog started his barking until Jim saw it was me.

He stopped peeling potatoes and peered up with a friendly smile.

"Mr. Phillips!" I called.

"Patrick, please call me Jim," he said as the russet skin began to curl away from its marrow again, finally falling with the dog's eyes following while his tail thumped against the planked porch.

"Jim, did you see or hear anyone come past your farm?"

His head shook while his lips formed a straight line. "No, I've been here a while working away at these taters for a warm soup. Monty hasn't stirred, either. Would you like some coffee, Patrick?"

"No, thank you. How would you like a rabbit to go with that soup?"

"Thank you kindly. You looking for someone?"

"A man came by the mercantile searching for Sean," I replied. "Just thought I'd find out who he was."

Jim stopped his peeling to look sternly my way. "Go home, Patrick."

I smiled awkwardly and waved goodbye.

As I moved westward, my body led the horse home; but my mind somehow angled the reins into the thickly wooded forest and the bank of the river. I considered hunting for another rabbit while Taffy drank from the clear waters.

It was eerily quiet as my eyes scanned the still trees and small, empty spaces for any sign of O'Flaherty. An eagle stretched his wings against the deep blue sky while the sun's descent coaxed me to glance at my pocket watch.

"We've got to make quick tracks, Taffy, or it will be my hide for supper. One rabbit will have to do."

Cautiously maneuvering Taffy around tall evergreens and cottonwoods, my trail unexpectedly ran into a dark suited man on his horse.

"Afternoon," Frank O'Flaherty spoke deeply.

"Afternoon," I replied as calmly as possible.

"I'm looking for someone, name's Sean Thomas."

I kept a straight face. "Name's not familiar."

He paused, tilting his head. "Do I know you?"

"No I…I don't suppose. Don't stray far from my home."

His probing eyes worried me until he said quite surprisingly, "Good day."

I smiled, tipping my hat.

As the horse turned and meandered away, I heard O'Flaherty mutter, "Virginia City boy."

Just as the words finished echoing throughout the dense forest, his horse spun around, pistol raised. There was a whizz, then another, and another. Four shots were fired, scattering the birds, silencing the trees, until….

My bow was falling to the ground as Taffy reared, screaming. Desperate to hold on, my left arm dangled from a bullet to the shoulder as her body fell, crashing thunderously to the ground, trapping my leg.

"No!" I screamed, her full weight snapping a bone. With head tossing fretfully, her barrel shook unnaturally over my crushed leg, sending shooting pains throughout my entire body.

"Taffy, get up!" I cried, trying to pull her away. My chest tightened and I squeezed my eyes shut, willing it to subside. "Not now," I pleaded, "not now!"

Frank approached, pistol still hoisted, ready to fire. "How the hell'd you get me with one of your arrows?" he charged bitterly.

I opened my eyes to see the white feathers, stark against an ebony vest, jutting from his abdomen.

"I should put a bullet in your head you lying son of a bitch, but I won't. It'd be a waste of ammunition. You're already turning blue," he sneered. "I will, however, do it for your horse," he declared before the round slug plunged into Taffy's body, silencing her raging cries.

"I forgive you," I gasped.

"Don't waste your breath, kid! Looks like you need every bit of it!"

As the sound of horse's hooves faded away, so sealed was my fate. Tears stung my eyes as I grasped at the ground. Handfuls of dried needles pierced my palms as I tried not to panic, willing my mind to take me somewhere else; where the air was easy to breathe; where I was free to move; and there was no unbearable pain. Told myself to be still, pressing my warm, bloody shoulder into the cold earth. I watched as the slivers of light came in and out from the swaying branches until I was shrouded in darkness.

****

As the golden sun sat perched atop the Rocky Mountains, Sean rode to the mercantile and tied his horse to the post. He found Rudy Smith behind the counter.

"Have you seen Patrick today?"

"No, I've only been here an hour," Rudy replied.

As silence filled the empty store, the store clerk sensed edginess in the gunslinger's demeanor and swallowed nervously, "Sam's out back. I'll get him."

Sean restlessly stepped onto the boardwalk and waved over Lilly.

She approached, smiling.

Touching her shoulder gently, he asked, "Have you seen Patrick, today?"

"He brought us some rabbits a while ago."

"Where'd he go, Lilly?"

While pointing east, Sam Tracey came barreling out the front door.

"You're searching for Patrick?" he spoke with dread.

"Where'd he go, Sam?"

"A man came looking for you. I asked Patrick to let you know."

Sean reached for his pistol and scowled. Heeling his horse into a hasty gallop, his heart filled with retribution at the thought of any harm to Patrick.

Joseph was on the porch when he stormed the house.

"What is it, Sean?"

"Patrick's in trouble," he said, stuffing bullets into the empty chambers of his colt forty-five.

"I'll go with you."

Anne watched with worried eyes as Sean and Joseph moved out of sight.

When they reached the Phillips farm, Jim was coming down the porch steps with his rifle.

"You trying to find Patrick? He went that direction," he stammered, pointing to the forest. "That's not all, Sean. I heard gunshots, four….maybe five of them. I thought maybe he went hunting for more rabbits."

"Patrick doesn't own a gun," Sean seethed.

Jim shook his head, deeply distraught.

Sean scurried to his horse, the old man quickly following.

Glancing at an anguished face, Sean spoke convincingly, "Jim, watch for Patrick from your porch. Let off a shot if you see any sign of him, hear me!"

"If you say so, Sean, but I'm here. I'm here if you need more manpower!" His words quivered desperate with emotion.

Voices emerged through the rustling of trees. I replied, but too softly, too weekly. Feeling for something to snap, I remembered my arrows. Moaning and twisting, my fingers crawled along the dried needles until I reached the smooth sticks.

Snap! I reached for another.

Horses approached.

"Patrick!" Sean cried with panic in his face.

"I'm…so…cold," I feebly trembled.

"Stay alive, Patrick. Just stay alive!"

Sean pulled back a corner of my shirt and the breeze seeped into throbbing wetness.

I saw relief in his face, which soon faded as my raspy breathing became more pronounced.

Joseph appeared, his serene face blurring and clearing, as he whispered, "Slow breaths."

Soft hands worked a woolen blanket around my heavy body.

I blinked, and he vanished.

It was taking so long, the dampness of the ground sent me shaking uncontrollably, the darkness of the night swallowing my light again.

I had no memory that my leg was trapped. Sean and Joseph were grunting and groaning as they pulled the rigid horse away.

Joseph's voice broke through my muddled mind. "We're going to take you home, Patrick. Just stay still."

I woke up on a galloping horse, and it felt like I was being split apart. My breathing went frenzied, so much so, I was panting louder than the horse.

"Patrick, just stay alive!" Sean commanded, his arms weaving around me, holding me together.

Consciousness came and went, though it was the voices that could always be heard.

It felt like I was audience to a play: Anne's doleful cries, Sean's heavy footsteps and even heavier breathing, lifting well more than he should have.

"Patrick?" he spoke rashly. "You're in your bed and Joseph's gonna make you better. Who did this to you, Patrick?"

I couldn't understand why it was so tricky to sound words, barely croaking out, "O'Flaherty…tip…white."

"Save your strength, Patrick."

"Sean, you need to get the doctor," Joseph ordered.

"I thought you could help him," Sean's voice oozed with discontent.

"We need chloroform, now Sean! Anne, bring boiling water, clean towels, scissors, extra blankets…"

I heard solemn talking, metal tools clanking, scissors cutting, water running, even though waves of darkness ebbed and flowed.

"Patrick, we're going to give you something to make you sleep," Joseph said.

My head swayed in refusal, the constant wheezing escaping my mouth the wrong answer to dissuade him.

"We have to…to control your breathing. You trust me, don't you?"

Tears rolled from my eyes as my control was given way to someone else.

"Give him my journal," I whispered hoarsely, "if I don't wake up." When I nodded, the cloth covered my face. Gripping Joseph's hand, I feared I would suffocate before falling asleep, my body going helplessly limp. It was the soft, distant sounds that put my mind at ease.

When Joseph forced Anne and Sean away, an eerie stillness filled the room despite the sounds of logs crackling in the hearth, my whistling chest, and more metal clinking against a china bowl.

"So much swelling and bruising in that leg," Doctor Andrews said. "I'd hate to have to amputate."

My mind silently screamed, *don't touch my leg!*

"We're not going to do that," Joseph averred.

The men argued over how to treat the swelling.

Doc. Andrews wanted warm compresses while Joseph wanted cold ones.

Joseph prevailed.

Joseph wanted my gunshot wound to remain open, cleaned, drained, and loosely bandaged, while Doc. Andrews wanted it stitched.

Doc Andrews prevailed.

When it came to my asthma, they differed again.

Doc. Andrews wanted to make a poultice with chloroform while Joseph wanted to make a balm with medicinal leaves, bark and roots.

I was a human experiment, and it made me feel so vulnerable, so fearful. Both did agree that my condition was grave: pulse very weak and heart beating faster that the buffalo charging the Plains.

The room became deathly silent again, except for the constant hissing as my chest rose and sank. It was Joseph's steady voice that sedated me when he began reading the Bible.

Sean paced the porch, wearing the floorboards thin as the minutes turned into an hour, maybe two. When the door finally opened, he held his breathe.

It was Doctor Andrews who approached solemnly.

"He's very weak and his breathing is.....its difficult Sean, but he's still alive. Joseph will stay with him in case he wakes, but I don't believe he will. His leg's in pretty bad shape. It's deeply swollen.....broken in at least two places."

Taking Sean's shoulder in his firm hand with soft eyes, he said, "I'm sorry. I wish it could be better news."

"I'll get Joseph some coffee," Anne said somberly.

As Sean watched the doctor depart, acrimonious contempt for O'Flaherty moved in. The kid never did an abject deed in his life and the thought of losing him like he did his father filled him with enmity.

Anne walked into the bunkhouse.

Turning, Joseph smiled sadly.

Her worry heightened when she saw how dreadfully frail I was, all of the colour drained from my youthful face except for dry burgundy lips, slightly parted as my whistling breaths escaped through them.

"Brought you some coffee," she whispered, her eyes unable to look away.

"Thank you, Anne," he said, shifting the Bible from his hands to the bed.

"Do you think that will help?"

"I think it already has. His breathing's relaxed some, so I will continue to read until Patrick says otherwise," Joseph paused. "Where's Sean?"

Anne dashed out the door but drifted in minutes later. "He's gone," she replied bleakly.

Sean was cloaked in darkness and gloomy trees as he entered the silent forest. When he reached the dead horse, he could faintly make out the bow and arrows, white feathered one missing. He hoped it was lodged into one of O'Flaherty's organs or main veins.

Continuing along a path to the river's edge, he figured the vindictive vigilante might stay near water if he was injured. His gut told him the man wouldn't go far. Patrick was just a lure.

Sean meticulously plodded through dull shadows, ears attuned to the rattling of fallen and dried leaves while eyes scoured for movements that gleamed or shined. It was well into the night when he saw O'Flaherty's horse, still bridled and saddled. Frank was leaning against a cottonwood tree, facing the black waters that shimmered under a crescent moon.

As Sean faced his foe, pistol aimed at his head, O'Flaherty snickered, "You're too late! Your son already did it!" The arrow had pierced his liver and black toxins were slowly flowing out.

"I tried to pull it out, but it's in there good," he swallowed, his pained face bringing no comfort to Sean. "I hope I'm not too late for the family reunion. Is she with you, too?"

"Who the hell are you talking about?" Sean growled.

O'Flaherty cackled, "The one you promised to reunite with at the creek. The one you vowed to come back to. Amanda Wilkes!"

His words wrenched at Sean's heart.

"Your timing of that letter was impeccable," Frank jeered, "just after the birth of that boy. It filled Henry with so much rage he paid me dearly to hunt you dead. But the most satisfying part was getting paid to protect her from you, watching her wash in that creek, skin so white, so pure; watching her laugh and read poetry under the shade of that willow tree, knowing you'd never do that again. Her skin," he recollected with garish pleasure. "It was just as soft as it appeared."

"You son of a bitch," Sean seethed, his finger pressuring the trigger.

"How many men does it take to destroy another man's life?" He replied caustically, "One! Is he dead?"

"No Frank, he'll live."

"Well, I hope he suffers 'till he meets us in hell!"

His loathsome voice forced stately trees to cower while inauspicious stars shone brightly over a pistol rising to kill.

"No Frank, he's not going to hell, but you are, now!"

The lone shot echoed across the tranquil river.

Frank's body crumpled as blood began trickling into vacant eyes.

As the seconds ticked in the silent gloom of night, Sean eyed the dead man with unrelenting malevolence, despite that relief should have prevailed. Worry for his son's condition took rampant hold. Wrapping arms around the dead man, he was set to drag when crumpled paper rolled from a gelid hand.

Sean squinted at the pale image of Mandy, the same image he saw of her years ago with her mother and father, hanging on their cabin wall. Squeezing anguish from his mind, he focused on disposing the corpse into a thicket of bushes.

After Frank's saddle, blanket, and personals were strewn over his lifeless body, his gelding was smacked into galloping away.

Mounting and spurring his own horse through the blackness, Sean's head filled with images of Mandy: her smile, her sparkling eyes and delicate touch, Frank's filthy touch on her. His stomach lurched as the flickering porch light came into sight.

With every step to the bunkhouse, he had to know, he had to find out, where she was. He had to find her.

Chapter 7

The sun was just breaking the horizon when Sean stepped into the room.

Joseph wearily turned and faced his friend. "Thank you for coming back. Did you take care of him?"

"How is he, Joseph?"

I was propped up in the bed with whatever was available…pillows, rolled up blankets. My body was bandaged, swollen, mottled purple and red in parts.

"The bullet went though his shoulder; the wound's been stitched. The condition of his leg is quite concerning," he swallowed. "It's a good thing we splinted it in the forest for the bone might have gone through the skin. I've been applying cold, wet cloths, and changing them once the heat has been absorbed. We can't apply a cast until much of the swelling is gone. It will give Doc. Andrews some time to find a firm dressing to keep the bones in place," Joseph said with a sigh.

"I want to go home and work on a balm that will help Patrick's asthma. I also have something medicinal that will help take the warmth from his leg, but he can't be left alone. If he wakes, he's to be kept still," he asserted. "Despite the splint, we don't know if all of the bones are properly in place."

"I'm not going anywhere. He's my son…I won't leave my son anymore."

Joseph nodded soberly. "Before I leave, Patrick asked me to give you his journal if he didn't wake up."

"He'll wake up, Joseph. He just needs time."

"Read to him. Let him know you're here. It seems to settle his breathing."

Sean pulled a chair closer to me as the door closed.

"Well, what would you like me to read? The Bible?" he asked in a shaky voice while leafing through the pages. "How about Dickens over there? That's one of my favourites. Was one of your mother's favourites, too."

A sliver of light appeared when I heard the nearness of him.

"Sean," I struggled to say, "had the craziest dream."

He inched closer to me, my voice so fragile.

"Strong Bull pulled…pulled horse off my leg," I mumbled, wheezing as the words barely escaped my mouth. "What foolish dream."

"You're gonna be fine, Patrick," he said delicately. "Don't talk just yet."

I wondered why everybody wanted me to stay quiet. Suddenly, painful memories flooded my mind. My eyes widened as I bolted upright, reaching for my leg. I gasped in relief.

"Patrick, calm down," Sean whispered, gently pushing me down against the pillow.

"I can't…can't feel my leg," I panicked, shaking.

"Your leg's fine! It'll be fine! That's not what we're worried about," he said fretfully when my breathing becoming too rapid, too short.

A wave of fear, then exhaustion, overtook me. I shuddered and the darkness swallowed my light.

I could still hear Sean reading the Bible despite the desperate rattling in my chest. Through whispers, he prayed for the suffering to end and for peaceful sleep to come.

****

His prayers were answered. I slept for the next few days. Despite being poked and prodded, I continued to stay heavy in stillness, my slumber undisturbed except for the soft voices.

The first voice I heard was Doctor Andrews speaking to Sean after his examination.

"Don't like the look of that leg. If we bleed him, the swelling might go down, as well as the temperature of his body."

"You do what you have to do to keep him alive," Sean said solemnly.

"Fine, I'll make two small incisions."

"Do you need me for anything?"

"For now, just get some clean water and two bowls," he advised. "I can do the rest. If I do save this leg and you want Patrick to walk on it again, I'll need to procure something to make a firm dressing. I don't think a mixture of glue and starch will suffice. It's not going to be easy to find but I'll do my best."

Sean paused, and the room went eerily silent again. "Would ah….plaster of Paris be more appropriate?"

Doc. Andrews stopped pressing on my leg to give Sean a look of astonishment. "Yes, that would do just fine. I'll not bother asking how you could procure such a thing."

When Sean returned with the steaming water, Doc. Andrews made one final comment as he took his lancet and placed it on the table. "He's showing signs of dehydration. Give him plenty of water if," he hesitated, "when he wakes up."

Sean walked heavily out of the room as the Doctor washed his hands and soaked his sharp, shiny instrument.

He placed a bowl under my leg above my knee, already propped up with blankets and rags, and made a small cut. I heard a shuffle, followed by a drip, drip that filled the room, sounding much like drops from fresh leaves after a spring shower.

It was sometime after when I heard a book scrape across the table, pages flipping, and Sean clearing his throat. I must have been in a bad state for he started reading the Bible again.

My body felt such heaviness, my mind as if it was spinning. Sean's voice was just a dull hum in a cloud of confusion. A little girl appeared. I recognized her as little Amanda, Colleen's youngest daughter. She wanted me to take her hand. I said I couldn't go. She waved me to a place that looked so wonderfully quiet and peaceful.

"Don't go," a voice whispered. "Don't go."

****

Voices filled my room again. How many hours passed, I do not know. Glasses were placed on the table.

"Any movement from our patient?" Joseph asked with hope.

"No, not a sound," Sean replied grimly.

A hand was placed on my forehead. "Still feverish."

All dry cloths were peeled from my leg.

"Still swollen. What are these small marks on his leg?" Joseph asked.

Sean swallowed, "Doc. bled him yesterday."

Joseph sighed, "How much blood, Sean?"

"I don't know."

"Everything Patrick needs is on this table" he said tersely. "Except for a better splint. It needs to be strong, but straight, light and thin.

He pulled the covers from my body.

"I'll get some fresh sheets," Sean stammered.

"Get Anne to bring the sheets. Go make me that splint."

"Patrick, I'm going to cool you down with medicine. You're going to feel a cold cloth on your forehead and along your right leg," Joseph spoke calmly. "What you feel right now is a balm that will help you breathe better. If you can hear me, let me know. I need you to drink before we splint this leg and we need you awake to do that."

I couldn't reply…..was too tired and too heavy.

When the room went quiet again, my mind dreamed wildly.

Joseph's voice brought me back. "I'm going to peel back your bandage."

As he reached over, I started choking. Soon hoisted forward, Joseph's light pounding against my back freed the plug in my throat.

The door creaked open, cold air rushed in, and I shuddered uncontrollably.

Panic and alarm filled Sean's face. "Joseph?"

"The balm's working. It's clearing his lungs," Joseph's voice denoted hope. "Look at his arm, Sean."

I was clutching Joseph in desperation.

"He's fighting, so let's get him all the help and energy he needs," Joseph urged, "by keeping the blood in his veins and giving his leg a better splint!"

The door opened gently this time. "I brought clean sheets. I'm sorry, I didn't realize…."

"That's fine, Anne. We'll change them and get him cleaned up once his leg is properly splinted."

"How is he?"

"A lot paler and his fever's higher."

"I didn't realize what Doc. Andrews was going to do, or I'd have said no…."

"He was only trying to do what he knew best. I just don't believe it's the best way to treat Patrick. I think he can hear us, Anne. I just wonder how much he can feel."

"Patrick, we must splint your leg again," Joseph spoke succinctly, his head still pressed into mine.

I was released to the softness of pillows and rags. A sheet was torn apart, but it was the painful squeeze to my leg that sent out an irrepressible jolt.

Joseph's response was that sweet distinctive smell of chloroform as it gently covered my nose and put my mind to sleep.

****

Sean's voice slowly crept into my mind. He was reading the Bible again. Maybe I should stay asleep, and he might just get through the entire book.

He stopped abruptly when the door opened, and Anne's soft steps came around my bed. My mind wondered when Sean would fix that squeaky door.

"Here, let me take something," he offered kindly to arms laden with fresh towels, cloths, and soup.

"I can manage. Please leave us alone," she beseeched with eyes, puffy and red. "Go get some rest."

I heard a deep sigh as boots shuffled heavily across the floor, ending when the door creaked closed.

The scent of her filled the room as her delicate hand combed through my greasy, heavy hair.

I sensed her sadness. I would have felt sad, too, if I had to look at my pale complexion, sunken eyes, and parched, swollen lips.

She cleared her throat and spoke lightly. "Well, Patrick, did I ever tell you I was a nurse before I came to this primitive land? I worked in a hospital, and we used to rouse sleepy patients by touching their lips gently."

She unscrewed the lid to a small jar of a jelly-like substance and proceeded to lubricate my lips with the tips of her soft thumb and fingers.

My eyelids fluttered as her name escaped my dry mouth. A soft smile formed on her face.

"I've got some broth that's going to make you feel much better, and you don't have to lift a finger for it."

She wasted no time raising my head with a rolled up rag and carefully feeding that broth.

"My husband joined the North West Mounted Police and moved us out here five years ago."

I could feel her eyes willing mine to stay open.

"He took me away from civilization. Away from a town called Toronto. This town had everything…three storey buildings, classy bookstores, fancy restaurants, dress shops, a University and library…"

I mouthed words, but the sounds were too faint.

Anne nodded like she understood. "In the end, my husband felt more suited to farming than police work. We filed for one hundred and sixty acres, paid our ten dollar fee, and toiled in the dirt until the day he died. He left me with a lot of work to do; however, he did manage to build the house before passing on."

I coughed and the warm broth went running down my chin.

Quick to wipe it up, the soft smile never left her exquisite face; and the soothing liquid was soon trickling down my throat again. That bowl would be scrapped empty before I was able to close my mouth.

She continued, "Part of the land agreement is that it be cultivated and have a fence. Thanks to you and Sean, I now own this land. Though I dare say my late husband's rolling in his grave as Sean the outlaw ploughs his fields," she laughed, but it soon faded.

"Sean and I are at odds with each other right now, so I'm extending you all the touch you think you can handle as long as you finish this broth."

She could see my hearing was still intact as I raised dark eyebrows.

"What?" I croaked, slowly nodding, willing to accept whatever she would offer me.

She was blatantly pleased. "Wait 'till I give you a bath, Patrick."

I nearly choked.

We laughed softly.

Knuckles rapped on the door and Joseph entered, contented with my improvement. "Good news all around. You're awake and the balm is helping you breathe better. I must put more on."

"Can Anne put it on?" I spoke shamelessly.

"I don't see why not," Joseph replied without speculation. "I'm going to refresh the cloths with cold water. Mind if we look at the other leg to see how much the swelling has gone down?"

If I had any shred of dignity, it was being tossed out the window, along with my usefulness and self-reliance, which left the house days ago. I nodded apprehensively to Anne's reassuring smile. He removed the blanket and sheets.

I was surprised to see I was wearing drawers, my eyes clearing and the white underwear seeming swaddled around my hips and held by a pin? My eyes didn't linger there for my splinted leg caused much more angst, my swollen ankle at an unnatural angle.

"Most of the swelling's gone down. In a day or two we will put the cast on," he said assuredly while shaking a white powder into a bowl of cold water.

Joseph doused a few cloths, breaking the floating clumps into nothingness, before amply squeezing and loosely dangling them from my leg.

"Cast for what?" I asked hoarsely while glaring at strips of reddened skin between the fair rags.

"Your leg is broken, along with your ankle," Joseph informed unequivocally.

"Two breaks?" I asked, barely coherently.

Joseph looked to Anne, then back to me. "As far as I can see, a break to the bone in your leg, and a broken ankle."

"How long….before I get out of this bed?"

"Once the cast is on, that's up to you. Until that time, you're to remain very still in this bed."

"Then I can limp out of here," my fragile tone mocked, hiding deep panic over a prostrate future.

"Why don't you find a nightshirt for Patrick?" Joseph asked Anne as he touched my forehead and promptly covered it with a damp cloth. "I also have a tea that I want you to drink as much as possible."

The nightshirt arrived. I was lifted, and my numb and cooled leg became hot and excruciatingly painful.

Anne clutched my hand, offering to use her touch to rub the balm over the skin of my hurriedly beating heart and irritated lungs.

I agreed, when suddenly the door swung open; and his big presence blocked most of the daylight from entering the room. I snatched the blankets and covered myself as he approached, his smile confident, disturbing.

Anne and Joseph traded worrisome glances.

"Why don't we go make the tea?" Joseph suggested. "You can give it to Patrick with the balm."

Anne was reticent. "Fine, but we won't be long."

I never felt so helpless and vulnerable in all my life when they left me alone with the man and his odd grin.

"I see Anne's done her job. Now it's time to do mine."

Sean moved to the bed and brought forth a glass of water. "I have to get this into you."

His demeanor was so domineering I felt the urge to kick his teeth in.

"Not thirsty right now," I said with as little emotion as possible.

"You have to drink the water. Drink it and we'll be right as rain."

I glared at him, feeling that there was no 'we' in this. It was just me, and I didn't want him to bark any orders my way, so I defiantly looked away.

"Drink the goddamn water, Patrick," he spoke loudly, his voice strangely desperate.

I hated his inflection. I hated it when he blasphemed, so I took the water, his smug face of satisfaction in my submission, and decided to wash it away. Releasing the glass, I waited for it to shatter.

Grabbing it in with a strong hand, he asked, "What did you do that for?"

Droplets ran from a face of utter disbelief to the collar of his grimy shirt.

"I'm not thirsty," I spoke vacantly.

"If you don't drink, you'll die!" he cried, driving more water from pitcher to glass. "What do you say about that!"

"I'm coming home."

Sean shook in frustration, water sloshing over the rim of the glass, showing great displeasure with my response. "You're not gonna die!"

I stared blankly at air. "It's not your choice. There's nothing you can do about it."

Anne walked in as he was clawing at my face, water spilling from my throat, arms swinging.

"What are you doing!" she fretted.

Immediately letting go of me, the glass finally shattered as I fell to the bed, gasping for air.

Sean spoke no words.

I assumed he was very furious with me, clearly indicated by the way he stomped out the room and slammed the door.

Anne slowly lifted me, the suffering and anguish obvious on her face, until my wet nightshirt seeped through her clothing. She carefully peeled it off and returned with a dry one; however, I had contorted my body to face a far and emotionless wall. The pain of my wounded shoulder and throbbing leg were so agonizing, I angrily gripped a pillow.

"Patrick!" she wailed, "oh Patrick, please don't turn away! Please let me know how I can help you!" Her voice sounded so deplorable, I finally told her to take my journal and leave.

Once alone, I closed my eyes and willed my body to depart this earthly place; to let the pain swell up like giant waves and swallow me whole until I could never be seen again.

Sean was thrusting a shovel into Taffy's stall when Anne slowly approached.

"Patrick needs your help," her eyes watered. "He's in a lot of pain."

"I know that, but he wants to die and I'm not gonna sit around and watch him do it!"

"You won't change his decision in this barn," she advised heatedly. "He needs you more than you know. Give him your understanding and support: no judgment, no pity. Read this.....it may help you to know him."

Anne offered the book in her outstretched hand. "It's going to get worse for you before it gets better."

He hesitantly took it and gingerly pulled at the letter that crept from the edges of the pages.

Before ripping at the seal of the envelope, he brushed a thumb over his name in Mandy's handwriting.

My dearest Sean,

Tomorrow we begin our journey to find you. It will be only a fraction the distance I have travelled to Montana, but difficult nonetheless. This land is still wild: unprotected from bandits, robbers and Indians. I have hired two escorts with whom I trust will get us safely to Fort Benton.

If you are reading this letter, something has gone horribly wrong.

I have never forgotten about you. You are permanently rooted in my mind. Though the hands of time have moved forward beyond days to months to years, it feels like you're still here.

Thoughts of your charming smile and soft caress still warm my heart. Some people live a lifetime and never truly find love. I found love. I found you. And my heart beats for you to my dying day.

That night, my passion for you was released; and I cared not for any consequence or judgment. I wanted you, needed you, had to have you, and have never regretted it. It took me a long time to realize we conceived a child.

Our son, Henry Robert Wilkes, was born April fifteenth, 1865. The day that so many were in grief and sorrow over our Dear President Lincoln, Henry was born and his presence filled me with lightness and hope. He has my eyes and your smile, my sensitivity and your will.

I wish you were here to watch him grow. I try to give him everything he needs, try to protect him from harm and ill-will. I should have taken him away from this house sooner, should have realized our boy lied to protect me. My inactions have caused Henry such pain. I blame myself for his suffering.

I now accept that his grandfather did not treat him like a grandfather should. Why he couldn't love Henry, or show him affection, or say a kind word, is incomprehensible to me. One night, my father lashed out at Henry in a horrible rage that left our son physically and emotionally scarred. I am left now to rebuild his strength, to help him forget those terrible memories, to see his beautiful smile again.

If you do receive this letter from Henry, please love and comfort him. Show him how a man can be strong but still compassionate, how a man can show affection and support without smothering, how a man can guide and discipline without hurting. Show him your true self, as you have shown me, how a good man can live.

I wrote a song, the song of my life. I play it everyday. It's a song of love, longing, fear, joy, sadness and hope. Give it to Henry, get him to play it. Then ask him to write his own song.

With all my love,
Mandy

While Sean glanced through Mandy's letter again, the journal fell to the barn floor. Still trying to cope with the loss of her and the loss of her love, the pages started flapping from cover to cover as a cool breeze blew through the open door. Lifting the journal, he turned to the first few lines: Patrick's name and date in a little boy's printing. As he flipped and skimmed through the copious written lines, words and names jumped out: Pa, horses, chores, Fort Benton…until he arrived at the end.

I was born under a Montana sky…...

Couldn't wait to enter this world, so I came early and gave Momma an easy delivery. My first vivid memory of her was when I was a toddler, and she was playing the piano so intently. I was calling for her, but she just kept on playing. I started crying, wondering how she could ignore me.

When she saw me I got scooped up in her strong arms and soothed. She said I was the most important person in her life. She showed me I was the most important person in her life.

She taught me as a schoolteacher would, to read and write. She taught me how to play the piano even though I thought being outside was a better use of my time. She taught me kindness, mercy and love.

My favourite time of day was the afternoon when we would go to Willowtree Creek, catch butterflies, play hide and seek, and wade in the cool waters looking for friendly rocks, slippery frogs, and speckled trout.

My first vivid memory of my grandpa was entirely different….

He had his hand around the back my neck under the kitchen table, making me pick up peas I had dropped from my spoon. His hands were so big, so strong, so calloused: they were the scariest hands I had ever seen, and when they came at me, I quivered.

Momma said he provided all the food including those peas, so we had to eat everything on our plate. He didn't have a lot of food growing up, so I figured I had to eat everything, whether it fell on the floor or not. I was three. What did I understand? It seems I was just a messy eater and had to be punished for that. It seems I had to be punished for a lot of things.

The last memory of my grandpa, lucid and blurry, was in the barn. His face was hard and red, though it was his eyes, black as coal, full of rage, I remember most. I lashed out at him for beating his horse, and he lashed back. It was a rage most uncontrolled, a forward momentum that could only be stopped by Momma's screams.

That night, her forward momentum began; and she got us out of that house for good. I believed we would finally be free, happy, and safe.

Sadly, I ended all of that; and felt my life was over, too. It was like I was trapped in the bottom of a well, struggling in the wet blackness, afraid and alone.

Bill and Mary Sullivan became my mother and father, reaching out and pulling me up. They gave me a warm place to sleep, food when I was hungry, a new name, and hope in a stable full of horses I could visit and care for any time I wanted. Bill gave me work to do, which gave me a purpose. He taught me how to break wild horses, and I could only do that when I had patience, strength, courage and will.

For once, I got to see what a real family was like. We always sat for supper together, had conversations and lingered longer than the customary five minutes I was used to. We talked about our challenges, joys, and worries. One of my fondest memories was of Pa humming a tune while he helped Ma with the dishes. They swayed together, their momentum equally in synchronization with each other: a perfect harmony. And it filled me with such happiness.

Pa led with a firm voice, not a firm hand. He was the first man to show me affection and hold me when I was sad or scared. He taught me that my thoughts were just my thoughts, as scattered as the winds off the plains; but my actions were the meaning to my life. He reminded me about God's forgiveness.

I was able to forgive myself and my grandpa, and that was the key to freeing my soul. My faith remains a strong force in my life. I am forever grateful to the man whose enduring love nourished my soul and was a salve for my broken heart.

I write in this book as a man unencumbered by life's doubts, loneliness, and hatred. I walk as open as a book, looking forward to my next journey, meeting people with a smile, a kind word, and a sympathetic ear. Pa once said 'you fall off a horse, dust yourself off, then get back on. Don't stop moving until you can't move any more.'

His legacy is now my legacy, and there's no room in my heart for hatred and anger. There are no weights to hold me down. I control my destiny.

Lying in the blades of grass feeling heaven's rain, I tell God how gratefully blessed I am.

I remember these words as I leave my wilderness home,
To a foreign land where I will roam.
In search of a man I have never known,
A father by birth right alone.
Though I greet this adventure with open arms,
I pray it will bring me no harm.
For I would rather face nature's bitter and cold embrace,
Or a wild animal's snarling teeth and fierce face.
Than suffer the wrath of man,
For that I know, I have often ran.

The bunkhouse door clicked open. I heard solemn footsteps, Anne's chair squeaking across the floor, then silence. If I had eyes in the back of my head, I would have seen their sign language: Sean's compassionate face, and Anne threats to shorten his life if he hurt me anymore.

"I'll be back soon, Patrick," she whispered with a touch to my shoulder.

When she was no longer in the room, Sean's mouth began to move. "Patrick…I want to say that I'm sorry for my behaviour. I was…upset because you wouldn't drink the bloody water, and I can't bear the thought of losing you because of that," he paused.

I remained unmoving, forgetting that I was exposed, my back telling its own scarred past.

He mumbled, "Son of a bitch…"

His words faded though breathing that became heavy and fast.

I didn't know how much the look of my marks threatened to tear him from the room.

"Jim Phillips came by to see how you were faring," he said with much emotion, clearing his throat. "He brought two cows. They're in the pasture," he hesitated, "guess I'll just have to work on finding those horses by myself."

Moving briskly to the door, he twisted the knob.

"I'll take the water," I whispered.

Sean's steps sounded more hopeful as he walked towards the bed.

"I'm warning you, though," he said with lightness, "you break this glass and you'll be drinking it out of a bucket."

Reaching out a hand, I let his strong arm turn me around while hiding my pain, my sounds muffled within a shaky body.

His grim eyes burrowed into mine. "I have to ask you something, Patrick?"

I swayed my head slowly, assuming too much, crying out, "He's dead! Died an unhappy, bitter old man!"

"That's not what I was going to ask," Sean remarked amid a face showing a twisted sort of happiness.

"Just get it over with!" I grumbled. "Ask me what you will because once I walk out that door, I'll never speak of that life again." Wearily, I rubbed my aching forehead. "Don't make me wish I burned that letter."

"I think you'll be happy you didn't burn that letter," he said, handing me the sheet of notes Momma had written long ago. "Your mother said you lied to protect her."

"So she knew." I shrugged my shoulders, wincing. "I'd lie awake when I was a little boy and hear him come in late at night. He was loud and cantankerous, tormenting my grandma!" I paused to swallow for my throat was drier than the High Plains.

"I could never understand how he could hurt her. When she died, I swore he wouldn't do that to Momma; so I lied to her. I couldn't stand the thought of him hurting her." I rubbed my head again. "So I hid moments from her….said I hurt myself when I could. Sometimes Mable and Jacob lied for me, too. He snatched me from my room, took the switch to me, and said quite…harshly that it was…it was never gonna be enough!"

My voice crackled and quivered as the memory became clearer. "He wanted to take me to the creek, but I struggled. That creek was a special place, and I didn't want to go there with him. He found water in the barn and…kept holding me down, saying it was for the greater good…it was for the greater good! What…what do you think he meant by that?"

Sean eased into his chair, shoulders sagging, "It can be hard to understand another man's words."

However, his look of abhorrence was obvious.

"You were a brave boy, Patrick," he said emphatically.

"I'm not so brave now, am I?"

Sean was speechless but only for seconds. "I've been shot and I know how hard it is to be brave when you're in so much pain." He continued, "When I was injured and riding to Helena, I fell off my horse. I lay there, and the cold, dark air sent me shivering. Too frail to move, there was this bush within arms length; so I lit it on fire."

Sean scratched his head at the memory. "Well, it seems that that bush was too close, for my coat caught the flames and it got really hot! Gave me a second wind, though! So I extinguished myself and crawled to the horse. Made it to Helena where some kind ladies took good care of me. I was days in bed, Patrick.....couldn't move. Had to rely on others to take care of me, Sean Thomas, and I'm alive because of that."

He glanced at my somnolent eyes while I rubbed my head in feverish confusion.

"It's when you're spitting up blood or your organs start failing, that you're a goner!" he said in a reassuring tone. "When you can't remember the last time you used the outhouse."

I glared at him in sheer dismay.

He quickly offered a glass of water.

"I think I'll take something that could ease the pain. It feels as though my head's about to burst and my leg…" I trembled, asking, "Could you open that desk drawer?"

He reached for the thin cigarettes.

"Is this the right time to be smoking?" he asked skeptically. "I have something that may be more appropriate."

"It's the right time for these smokes," I murmured, eagerly awaiting the lit match to burn the potent leaves. "I have to warn you, though, they can cause strange dreams."

"Is that right?"

"Yep," I puffed the medicine deeply. "Last time I had one of these," I stuttered, "dreamt most vividly that I was in Fort Benton crossing the gritty road, and there was this long line of people like a parade was going on." My quivering continued. "Tried to get through but they were wagging their heads, telling me to shoot him."

I inhaled too deeply and coughed out grey clouds.

"Patrick, you don't have to talk."

My ears played deaf. "I hollered 'Who am I supposed to shoot?' The crowd pointed to a tall, darkly swathed figure maybe thirty yards away. I refused, even though I had a pistol holstered at my side and the crowd cheering me on."

I was beginning to feel the effects of the cigarette as my headache waned. "I just kept saying 'no' and the crowd got angry and started….they started throwing candy at me."

"Who was the dark figure?" Sean asked curiously.

"I don't know…some outlaw, maybe Bill Hickok," I replied with a dopey gaze.

"How long ago was this?"

I vaguely said, "Maybe six months ago."

"Well, it wasn't Bill Hickok 'cause he's been dead five years," Sean corrected plainly. "Shot in the back during a poker game."

"Oh," I said, averting my deceitful face.

"It's fine, Patrick."

He walked over to the stack of books while I desperately tried to keep my heavy lids from falling over glazed eyes.

"I can't believe she kept it all these years."

I peered at the book. "Good luck with that one."

He opened the cover of 'Great Expectations' to discover the hole in the centre of the pages and his pouch of gold stashed inside. Shaking the pieces into the palm of his hand, a flood of gold-digging memories came rushing in.

"I remember the day your grandfather and I found this gold at Alder Gulch. It was a great day," he spoke reminiscently.

"What was he like?"

"He was a very strong, confident man. We have his smile, though I think his dimples were even bigger. He was about my height, had dark wavy hair, and hazel-green eyes that lit up around family and friends. I kept him busy the last few years of his life. He was constantly putting out my fires. Always willing to lend a hand, though; and that's how he died, helping someone retrieve his stolen horse."

"You went after his killer."

"Yes, I went after that cowardly O"Flaherty. Shot him dead."

"Did you feel better after you killed him?"

"I don't reckon I felt much of anything. Well, that's not entirely true," he recollected. "I guess it released some of the anger and revenge I had pent up inside. I also figured I was ridding the world of a spineless malefactor who didn't deserve to take another breath."

I watched as he slid the gold back into its pouch.

"Killing a man always comes with repercussions, though. Those O'Flaherty brothers never wanted to let it go. I guess it didn't help that I killed another one in Virginia City. Never did get the third one despite that I had my share of chances."

While he walked the book back to the desk, I let the heavy lure of sleep win until his voice bolted me alert.

"Left that one for you, son; but in the future, stay away from anyone comes looking for me. You'll live longer."

"Just wanted to convince him to leave……go away from this place," I said, feeling most gullible.

"They don't listen very well," he replied, pulling a chair in close. "I've been chased all over Montana. Finally moved to Canada and was left alone for a while. Then I came back to Virginia City to see your mother."

I was now higher than a kite, without inhibition, so I figured I'd do the asking, "What's that in your hair?"

"Pardon?"

I pointed to it, looking like a rolled up maggot. Even thought I saw it moving.

Sean ran fingers through his long hair and eyed the white clump. "It's just flour. It's a long story."

"Do you have an aversion to bathing?"

"No! I'm a little remiss about bathing once a week, but things have been crazy around here lately! I just haven't had time!"

"That's no excuse," I scolded like a parent. "Heck, I don't know how long it's been, but I can't hardly stand the feel of myself." My fingers madly scratched at the sore and itchy bandaged shoulder.

"We can remedy that."

"Why didn't you see her?" I blurted out.

Silence filled the small room.

"I tried to," he said while smoothing the creases in his forehead. "I saw you running through the pasture until a tall man called after you. When he scooped you up, I figured he was your father. Who was he!" he asked acrimoniously, but shook apologetically.

I was confused, my fog-filled brain trying to conjure up the memory. "Tommy?"

"Colleen's brother, Tommy?" he asked in disbelief. "He was such a small boy when I knew him."

I hid how distressed I had become by this knowledge. "This smoke's not working fast enough. Can you get me some whisky?"

"Sure. Drink that glass of water while I'm gone."

I sucked deeply on the cigarette, wishing for dark sleep to come before he returned. Somehow, I felt responsible for my parents never re-uniting. If I had gotten closer to Sean, or if I hadn't been in that pasture at all, maybe things would have been different…..been better. As I drifted off, I wallowed in regret, wishing I'd never been born.

Sean was reaching for the whisky when Anne came into the house with a bucket of water. "How is everything with Patrick?" she asked nervously.

He turned with softness in his face.

"We talked for a while. I couldn't tell him everything, Anne. Just what I thought he should hear, but he still seems to be in a painful way."

Then it clicked in his mind like the sound an empty chamber makes when the trigger is pulled. He rushed past Anne.

As Sean entered my room, I heard his voice just an echo…..too far away to answer.

Slumping in the chair, Sean glared at the butt of the cigarette floating in the water. His response was to pop the cork and let the whisky burn down his throat.

"You must know it's not your fault, Patrick. I was never gonna be able to stay," he lamented, his head wagging vehemently with eyes regrettably on murderous hands. "It's not your fault I left."

Lifting the picture from a pocket, his insatiable need to know Mandy's whereabouts would not be quelled. Tightening lips around the rim of the bottle, he drowned his deep discontent.

Starting to stir, I was flat on my back, complete darkness surrounding me. A slight breeze and the moist ground sent me shivering as I grabbed at loose dirt. I could only figure I was in a shallow grave, cold, naked and alone. My eyes searched the black hole as I cried for help.

Footsteps approached, metal broke ground, and dirt began showering upon me in relentless heaps.

They awoke, slithering and hissing around me. I started to panic, gasping for air. Dirt filled my mouth, choking me, crushing my chest, as I desperately tried to move.

A voice echoed in the night, Sean's voice. It got louder as I tried to focus on his words, tried to understand what he was saying.

"Patrick!" he bellowed, clutching me tightly. "Breathe Patrick! Calm down. Breathe!"

I forced my mind back to that wilderness home,
Where wild mustangs freely roam.
Where I no longer struggled to breathe,
Where air filled my lungs and my chest didn't heave.
Where I prayed to God above,
For his sweet mercy and love
Where heaven's rays shone on my skin,
Took the cold and hollow darkness from within…

My breathing slowed and arms went limp, falling away.

"Oh Patrick," Sean cried, his sigh heavy on my head.

He didn't linger long over me when he said with much emotion, "Patrick, you need the bath, son."

Chapter 8

Joseph stepped quietly into the bunkhouse and approached the bed. With a light tap, he stirred Sean, who jumped up and rubbed his eyes.

"He had an attack last night. Used your balm and that seemed to help."

"You can also give him the chloroform," Joseph said, removing a dry cloth from a hot forehead. "I think we should set up a cool bath for Patrick. It will be tricky with his leg, but we should try."

"I'll bring over the tub and get some coffee made."

Joseph continued peeling away the rest of the cloths and blankets. "I'll get him ready to move."

Sean walked gingerly to the house, taking in sharp breaths of cool spring air. Entering the warm kitchen, he sat heavily in the chair.

Anne turned as she stirred soup. "Would you like some coffee?"

He nodded wearily. "Pour Joseph a cup, too."

She placed a mug within his reach before pressing strong fingers into throbbing, tense shoulders. "What are you thinking?"

"I'm thinking how fast things can change. One day, you're going about your work, and the next, you're fighting for your life, struggling….struggling to…"

"I know…I know."

"How long can he survive like this?"

"He survives as long as the Lord doesn't take him, and I pray that's not too soon."

"We're going to take the tub in. See if a bath can help with the fever."

"I'll bring some towels, soap, and my touch."

"You rub him like you rub me and I may never get you back," he moaned as she dug at the kinks in his neck. "I think it's time to take that measly beard off so don't forget the razor."

By the time the huge tub was placed in the bunkhouse and filled with cool water, I was awake.

"Well, Patrick, whenever you're ready, the bath is waiting," Sean spoke softly, though he hovered too closely to me.

"You don't think I'm having a bath with you two standing there, do you?" I asked, shaking my woozy head. "Just give me a minute or three to catch my breath."

Sean wagged his head. "No."

Before I could complain, my naked body was quickly hoisted, both men trying to get me in the bath without breaking my other leg.

Joseph and Sean were standing outside when Anne walked over, arms filled with towels, soap, soup, razor, and scissors. "What are you two doing standing out here?"

"He's very angry with us," Sean said.

Joseph concurred. "He slapped my hand when I tried to take his bandage off.

"Will you open the door for me if it's not too much trouble?"

The door creaked open and I howled, "If you think you're gonna wipe me down….."

"Calm down, Patrick," Anne snapped.

I instinctively covered myself.

"Don't have to be shy with me. I've already seen it."

"You did?" I asked, so very confused.

"It's not a big deal for me," she said unabashedly. "I've seen…I worked in a hospital, grew up with a brother, and believe me when I say it's not the most attractive part of the male anatomy, so I didn't pay any attention to yours, but I have…."

"I get it!" I said grumpily. "You saw it and it's no big deal."

"Then sit up and let me clean your back," she replied rather impatiently.

My feelings of inadequacy didn't last long as Anne gently moved that cloth up and down my rigid back, putting pressure on every aching muscle, and I had plenty of them.

"When I met Sean for the first time, he was filthy, clothes torn; and he smelled…. horrible, like an outhouse overflowing with feces on the hottest summer day."

"It's probably all of that rotting flesh," I muttered crankily.

"He's not that old!" she retorted tartly. "He just stank, but despite that and his surly behaviour, I graciously took him in. It's slim pickings out here, and he offered free labour in exchange for room and food."

I mumbled, "I'm glad you didn't pay him. At the speed he works, you'd be broke and still have a broken down farm."

"Sean loves it when I rub his back," she boasted while her hand moved the cloth along the protruding bones of my spine.

"Can we pretend that Sean doesn't exist!" I spat out. "That it's just your hands on my body." I whined out the words and wasn't inclined to rescind them anytime soon.

"You just tell me if it ever hurts too much. I can't tell if those moans are moans of pleasure or pain."

"I think I'd call it painful pleasure if that makes any sense, Anne."

She smiled, seeming happy to bring pleasure to such a pained person. Guiding me against the tub, she proceeded to scrub my neck, taut shoulders, and lean arms all the way to limp hands and fingertips.

"Now this is the area I most enjoy on a man," she purred, being ever careful with my wounded shoulder before gently going over every rib that by now was sticking out from a thin frame.

"Do you want me to take off the bandage?"

"No," I managed to mumble through easy breaths.

Her touch was so soft it tickled, so much that a chuckle escaped when she reached my concaved stomach.

That unwavering hand continued its southerly journey into my groin area. I peered at Anne, who seemed focused on her task, paying me no mind; and I couldn't get her off of my mind.

"Did you know that young men have more vitality and stamina than older men?" I advised.

That hand stopped moving. Maybe I chose the wrong time to have this conversation because that hand sadly moved on to my healthy leg.

"Older men tend to have more experience."

I pondered her answer for Ophelia said I possessed that trait despite that it was my first time; however, she was paid to make men feel good, and she did make me feel good.

I felt a melancholy twinge, thinking I may never have a good feeling in that area again the way my leg ached from hip bone to ankle.

"Patrick, I'm going to wash the upper part of your right leg," she spoke delicately. "Sometimes an injury feels less painful in water."

I agreed with a simple nod.

She clasped my right hand while her right hand washed my leg, but the searing pain forced me to let go and grip the edge of the tub firmly.

Anne continued washing until I was so tense, water started quaking.

"Patrick!" she stopped.

"What?" I asked, exasperated.

"You have to tell me when the pain is too great."

"Anne, I'll take the pain if it means I move my leg again. I have to walk again. I have to ride again. I have to tame horses again…"

She put fingers to my flapping lips. "Small steps, not giant leaps, or you'll find yourself chewing on dirt or worse."

While I lingered in the tepid water, she offered me a bowl of soup.

"Has that soup got anything it in?"

"No."

"Then it should be called broth, and you can just put it in a glass and I'll drink it. Free your hands up for more important….what do you call it?"

"Therapy."

"Yep. I need more therapy."

Anne was so sweet and very obliging. She washed my hair with the smooth pressure of her slender fingertips, so soothing and deeply relaxing that I fell asleep, my mouth agape.

"Patrick, I'm going to call the men in to get you out of that tub."

"Nope," I said dopily.

"I don't think I can do it on my own."

"Bring the chair over and we'll do it together."

"Put your arms around me and hold on tight."

She managed to keep me steady on one leg, whisk a towel on me and swivel my body to a chair without the help of any men. She was a wonderful woman and I was completely envious of Sean.

"Nothing I like more than shaving a man," she smiled, covering me with a thick blanket. Lathering soap into my pathetic beard, she said, "Nothing I like less than cutting a man, so hold still."

"Anne, has Sean ever told you how beautiful you are?" I wistfully gazed into her sparkling blue eyes.

Her cheeks went rosy. "I'm sure he thinks it everyday."

"I would tell you everyday if you were my wife."

After the measly beard was scraped off, she wiped my face with a wet towel and peered into my eyes. "You smile at me, Patrick Sullivan, and I just may take you up on your offer."

I grinned as fully as I could. With gentle hands on my smooth cheeks, she kissed my warm forehead.

"How short you want your hair cut?"

"Cut it real short, Anne. I can't be bothered with it right now," I slurred as a heated wave of exhaustion smacked me in the face.

"Fine. Do my best, but can't promise you it'll come out even…short. Well," she contemplated, "we can always shave it off if it doesn't look right."

She cut, and she cut, and she cut.

While the scissors snipped hair over my nose, I told her a story that came to memory.

"My pa, Bill, had a way of telling a story that made you feel like you were there. During the two month journey he took with his family by steamboat, people were sick with cholera. As he and his brother passed a cabin, they saw a man rocking his child on the bed from side to side in an unrelenting grip. The crew was trying to separate them, but the man wouldn't let the boy go for fear that if he did, he would die."

I swallowed, my dry throat making my voice croaky, almost incoherent.

"The man had already lost his wife and daughter; his son was all he had left. After much convincing, the two separated and were given food and water. By the time Fort Benton was in sight, the man had succumbed to the virulent disease. Bill and his brother, John, buried the man and took the boy with them. His name was Trey."

I paused because I knew that boy. I knew how he felt and believed that it was he who was holding his father so closely.

"Hold steadfast to the ones you love for they will surely die. Hold steadfast to the ones you love, to keep them alive, to try. I don't long for the years, Anne. I live for the sweet moments."

She was quiet, except for the sniffling, like she was shedding tears.

"Anne, there were some pretty sweet moments in that tub for me. If you ever tire of Sean, I'm your man," I spoke confidently.

She laughed. "I'll keep that in mind."

With fuzzy eyes, all of the dark hair on the milky coloured towel appeared like an emaciated rodent.

"Is there any left on my head?"

"Let me get a mirror."

Gawking at my reflection, I repeated 'shuck' under my breath endless times for my face was not my own. I was pale and gaunt, eyes sunken, lips hugely swollen and grossly fissured. Then I peered up at short lop-sided hair, tilting my head to correct the obvious unevenness.

"Do you want me to cut it, make it more even?"

"If you cut any more off, I'll be bald," I stammered, until her worried face came into focus. "Thank you, Anne, for everything," I smiled appreciatively.

She scooped up the loose hairs and tucked them in a glass dish.

"What are you gonna do with that?"

"I'm collecting it to make a wreath. Don't have any family out here but Sean and you. Does that bother you?"

"I don't want it back. Is it enough?"

"It's ample, though I can't wait to get my shears into Sean's hair."

"I'd wash it first," I mumbled.

"Pardon?" she asked.

"I'd wish supper at the house first," I corrected. "This room is becoming too confining."

"You're not going anywhere until the cast is put on."

"Then get Joseph in here and let's get it done."

After slipping me into a nightshirt, she disappeared and I foolishly hopped to the bed, deeply regretting it. Even the touch of the mattress sent a searing pain through my entire body. I was still shaking like a dainty leaf when the men walked in.

"So you think we should cast your leg?" Joseph asked.

"Maybe not today," I pleaded. "Maybe tomorrow."

Joseph uncovered my leg. "Best to do it sooner than later, especially if you're going to foolishly walk on it. Sean, go and get Doctor Andrews."

By the time Sean returned with the Doctor, I was amply dosed with fever reliever and asthma balm, which faintly smelled like stinking skunk and musty earth.

"Are you sure you're both up for this today?" I asked wearily.

Sean sat on the bed lightly. "It's gonna get done today, Patrick."

I hated him.

"Where's Anne?" I asked nervously.

"We can give you morphine," Doc. Andrews suggested with a look of gratitude to Sean.

"Or chloroform," Sean added in.

"No!" I replied defiantly.

Doc. Andrews was at the end of the bed, tying on his crisp, white apron while Sean and Joseph were at my right side, hovering too closely, making me feel like a rabbit in a trap ready to be picked apart by ravenous wolves. I swallowed back a horribly queasy feeling.

"Where's Anne?"

"I'm right here, Patrick," she calmly answered, entering the room with a pitcher of boiling water, clean cloths, sheets and towels.

When finally empty, her hands took mine.

I lay with my back against the bumpy mattress, staring at the dull ceiling while metal scraping a bowl and sheets being torn filled my ears with dread.

My own blanket and sheets were pulled away as I focused on Anne's peaceful face and blurred out Sean's overbearing presence.

I had always been a strong and patient man. Could endure almost anything, but I was so tired, my body so frail, my emotions too hard to control. I felt like saying, *just leave me; I'm worth less than a tattered shirt.*

"We just have to lift your leg a little," Doc. Andrews advised. "The plaster from this casting can get quite messy. We want to keep your sheets clean."

"Don't want to know what you have to do!" I said through clenched teeth. "Does he have to be here?"

"Sean, why don't you go and make Patrick some oatmeal?" Anne suggested.

"Sure thing," he said with obvious disappointment.

"Anne," I said, my voice rushed. "Take me to that busy town 'Toronto'. Take me there, now."

Joseph had already removed the splint and was poking at my leg.

"We're walking along King St. West from Bay to Simcoe. The sun brightens the busy town, making it feel more alive. The wide streets are filled with fancy carriages and open wagons. A stagecoach arrives. Its passengers look up at the three and four story stone buildings with wondrous awe. The businesses are replete with customers because it's Saturday. People are smiling and gay."

I squeezed Anne's hand too harshly when Doc. Andrews pushed on a broken bone.

"Sorry, Anne," I croaked.

She gently squeezed back. "We are strolling along the wide plank boardwalk. My arm is in yours. You're wearing a nicely tailored jacket, vest, white shirt, and tie. I'm wearing a silk ruffled blouse and brightly coloured plaid skirt. We hear the sounds of the large road: horse hooves clopping and wagon wheels creaking, as dust and debris swirl into the air. There's a strange mix of smells: sweet, heavy, dry, and bitter. Passing a classy bookstore, we glance at the bay window to see the latest novel by Mark Twain. Continuing along, your heels click the planks until we arrive at a bakery. As you politely open the door, the sweetness of sugar fills our noses and intrigues our taste buds."

As Joseph was wrapping, Doc. Andrews held the bones in place; and I felt myself sinking into the centre of the bed, wishing I could leave my leg behind.

"Patrick, they have everything: frosty cakes a mile high, fresh fruit pies, raisin butter tarts, lemon loaves, and flat and flaky butter cookies."

I take my mind to the display counter, eager to escape my dark and sickly smelling room.

"I offer you a taste of anything your stomach desires, and you point to the apple pie. It has a special crumble top which is lighter than traditional crust, and you're eager to try it."

Jacob continued to wrap, however, I now felt the pressure of the splint against my sensitive skin. Ready to jump off the bed, Anne stroked my shaky forehead.

"I order half that pie for you, Patrick, with huge dollops of whipped cream and a slice of cheese on the side."

"Half the pie, Anne?" I asked, my voice feeble.

"Oh, yes. You deserve half of that pie. It comes all fancy on a plate with spiral mounds of fluffy cream on top."

She put a hand to my thumping chest and called out abruptly, "Stop!"

Joseph and Doc. Andrews gave her a sharp look of concern.

"Patrick, you have to take something…whisky, chloroform, or morphine. Your heart's beating too fast. You have to take something. If you don't choose, I will."

"Fine, Anne. I'll take the whisky."

She nodded and briskly left the room.

Joseph walked over and listened to my racing heart.

"Women," I said fearfully, "always overreacting."

"She's a very perceptive woman, Patrick. You're a true warrior, but even warriors need help from time to time."

The door to the house slammed shut. Sean turned from the stove, his wooden spoon dripping oatmeal onto the floor.

"I'll never understand men!" Anne cried emphatically. "I used to have to sedate them to take large slivers from their hands, and your son won't take anything and it's killing him."

She pounded a glass on the table, filled it with whisky, and emptied it like a thirsty drunkard.

"I'll never understand men!" she cried, shaking her head.

Her light feet thudded out of the house with the bottle and a book.

"Oatmeal's ready," Sean informed the empty kitchen.

When Anne entered the bunkhouse, Jacob caught her arm, whispering, "We're going to give him the morphine. Patrick's not in is right mind. The fever still rages, and his heart is beating too fast. You give him the whisky, and we'll give him the morphine while we tend to his ankle."

"I'm back, Patrick," she whispered as the whisky was brought to my lips. "Where were we…the bakery? Are you ready to take a bite out of that pie?"

"I'm tired, Anne," my eyelids fluttered, "I'll try it another time."

"Sure thing. That pie will be waiting for you whenever you're ready. Why don't I read you some of Mark Twain's book 'Adventures of Tom Sawyer'?"

Feeling a sharp pain, I stiffly shook my head with the last bit of energy I had. "Could I have another glass of whisky?"

Anne started pouring, and my mind began taking me from a caged and heavy body. Green grasses traveled beneath me as Lincoln charged toward the wall of pines that lined the hill to the river. We cut through a strong easterly Prairie wind, the beating of horse's hooves heavy against Montana soil, until the sounds of the Missouri rushed in.

****

I awoke and Anne was smiling down on me.

"You have that whisky ready?" I whispered.

"Patrick, that was yesterday. Your leg is casted," she spoke softly.

"For how long?" I asked somberly.

"It'll be a month, maybe more, before that cast will come off."

"I can't wait that long to get out of this room. I want to come to supper, tonight."

"Well, that's not wise. You're still feverish, and you haven't even stood on that leg…."

Anne couldn't stand the way my deep blue eyes implored her, besides I found out it was Sunday; and I knew how much she loved everybody together for Sunday supper.

"I best get moving Anne before I fall asleep again."

"You're not going out in your twisted nightshirt."

"No, bring me clothes from there." I pointed to the pine chest of drawers.

"Only if you let me help you dress."

"Only if you promise to undress me later," I grinned feebly.

She was tossing her head while peeling back the covers to reveal the white bandaged cast that began just below my knee to the tip of my toes.

I couldn't hide my forlorn face.

"You're lucky, Patrick," she said. "One simple break to the bone in your leg and ankle."

After my cast was slowly swung to the ground, she nonchalantly passed me the chamber pot.

"What you want me to do with this?"

"I want you to use it. Joseph's collecting it."

"I've heard of collecting rocks before, and hair, thanks to you. What's he gonna do, soak clothes in it?"

"I'm not sure. You can find that out when you give it to him."

"This image won't go well with the other images I have of us together, Anne. I just said that aloud, didn't I?"

"I'll blame it on the fever. Patrick, the only image I want you to hold onto is the one of you walking out of this room alive," she cried, her eyes watering.

"I'm gonna be fine, Anne," I said, patting the top of her head.

"I'll get your clothes."

"It's not happening for me," I said impatiently.

"Think of running water, Patrick."

She took her time picking out warm clothes while my kidneys took their time functioning again.

"It's been too long," I said, struggling to have that feeling again.

"Not that long ago. You just have to relax and don't expect much."

When she came over, I looked at her glumly. "It looks the colour of molasses."

"It's the constant fever. You need to keep drinking."

After placing a full glass of water in my hand, she gathered undergarments.

"Forget about those," I mumbled with eyes struggling to stay open. "Just don't clothe me in wool. It makes my skin itchy."

Taking my softest flannel shirt, she draped it around warm shoulders.

"I'm going to get your father to carry you over."

"Over my dead body!" I warned. "I'll walk. I just may need more time. Well, a lot more time."

She was shaking in disapproval, gingerly pulling pants over my good and useless leg. After wriggling them over my hips and fastening them, she reached for a pair of suspenders and my boot.

"Where's my other boot, Anne?"

"You only need one, Patrick."

I foolishly nodded. "Where's my other boot, Anne?"

"It had to be cut away to get your leg out safely."

I gasped, trying to erase away her words. "My pa picked out those boots."

"We'll get you another pair." Her fingers felt my flushed cheek. "Patrick, I think you should stay in this bed."

"No, Anne…I have to get moving or else I'll never get back on Taffy, again."

With a face full of pity she eased me back on the bed and covered my fiery forehead with a damp cloth.

"I brought you a book about Tom Sawyer's Adventures. Read it or get some rest. I'll bring your father around when supper's ready."

I didn't need any encouragement to sleep. My eyes were closed before she twisted the door knob.

The late sun was streaming through my room when the door slowly creaked open again. I thought I could hear Sean's voice but was too tired to answer.

"Patrick?"

I remained stone silent.

"Patrick?"

He touched my shoulder.

I gasped.

He jumped.

"You ready to go?" Sean asked as his heart stopped thudding against ribs.

I shook my head of the wretched drowsiness and found both he and Joseph staring at me. I faintly remembered being in this position before without a stitch of clothing on.

"You can keep your hands to yourself," I grumbled. "I'm walking."

Sean was impressed by my feigned fortitude.

Joseph was warily concerned.

"Take this," Sean offered proudly.

It was a wooden cane he had whittled once he heard I wanted to come to the house for supper.

"You sure you want to do this?" he asked.

I ungraciously took the cane. "Keep moving forward, Sean. Besides, I've got a pasture to fill with horses some-day soon." It came out as a question more than a statement as I pushed my casted leg to the floor.

Apart from feeling very weak, I rose with little diffi-culty, sliding the injured foot slowly along the pinewood planks with ease.

"That's not so bad," I smiled.

Sean nodded with great encouragement.

It was when I put weight on the broken bones that I let out a stifled cry and lost my balance into Joseph's waiting arms. With lightening speed, a chair was slid under me.

"You've done well, Patrick. Now let us do the rest."

Wiping dry brows with a quivering hand, my voice balked, "Didn't know it'd be so hard to balance on the darn thing. I just want to get out of this room," I griped as the four walls moved ever closer to my being.

"Since that's what you want, that's what we'll do, right Joseph?"

Sean draped a jacket over my sagging shoulders.

"Under my better judgment, that's what we'll do," Joseph replied, winding my torso in a heavy quilt.

Both men lifted me in the chair towards the house.

I asked what was for supper, though Sean didn't have a clue. I just prayed it wasn't broth. Secretly, I was happy I wasn't walking. The house seemed miles away. My body of bones rattled, even twitched, despite being wrapped like husk on corn. I prayed I would breathe freely this evening. I should have prayed for more.

As we entered the warm kitchen, Anne was already seated. Sean stripped my layers like he was peeling an onion. I must have been hungry for I kept thinking about food. My chair was anchored furthest from the door. I looked to Anne, who was staring blithely. Then I glanced at Sean, who was staring oddly.

A small smile crept across his face. "It's good to finally see that face without the fur." His eyes went to the top of my head. "Is your hair unevenly cut?"

"My head's a bit crooked. It happens with early babies, sometimes," I smiled subtly with a wink to Anne.

My smile faded when I looked down at the…soup. Not just any soup. It was a paltry soup, consisting of three floating carrots. I couldn't hide my dismay.

"What is it, Patrick?" Sean worried.

I glimpsed everybody's soup and there was little in their bowls, too.

"What do you have in your bowl, Sean?"

"Well, I have potato, carrots, and this brown thing."

"It's a mushroom. The brown thing is a mushroom," Anne stated.

"Joseph?" I asked.

"Well, I have potato, carrots, and onion," he smiled.

Sean piped in, "You got onion, Joseph. Well, Patrick, you can have my potato and mushroom if Joseph gives me his onion."

"Hold your horses!" Anne exclaimed. "I have more vegetables in the pot! I just thought it best to make a light meal for Patrick. Don't want him to feel uncomfortable. He hasn't...." Her words halted hastily while snatching Sean's bowl.

I looked at my sad bowl of soup with the carrots, potato and mushroom, and chuckled. I did it again when I pointed to Joseph's sad looking bowl, now missing the onion.

"I thought I was lying in the bed so long, famine started," I continued to chuckle.

Sean and Joseph joined in.

Anne finally laughed, too.

My laughter stopped and started like that of Scrooge on Christmas day when he got the boy to get a large turkey to take to Cambden Town. That got me thinking about...turkey, beef, roast venison, pork chops and.... and bacon...oh bacon.

"Anne, do you have anything else to eat? I'm starving?" I growled like a hunger-starved grizzly bear.

"Oh, I forgot about the biscuits still in the oven."

Sean said, "Yippee!" And that got us howling again.

"I'll finish my soup. It should take all of five seconds," I said, chuckling again. Taking one of the steaming biscuits, I tried to break it apart; but it was hard like rock. I couldn't even get my mouth around it.

"Anybody got an axe or something." I knocked the biscuit off the table, and it bounced from the floor, disappearing without a trace of crumbs.

"I think we'll find that in bed tonight, Anne," Sean said with humour. He took another biscuit, broke it apart, and plopped it in my soup to soften up.

"What kind of biscuits are these supposed to be?" I asked, scratching my head.

"Lead!" Sean replied too loudly. "Ow!" he cried as Anne stomped on his foot.

"I have pemmican," Joseph chimed in.

We broke it into the soup, hoping it would re-hydrate; but it didn't. The hard bits got mixed with the crunchy biscuit, now mushy, and still got stuck in my dry throat. My soup no longer palatable, I dropped my spoon and looked about the room for something raw to gnaw on.

The chewing and popping of jaws got so loud I snorted, saying, "You all sound like you're munching on bones!"

I coughed and my throat disgorged a stubborn sliver of pemmican while Sean patted my back, putting me into agony again. At one point, I seized my shoulder, feeling much like I was being shot again.

Joseph witnessed my pained face. "You hurting?"

"Think my stitch is a little too tight." I forced a grim smile.

"How long has your stitch felt that way?" he asked in a doctoral way.

I felt too conspicuous with all eyes set on me.

"It just…now," I lied, my face feeling as red as a setting sun.

Joseph gave me an unconvincing glare. "Anne, what happens when a wound gets infected?"

"It can lead to blood poisoning."

I ignored that comment. "Can I have a glass of broth?"

She rushed over and eagerly gave it to me.

I was barely finished that broth when it warmed me to an uncomfortable temperature. While I pulled at my shirt collar for relief, my vision distorted. Everything and everyone went a golden brown hue. I kept blinking, but the odd colour remained.

Joseph shot concerned eyes my way. "Sean!" he called out quickly.

"Patrick?" Sean cried warily.

My mouth opened, but filled with empty words. When the light in the room extinguished, I was floating.

My body twisted and contorted until I was finally on a flat plank, the scent of my room very familiar.

"He's burning up, Sean," Joseph's voice was shrill.

"What does that mean?"

"He could have an infection," he replied. "Let's turn him around so I can get a better look.

My shirt and bandage were peeled away.

"I should have caught it earlier. Redness around the wound is not a good sign."

"What will you do, Joseph?"

"I'm thinking I have to cut into that shoulder again and I'm hoping it's not too late," he said. "I need you to bring over some boiled water."

"I'll go and get Anne," Sean offered.

"I don't think we need Anne," Joseph believed. "You and I can handle this."

He removed a scalpel, forceps, and a few more vials from his satchel.

"We need more light, though," he requested. "Bring over another lamp and the water."

Sean filled the bowls amid a yellow glow from two kerosene lamps.

"Wash your hands well with the soap," Joseph commanded. "Then bring me the morphine."

When he extracted the drug from its sealed vial and brought it to my arm, Sean trudged over to the already roaring fire and added more logs.

"I think we've got enough heat in this room!" Joseph spoke with agitation. "Wash your hands again!" he demanded while cleaning his metal tools.

After my shoulder was dabbed with a light brown paste, Joseph asked, "Are you ready to see the destructive path a bullet makes?"

"What's that supposed to mean?" Sean griped. "I'm supposed to see the kind of damage I've inflicted on those who really deserve it?"

"I'm not your judge and jury," Joseph cried in frustration. "I'm a healer. I heal people. Let's heal your son."

"You ever do this before, Joseph?"

"Once," he admitted with sadness. "And this is the only way we might keep him alive."

The shadow of his small frame loomed large over the bed.

"After I cut open the wound, I want you to hold both sides apart," he advised. "I'll show you how. Ready?"

Sean nodded dourly.

The stitches were snipped, the knife sliced along the red scar. As deep red blood flowed out, Joseph placed Sean's nervous fingers across both flaps of skin and pulled. Joseph quickly compressed the opening for a few moments, then re-compressed, until red liquid stopped oozing out. His fingers followed the bullet's path through sinewy muscle.

"What are you looking for?" Sean asked, his eyes fixed on the burning embers in the hearth.

"Anything that shouldn't be there….a bullet fragment…" Reaching for the small forceps, he plunged them into the wound and grasped a small piece of fabric. The red-soaked fibres were released into the bowl amongst soapy bubbles.

"I tell you, Joseph," Sean uttered in awe, "I may have the fastest draw in all of Montana territory, but you have the fastest hands doctoring to Patrick's wounds."

Joseph reached for the needle.

"What are you gonna do with that?" Sean swallowed.

"Hopefully thwart infection. The affected muscle has been removed. Now I'll flush it clean," he replied, glancing up. "You look a little pale."

"I'm fine. Everything's fine."

Joseph gave an unconvincing nod. As he plunged the needle into the affected spot, Sean's fingers fell away, followed by a thud.

He opened his eyes to Joseph's grinning face.

"What happened?"

"You fainted, Sean."

"No I didn't."

"Yes, you did. You have a big bump on your big head to prove it," he said, pointing.

"You never tell a sole about this, you hear me!"

"Actually, I think it'd be a relief for Patrick to hear you're human and afraid of something."

"I'm not afraid of anything, especially your needles!"

"Sean, I'm pretty tired. These Sunday night suppers are lingering way too long in the night. My arms hurt because you are two times heavier than your son, right now. I'll be back tomorrow to check on him and you."

"Why so soon?" he asked, rubbing his goose egg.

"Patrick's still warm and mumbling in delirium. You have to keep an eye on him and cool his forehead."

"Of course," Sean said, thinking he could do another night without sleep. "Should I read to him, Joseph?"

"He won't hear you, now. Just lie back down on that pillow until he starts to stir. The morphine will wear off, and you may need to give him more."

"Thank you, Joseph. Thank you."

Sean turned out the lights, hoping the fire would keep emitting its soft glow into the room.

"You're giving me ample opportunity to know what it's like to be a nervous parent. Just get better, Patrick," he said with a touch to my hand. "Just get better."

Laying his throbbing head into the pillow, he assumed sleep wouldn't come, but it did.

"Water, water, everywhere, but not a drop to drink," I spoke in a grainy voice.

Sean gingerly lifted his head. "I've got water. Just hold your horses."

Rolling off the bed, he stumbled half conscious to the bedside table.

I stared blankly at ceiling.

"I guess I have to pour it in your mouth," he asserted.

As the liquid reached my lungs, I gasped and choked. Suddenly, I was back in Grandpa's barn, still a scared child, but ready to use my voice.

"I don't want to be here," I panicked, desperate to move away.

"Why, Patrick, you're safe here," Sean assured.

"Don't touch me," I recoiled, flailing arms wildly. "Don't touch me!" my voice wailed. "Let me outta here!"

"Patrick, you're safe in your bed," Sean voiced in desperation as my arms thrashed his face and chest.

I tried to wrestle free from his mighty hold, wriggling my body; but it was too hard, his brutish hands putting me in such pain. It felt like his entire weight was crushing my bones. I panicked in utter helplessness.

"Let me outta here!" I wailed. "Don't touch me!"

I shrieked as something pierced my arm.

"I'm sorry!" Sean exclaimed.

As he held me down, my voice began to fail, weakening to small whimpers. My arms had no strength left to fight, and I felt so afraid.

"You're safe, Patrick. No one can hurt you anymore," Sean cried vehemently.

It felt like a torrent of water rushing through my body, paralyzing my limbs and numbing my brain. All feeling was uprooted and thrust away.

"Let me go," I whispered softly. "Don't wanna die."

Sean knew he would never forget this night. He prayed his son would never remember it.

Chapter 9

The fever finally broke a few days later. I was on the road to recovery, though the trail I took was tangled with alders like the gold-filled gulch of Virginia City. It almost broke my strong and unwavering spirit.

The weather battled me too, as rain and thunder pounded my bunkhouse, shrouding me in damp darkness.

Sean tried to cheer me up on several occasions. I felt so downhearted, I wanted to knock his lights out; but he still had a loaded gun somewhere in that house.

Instead, I lashed out with insulting, terse words....

Opening my groggy eyes, he appeared, sitting at the table reading 'Through The Looking Glass'. At any other time, I would have laughed at the outlaw reading a children's book; but I was very itchy and uncomfortable.

"How long have you been here?" I swallowed.

"Not long. Just added more wood to the fire and saw this book on your table. I thought maybe we could play a game of chess or checkers."

I loved games, but knew I wasn't going to love playing them, today.

"Checkers," I offered. "Chess takes too long."

"Why? You have somewhere to be?"

My body squirmed as I scratched my head. "Can you take this sticky stuff off my back?"

Easily lifting my shoulders from the bed, he somehow forgot that the left one with the bullet hole was still sore.

"Just wipe it off," I beseeched as he struggled with my bed clothes.

"Just give me a second," he replied impatiently, yanking until I felt airiness on my back.

"Please, just wipe it off."

"Where is it, here?"

"No, what's that you're pointing to.....it's up a little farther....do you want me to draw you a map?" I stammered.

"You know, glue's transparent," he muttered, his voice strangely wavering as he dabbed my protruding spine with a damp cloth.

"That's much better," I moaned, forgetting he was in the room.

I shuffled to the table. Sitting my protruding bones against that hard chair was a bad idea as I fretfully clawed the back of my head.

"You move first, Patrick."

"How long have I had this cast on?" I asked, glancing at the wooden board and glass of water eagerly placed within my reach.

"About two weeks," he answered, sliding the black checker up the centre of the board."

"Two weeks," I grumbled. "How much longer?"

"Two weeks, maybe more," Sean replied dryly.

"I broke my arm once and was told that the cast could be removed for a spell to give the limb some fresh air." I spoke as professional as a doctor.

Sean looked up. "Is that so?"

"Why don't we try it with my leg? I have a knife in that desk drawer. Pass it to me and I'll do the cutting," I offered, scratching again.

"Do you have bugs in your hair?" he asked, reaching for the knob of the drawer.

"Just an itchy scalp. Get the knife."

"This is one sharp blade," he said, brushing his thumb over the steel edge.

I smiled, "It'll work just fine."

Slowly, his arm stretched back to the desk and the knife was released. "We'll speak to Doc. about the cast. Make your move, Patrick, and have a sip of that water."

I contemptuously shoved the brown checker into harm's way, squirming in the chair one last time.

"I don't want to play anymore! You can take the book, game and leave!" Shoving the board at him, my arm swung slovenly, shattering the glass against the floor.

"Shit!" I uttered irately.

Sean was speechless for once, though I swear I saw him grip the table.

"Can you ask Anne to come here?" my voice pleaded.

"Anne's not here right now. She'll be back in two days. Anything I can do you for?"

Irritably, I shook my head and dragged my flaking corpse back to bed.

Sean offered his hand, but I shrugged it off.

My sore back screamed not to lie down, but I had no choice, wanting to feign sleep so he would depart.

After the door closed, I went for my knife, which was gone, just like all hope of getting any sleep.

****

Joseph was pulling a pork roast out of the oven when he heard a light tapping at his door. He peeled back the curtains to see Sean's brooding figure against the somber, grey sky.

"Morning Sean," he smiled.

Sean replied in his usual grim 'uh-huh' fashion while unknowingly biting his lower lip.

"Come on in. You're just in time for breakfast."

"I can't stay long. Left Patrick with Mr. Phillips. Don't want to burn too much of the man's energy. He's ancient."

"Oh, I think he'll be fine. It'll do him good. He felt so poorly about Patrick's predicament."

Joseph grabbed another plate and spooned fried potatoes from his skillet atop the stove. "Would you like me to make some coffee? Right now, all I have is tea."

"No, tea's fine," Sean replied, sitting down. "That's a fine looking ham. What's it coated in?"

"A cornflour. Seals in the brine nicely," Joseph remarked while slicing three pieces onto Sean's plate.

"I just realized I don't know much about you, except that you're a loud hunter."

Joseph reticently handed Sean a basket of warm biscuits.

"Tell me about your parents."

"My father was a trapper. He began trapping beaver along the mountains to Calgary and south of the border into Western Montana. When the demand for beaver pelts ended, he began hunting buffalo in the high plains."

Sean nodded, stabbing at crispy potatoes and hastily devouring them.

"He lost his bearings during a sweltering heat in Dakota Territory. Was days without water and had to drink his own urine to survive. When his horse got too tired, he was forced to walk. Got blisters all over his feet and cleansed them in urine, horse urine."

Sean stopped chewing. "He must have been in dire straights. Hell, I've been without water. I think I'd die before drinking my own bodily fluids."

"Funny, I take you as a man who'd do anything to stay alive," Joseph spoke cunningly. "When my father reached my mother's camp, he was barely breathing; and I doubt, smelling too pleasantly. Her people restored his health, and in return, he offered the remaining tea, coffee and sugar he had. While recovering, he fell in love with my mother. They married and slowly moved back to this cabin. My parents were older when they met. I was a happy surprise to them."

He sipped tea, watching Sean devour the tender ham.

"The last time I saw my father, he was heading into the mountains. He had forgotten his snowshoes and was having difficulty stepping through the three feet of heavy snow in his path. The Nakoda man following him described it as a fast moving ball of snow that came from the mountains and swallowed him as he struggled to get away. I was fourteen when he died. As I grew, I searched the forests and prairies for leaves and roots, concocting medicinal teas my ancestors have made and still make to this day."

Joseph sliced more ham onto Sean's plate. His friend had a good appetite.

"One day, I left my mother for a week to search out new plants and willow bark. I took too long," he said forlornly.

Sean glanced up from his voracious cutting.

"My mother was chopping wood when the axe slipped. It was a big cut in a bad spot…slit a large vein. She lost a lot of blood but was able to tourniquet the leg. When I arrived home, her ankle and foot were swollen….and black. I guess I know a little something about leg injuries. She didn't want me to amputate. The spirit of a tree had spoken to her, saying it was….her time to die."

"It's too bad you couldn't save her," Sean voiced with great sympathy. "You've done wonders at healing Patrick."

"Speaking of Patrick, where did you get the morphine and plaster from, Fort Benton?"

"Hell, no! I'm a wanted man there. Truth is, I didn't have to take the risk. Not when I had access to a perfectly good hospital in Fort MacLeod."

"You went to the barracks of the North West Mounted Police?"

"Yep. Went right to the recruitment office, said I wanted to join."

"You're too old."

"No, they'll take anybody…..."

"Obviously….if they considered you."

"I was going to say anybody not over forty, and I'm not quite over forty."

"By six months."

"I flat out asked them if they wanted someone who could shoot. They took me out to their range, asked me to shoot a bull's eye on a tree maybe two hundred yards away. I said I'd do better than that as I took the Winchester Model 1876 they offered. Now, don't get me wrong, the Winchester is a fine rifle; however, I much prefer the Sharps Model 1874, 'cause that's knock down power. But beggars can't be choosers, and at that range…."

"Please continue with the story," Joseph interrupted.

"That's what I'm doing, Joseph! There was this flag of the Union Jack, maybe two hundred and fifty yards away, which is an easy target for any rifle." His eyebrows flared up. "Well, I aimed, waited for the wind to die down, and took my shot. That pole snapped like a dried twig: flag went horribly limp. I had one Mountie running to the distraught pole, and the other one quickly removing the rifle from my person."

"You don't say," Joseph spoke skeptically.

"Then I told them I was a Doctor. Hell, I've been tending to my own wounds for years, so it wasn't a bold faced lie. They ushered me to a Dr. George Allan Kennedy, Surgeon of the North West Mounted Police."

Sean sipped his tea. "It's very…" Pursing his lips, he stated, "Minty."

"That's because it's made with peppermint leaves," Joseph answered plainly.

Sean pushed the cup aside and continued, "As I waited in his office, my eyes focused on the glass medicine cabinet filled with the whole kit and caboodle: morphine, pristine white bandages, and plaster of Paris. The surgeon rushed in between two operations, and with a simple nod of his head conducted the interview. Asked where I schooled. I replied, 'from my books.' Asked where I got my medicine. I answered, 'from the trees and leaves' and from a bottle of whisky which I promptly removed from a coat pocket. Dr. Kennedy said he couldn't indulge….had surgery in ten minutes. I said I performed my surgeries after I indulged, removing all shakiness from my hands."

Joseph sat back in his chair and listened to the incredible tale while savouring his tea.

"Well, the doctor finally acquiesced, had a small drink or two, and informed me that to be a Surgeon for the mounted police, one must have a degree. He boasted schooling at a University in Toronto and kindly said I would be best suited to keeping the peace in this wild frontier, going after murderers and thieves. But he did end by saying that he was opening up a drug store in a year or two, and that I might want to bring my medicinal expertise of plants and trees to the table. I said I would gladly bring a deck of cards to the table, as well, and that sparked deep interest in the man's intelligent eyes. Seems our Dr. Kennedy is a renowned poker player. I offered a game with the man any time, as long as he didn't mind loosing his metal instruments. He laughed, escorting me out of his office."

Joseph's head wagged at the audacity of his friend.

"It was foolish of me to leave my hat in that office. I winked at the pretty, little lady sitting behind a desk; and she waved me back in there to get it. Got my hat, raided the cabinet, but left my whisky, so I think it was more of a trade than stealing. Besides, Dr. Kennedy said that anyone coming injured to his hospital would be seen, get treatment, drugs, whatever necessary….."

"So, are you a Mountie, now?"

"Nope…….Filbert Cunningham got caught on a few small hang-ups."

"What…that you're American?"

"No, they'll take Americans. For one, I'm just too much man for them, Joseph."

"You're too…..fat?"

"Seems they only want tall and lanky one hundred and seventy-five pound men. I can't remember the last time I was that weight. For two, they prefer their Mounties be fluent in French. What's happening in this country when you have to know two languages to get a job? Heck, most of the people out here don't even speak English, let alone French."

"Well, I don't see them hiring Indians anytime soon to speak with the Indian population."

"Maybe it's because they think you'd want to wear your headdress. Ruin the whole image they've created."

"Sean, you want some more………PIG?"

"No, I couldn't stuff another piece in this mouth."

"Oh, I think there's room in that mouth for one more piece."

Sean shook his head, looking rather soberly. "I'll do anything for my son, Joseph. He, ah, he has sores all over his back, over his scars."

"Red sores?"

"Most of them. One blistered and caused him some discomfort."

"I imagine he's in a lot of discomfort. They sound like bed sores similar to the saddle sores you get when you've been riding too long."

"I guess so."

Sean felt some relief, though he knew how easily saddle sores could fester.

"He's been in that bed, too long. I've got something that can help. You can help me make it if you like."

Joseph led Sean to a table in the corner of his small cabin.

"I have lots of dried leaves, roots, pine needles, inner bark, wild onions, animal fat, and, of course, urine. This here is your son's dark urine," he said, handing the jam jar to Sean.

"What are you gonna do with that?"

"My father believed it had healing properties. That's why he drank it every day. That's why I drink it every day with my morning tea."

Sean's look of disgust was all over his face as he scurried to the door and spat out the saliva in his mouth.

"Good God, Joseph!"

"Relax," Joseph grinned. "I didn't get a chance to put it in this morning's tea. Let's get working on this balm."

Sean wiped his moist lips, trying to forget the unusual taste in his mouth. "What do you want me to do?"

Joseph handed him an empty jar. "I want you to give me your urine. This balm will be distinctively yours, solely for your family."

Sean snatched the jar. "Just for the sake of my son."

****

The door opened. I squeezed my eyes shut, praying that he would just leave. My prayers were answered when the door opened and creaked closed again.

"Patrick, how are you feeling?" Joseph asked as he sat on my bed.

"Where's Jim?"

"He just left."

"Oh, I thought he was asleep."

"You were asleep."

"No…I don't sleep; and I don't want to trouble you anymore, Joseph. I don't want to trouble anybody, anymore."

"If healing people was so much trouble, I wouldn't be doing it. You look to be uncomfortable?"

"There's something on my back. It just sticks to my shirt. Sean did a lousy job of wiping it away, and he took my knife. What if someone comes in here! I won't be able to defend myself! A man has to be able to defend himself!"

"Well, why don't I take a look at your back? I think I have something that might remove the stickiness."

Sean stormed in.

Anxiously, I turned away as he handed Joseph a jar.

"Thank you. I'll call you if I need anything else."

"I'll just be feeding the horses."

When the room was quiet of his footsteps, Joseph lifted my shoulders from the bed.

"I hope he doesn't give my horse too much food or I'll be spending the night."

He gingerly pulled the crumpled nightshirt over my itchy head.

"I'm going to put you on your stomach. Make it easier to apply the cream and let it dry."

It was no small maneuvering to spin me around with the awkward cast, which he propped up so my toes wouldn't be pressed into the lumpy bed; but Joseph did it.

Hugging a pillow, I already felt better.

"Patrick, you have bed sores. Thankfully only one has blistered. I know it's awkward to talk about your afflictions, but you best get over that because once an infection sets in, it can be too difficult to treat."

I didn't care for the advice he was giving, wondering why God didn't just give me an infection and end my life promptly.

"I've always had sensitive skin. My pa brought home a sheepskin to cover my mattress during the cold and dry months."

Joseph began to wipe the all too familiar jelly over the reddened bony parts of my body.

"My momma had this sensitive skin, too. She grew up surrounded by cotton fields with a slave named Naomi, who collected the balls, spun the fibres into thread, and wove them using a hand-loom. Then she sewed the softest quilt for Momma's mattress. Momma loved Naomi. She was like a mother in all respects. When

Naomi was dying, Momma wrapped her gently in that quilt. That quilt was also used to make a soft bed for me when we journeyed to Helena. It was taken from the wagon as I held her in my arms."

"I'm going to put the balm around your sores, now."

"It's in my hair, too," I confessed sadly.

"Is it anywhere else?"

There was a lengthy pause in the room.

"They say 'that which does not kill you makes you stronger'. I don't feel so strong," my voice whispered sadly.

"Did I ever tell you about the time I went hunting with by bow and arrows because I was out of bullets?" he asked.

"I don't recall."

"Hit the buck at around fifty yards and waited for him to bleed out. Took in the tranquil and green forest, ate some pemmican, and when I searched for him, the buck was gone. I moved a few yards in each direction until I tracked the blood. Found him leaning on a pine tree. He had rubbed his antlers into the bark, ready to attract female deer. Maybe he didn't feel he was hurt. Maybe he just had to keep moving. We move as long as we can until our heart stops beating. You have to keep moving, even if it means changing your position in this bed. I'm going to have a thorough look at the rest of your body. Make sure you don't have any more sores that could worsen. Is anything else troubling you?"

"You got other balms in that bag?"

"I have balms and teas. Some of the plants I have used to treat your asthma can also be used for other ailments such as coughs and sore throats."

"Uh-huh."

"Another one here ails upset stomachs and diarrhea."

"Uh-huh."

"This tea here ails constipation."

There was a lengthy pause in the room.

"I can prepare some tea unless you would prefer a treatment with faster results.

There was a lengthy pause in the room.

"I can make you more comfortable," he said with confidence. "Just stay still."

"I just want to sleep, Joseph," I cried, mumbling. "I just need to sleep."

Joseph did what he had to do. I felt like an eagle spread in flight when he was finished, but I was no longer uncomfortable; and sweet sleep finally came. I dreamt I was in a deep forest eager to search out new rivers as the sunlight flickered through the leaves of creaky trees.

As Sean closed the door with two steaming mugs of coffee, Joseph was washing his hands.

"You've been in here a long time," he said, glancing at the bed. "I can see why. That's a lot of bed sores! Puts my saddle sores to shame!" He angled his head.

"Quiet, please," Joseph requested. "Getting a good look at your son?"

"I just see something familiar."

"Best we go outside. Patrick's barely clinging to an ounce of dignity. If he knew you were ogling him, it would send him over the edge of a cliff."

"I don't see what the problem is. I'm his father."

"He's a grown man. Let's give his wounds some air and his body some privacy. Oh, and since you are his father and Anne's not here, I take it you'll be doing the washing," he smiled, passing Sean a bundle of dirty nightshirts and linens. "And you'll want to clean the bed pan, too."

Sean grunted out a look of displeasure with one last glance at the bed.

****

Anne came back and so did the sponge baths. I wished Sean would visit someone for a few years, but he didn't.

He towered.

I shrunk.

He smiled.

I scowled.

He was strength.

I was weakness, finding it wholly inconceivable that the blood coursing through his veins also flowed through mine.

"How are you feeling?" he asked.

"I'm fine. Everything's fine" I said blankly.

"Patrick," he smiled. "I have a joke."

"I see you've found your sense of humour," I mumbled amid an empty stare.

"I see you've lost yours," he replied cunningly.

I diverted embittered eyes to the door, willing him to walk out of it.

"Why don't we play a game?" he offered, taking a deck of cards from his pocket.

"We tried this before."

"Well, we can try it again."

"Poker," I sputtered out. "Just do me one thing. Grab the sling out of the top drawer."

He brought it over and tried to put it on my arm.

"Don't touch me," I growled sourly.

Snatching the cotton sling, I maneuvered it around my arm as Sean watched intently.

"Don't you have something better to do?" I roared.

His face became so livid I could feel the heat steaming off of it.

"I'll go shuffle the cards," he spoke crisply.

I hobbled the three steps to the table and sat down with an awkward thud.

"You planning on getting dressed, today?"

"What's the point?" I said matter-of-factly. "By the time I'm fully clothed, I'll just be taking them off again. Sounds like a heck of a lot of effort and waste of energy. My coin's in the desk drawer."

"Oh, we're playing for money?"

"What else would we be playing for, soggy twigs?" I spat out.

"I'll have to go to the house," he muttered, "and maybe not come back."

"You can borrow my money. Pay me back later. Let's get the game started before I fall asleep in this chair."

Sean got the coin, separating it evenly, and dealt out the cards. I anted up a nickel, tossing it in the centre of the table.

Casually perusing my cards, I said, "Raise you ten cents."

"I'll match that and raise you another ten cents," Sean said remotely.

Filling my hand with two new cards, I grinned. "I'll raise another twenty cents."

Sean wagged his head, tossing in the coin.

"Call….what do you have, Patrick?"

"I have three of a kind."

"I have a full house," he boasted.

I threw my cards on the table.

He dealt for me.

More coin slid into the centre of the table.

"How long have you been playing poker?" I asked.

"Too long," he replied, throwing in coin. "And you?"

"This is my first time. Pa didn't care for cards. And the ranch hands…well, they wouldn't take my gold."

"You mean my gold," Sean corrected.

"Well, it's in my possession, so it's my gold!" I proclaimed, but thought how easily he could take it, my pathetic body offering little struggle.

Sean asked me to concentrate on the game.

Meanwhile, his concentration seemed to wane as he peered at the chamber pot sitting under the bedside table.

"I said I want two more cards!" I grumbled. "Why are you more interested in the floorboards than this game?"

Sean dealt two cards my direction and I cringed at them, feeling I'd have scratched the back of my neck if I had a free hand. Instead, I just twitched my head from side to side.

"You got more bed sores, Patrick?"

"No!" I yelped.

"Then I'll raise you fifty cents!"

I threw all my money in, figuring maybe I'd bluff my way through this round.

"Call," Sean uttered, putting down his flush.

Shaking in disappointment, I laid down my cards. "All I have is two pair of fives," I mumbled solemnly.

"Patrick, that's four of a kind and that beats a full house!"

"Oh!" I grinned boyishly, scooping up the loose coin.

"What does your God say about gambling?"

My grin faded. "My God? Well, I'm not too sure what he says about a friendly game between a man and his…..his son, but my God says it's better to give than to receive, to give charity to the less fortunate." Pushing the coin towards Sean, I raised eyebrows. "Maybe this will pay for more glasses."

Sean shuffled the cards one final time. "So you want to hear that joke?"

"Sure," I said, my voice dull.

"A peddler was coming along a dirt road, cut a corner too quickly, and fell into a ditch. Horse was lying on the ground, injured leg. Luckily, a farmer happened by with a big old horse named Charles. The peddler asked for help. The farmer said Charles could pull the peddler's wagon out."

"Is this going to take long?" I cut in. "Want two more cards."

Sean flung cards my direction and continued, "He hitched Charles to the peddler's wagon, and then he yelled 'pull Seymour pull.' Charles didn't move. Then the farmer yelled 'pull Fred pull'. Then the farmer yelled 'pull Charles pull' and the peddler was pulled out of the ditch. The peddler was very appreciative but curious. He asked the farmer why he called his horse by the wrong name three times."

"Two times," I said wearily, holding up two fingers.

"Fine!" he hollered, "two times! The farmer said Charles was blind, and if he thought he was the only one pulling, he wouldn't even try."

I didn't laugh. Instead, I thought of something better to say. "Maybe that's what's wrong with your horse. Maybe he's deaf."

Sean didn't react. Maybe he was hard of hearing, too.

"I have something for you, Patrick."

I hoped it was my knife. I couldn't wait to slice this cast open.

"I missed seventeen birthdays and wasn't gonna miss giving you this for your eighteenth."

He handed me the parcel wrapped in brown paper.

I took so long opening it with one hand that Sean's fingers started inching across the table. It was a soft leather journal.

"I saw your old one was full. Thought you might need another one so you could write more....more words."

As my fingers moved along the soft brown covering, I was speechless.

Sean smiled, easing into his chair. "I have something else that I should have given to you sooner."

He walked to his jacket pocket and returned with a pistol. It scrapped across the table and stared at me coldly.

"You always bring a gun to a card game?" I asked nervously.

"Actually, I do but this time I brought it for you," he replied. "It's not my first gun. My first gun was a Navy Colt thirty-six caliber."

He didn't see the trepidation on my face, his gaze reminiscent while continuing to speak, "My father gave me the Colt before we left for Colorado. He said that we were going to a place where lawmen didn't exist, so we had to defend ourselves. The…ah, Navy Colt took a make your own kind of ammunition which consisted of a ball, powder, and percussion cup. When I got the Colt, I practiced with it every day until I could throw lead 'quick and straight'. The trees around our property had more slugs than birds in them. I switched to the Colt forty-five for practical reasons."

Sean glanced at the gun. "The thing about these pistols is that they're only accurate within short distances. Once, I had…two men no less than forty yards away, and I just knew by their posture that they were gunning for me. Brushing my frock coat back, I let them know my intention should they come any closer. They started marching and shooting, and I just….just stood my ground. Their guns ran empty at about thirty yards. I didn't have a scratch on me."

Sean recollected his bravery with fondness.

"Then I began walking until I was twenty yards away. Fired once. Man on the left went down hard. I let the dark smoke clear as the last man standing came into focus. He was shaking profusely while loading his gun, dropping bullets like they were steaming. I kept walking towards him, though I felt like screaming, 'run away, I won't shoot you'! When he raised his pistol, I fired a shot, then another. My second shot wasn't needed. First one punctured a lung. His face was unforgettable as the air leaked from a deep hole. He made such horrible, suffocating sounds."

Sean's reminiscent gaze dissolved as his eyes centred on me.

"I….I don't want it," I said frankly, sliding the gun back to him.

"You need a gun to protect yourself especially if you're going after my lawmen."

The gun slid my way again. "If I had that gun, I'd be dead," I cried, thrusting it away.

"I'll teach you to use it so you'll never miss your target!"

And that gun was staring coldly at me.

I closed me eyes. "You're too late."

Sean's chair creaked as he sat back with a deep sigh. "You said you never shot anyone."

"I said I never shot a man," my voice quivered, my body instinctively following.

He looked perplexed, but that soon changed to shock and finally…recognition. Sitting up in his chair, he asked, "How did it happen?"

"Doesn't matter," I mumbled sadly. "Result's still the same. I made my peace. Had to….a long time ago, but I'll never touch a gun again." And that cold, metal piece slid across the table one final time.

"My pa had a game called dominoes," I said. "The pieces could be arranged so that if one fell, the others would follow. That's exactly what my life's been like since the day I was born. One after the other until everything was lying on the ground including Momma."

The room went silent. I waited for a vindictive response; however, he seemed troubled, conflicted.

I tried to make out his reaction. It could have been a number of different feelings or all of them coming together at once…..anger, regret, disappointment, in his son.

Finally, he said helplessly, "Tell me what I should do? What can I do?"

"Momma always wanted to see us fishing at Willowtree Creek. Maybe we go fishing," I offered with feigned optimism. "She'd want that."

Sean nodded heavily before grabbing his pistol and jacket. With a profound sigh, he said, "Night."

Once on the porch, he gripped the railing and sank heavily onto a wooden chair.

"Mandy," he whispered solemnly.

Removing her image from his pocket, a memory of long ago emerged. She was eagerly waiting in her pink dress under the shade of the giant willow when he arrived.

Making quick strides, she was soon in his arms, his strong hands moving tenderly through soft hair, freeing tresses from a tight comb to flow along her slender back.

"Sean," her voice echoed softly through the trees.

"I don't want to let you go," he cried softly.

****

I sat at the table long after Sean had left the room, my heart in such torment. My spirit was languishing in such a dark place that I turned out my lamps so I could physically be there as well.

Though I no longer wallowed in guilt and shame over Momma's death, I could only wonder what Sean thought of his only son. How he looked scornfully at me; how he shook with ire. I wondered how long it would take before he lashed out at me.

There were no rays of hope shining through my window: just ominous sky and ample tears flowing from the clouds.

After the room became silent and dark, Sean re-entered. He struck a match and lit the kerosene lamp at the desk, rekindled the fire in the hearth, and walked over to the chamber pot.

There was no need to empty what little there was, and its dark colour gave him more cause for worry. He would sleep another night in the bunkhouse and call upon Joseph when the sun began to rise.

I awoke to hear what sounded like a barnyard pig in my bed. The room was pitch-black, I couldn't see two fingers in front of my face, and my kerosene lamp was out of reach. I gingerly tapped Sean; however, he continued breathing raucously at my face.

Jabbing him with my elbow, he scowled, "Do that one more time and I'll pull your arm out of your socket!"

I shook nervously. "Just trying to get better! I can't sleep with your incessant snoring."

"Well, Anne says I have two choices: the barn or your room, so here I am! Besides, I have to keep your fire lit and make sure you're drinking water! Drink your damn water!"

Pondering how I could get this room to myself again, I came up with the only solution.

"Well, we have a third choice," I began slowly. "The way I see it, I don't snore, Anne doesn't snore, and you do snore."

I waited to see if the words needed further elaboration.

Nope. I never saw Sean gravitate so hastily to his house as I welcomed the silence of my room again.

Chapter 10

When dawn arrived, the damp air rushed in as Sean rushed out to Joseph's cabin in the woods. It would take twenty minutes west of the Taylor ranch until he was at his friend's door, anxiously banging.

"Sean," Joseph answered, his white shirt still unbuttoned, hanging loosely over trousers. "You're too early. Breakfast isn't ready yet."

'That's fine, Joseph. I wanted to bring you this."

"What's this?" he asked, staring at the jar.

"It's Patrick's. That's all he had in his pot yesterday."

"You riding with your Sharps rifle, Sean?"

"Of course. You live in the wilderness, Joseph."

"And you have this precious urine to protect."

"I'm not laughing. Is that normal or is there a problem?"

Joseph eyed the jar. "It's a better colour, but there should be more of it. I'll get my satchel. Go groom and saddle my horse."

Joseph's horse, Pepper, was voraciously munching on his morning hay until a bridle was forced into his mouth. Pepper madly whipped his tail while Sean pulled the toe pick along the inside of his hind hooves.

"You can eat at my house, you pig!"

Joseph arrived as his horse was being cinched. "I'm sure Patrick's fine," he spoke sanguinely. "It just takes time for the body to heal."

"He was just acting strangely yesterday. It's not like Patrick to be so angry and grumpy."

Joseph glared at Sean, his face expressing what his tongue couldn't. *He's your flesh and blood, angry and grumpy are in the family.*

They trotted back to the Taylor ranch. Pepper wouldn't gallop.

"I need Patrick to heal and get me a new horse," Joseph said.

"I don't think he'll ever be strong enough to do that again," Sean spoke pessimistically.

Joseph looked at his friend with great thought.

Once at the farm, he went directly to the bunkhouse, waving Sean away.

Sean took a quick glance at the worn floorboards, and rather than wear them out further, took the horses to the barn and fed them.

When Joseph entered the darkened room, he pulled back the short, brown curtains to find me awake, pulling at frayed ends of my cotton sling.

"Patrick, how are you feeling?"

"I'm fine. Everything's fine," I replied vacantly.

Approaching the bed, he asked, "How long have you been awake?"

"It's hard to say. Time moves differently when the sky is dark grey and sunless. I can't tell when night falls and day begins."

"How are your bed sores?"

"They're almost gone. Anne's been treating them everyday since she's been back, and this feather tick is quite soft. I almost never want to get out of bed."

"I've heard about the sponge baths. I almost want to get injured myself."

A smile formed at the corner of my mouth.

Joseph sat on the bed. "Patrick, how many horses you say you broke on that Montana ranch?"

With a hint of interest in my blue eyes, I said, "Oh…let me see…seems like someone else's lifetime ago…but I think…"

As I tried to calculate the number, Joseph held my wrist and felt my pulse.

"And how would you begin to break a horse?"

"Oh…well, firstly I'd observe the horse….."

He lifted my nightshirt and poked and pressed on my abdomen.

"And where did you say you found these wild horses?"

I smiled, replying, "High Plains of Montana."

Peeling back my bandage, he revealed a healthy stitched wound. Then his hand rested on my beating chest. "It takes a strong heart to do that kind of work, and you have a strong heart. I should find your father and tell him you're well. He's probably pacing those floorboards as we speak."

I glanced away. The mention of him sent a pang of melancholy I didn't want lingering in my darkened room all day.

"You know you can tell me anything. The words you speak will stay within these walls," he assured softly.

Looking into his eyes, I saw a peaceful calmness and willingness to listen without judgment.

"I don't…..I don't know how to say it. My grandpa ….he used to, he used to discipline me at supper. It was a normal thing in my house. So normal I gave the punishment a name 'snapback' on account of the way my head lunged forward and snapped back. It started when I was really young, so I learned it, like I learned my printing and math."

I swallowed, and Joseph smartly gave me a glass of water which got gulped down to its empty bottom. "I learned it would come when I let a fly linger too long on my plate, or when I dropped food on the floor, or spoke at the table."

My eyes focused on the sling as I pulled more threads from its open seam.

"Slowly I moved my chair away, making him take longer reaches until one day he noticed. Never looking up from the food on his plate, fork still in hand, he grabbed my chair. I can still hear it scrape across the pinewood floor, leave two deep scratches. With harsh eyes and a grim smirk, he said I was too far away. Squeezing a hard hand around the back of my neck, he said 'boy will never be that far away from his grandpa'."

My eyes went gloomy. "Sometimes Sean walks in here and towers over me. I'm lying like a bird with broken wings, and he has this peculiar grin. I feel….I feel…" My mind wanted to concede vulnerability, weakness, fear, but instead I admitted, "uneasy….I feel uneasy. I look into his eyes and see my grandpa staring back at me."

Joseph took his time to respond.

"There is one way to overcome this uneasiness," he suggested while uncovering my broken leg.

"I walk on it three times a day! Go over to the hearth and I, well, sometimes make the fire smolder. Sean comes thumping in 'why are my logs all wet?' I just don't care to use the chamber pot. Sorry, I know you like to collect it."

"I admit I might try it in a balm, but I don't drink it," Joseph confessed. "That's just gross. I just said it to goad Sean."

"You obviously don't worry about him clobbering you!"

"Patrick, your fears are very real. He has a short temper and can get very irate."

"I can't go far on this leg. I stumble into the table and it...it hurts when I put my full weight on it."

"Then move it while you're in bed. Keep the upper part of the leg strong so that when that cast comes off, your whole leg isn't weak."

Joseph gently bent my knee and slowly slid my foot up the mattress. He moved it from side to side and finally lifted my entire leg.

"You do these movements as often as you can and your leg will be stronger," he spoke confidently. "When you're ready to walk, wear these." He pulled a pair of soft moccasins from his satchel.

"Thank you, Joseph.....for all of your kindness."

"Just keep moving that leg. Make it stronger so you can get out of this house and find those wild ponies. Find me one so it won't take me all day to get back to my cabin."

I nodded, greatly appreciative. Joseph was a very thoughtful man.

"Once I can walk again, would you show me more of this wilderness country?"

"I have a place in mind, Patrick...

Along the Highwood River, west of here,
So fondly remembered, it eases my fear.
I'll take you to the lake's shore,
Where I've so often been before.
Its pristine waterfalls, foamy bottoms,
Turquoise waters in the cool of autumns.
We'll cast off in my bark canoe,
Glide along the smooth, clear waters and through,
The reflections of majestic mountains, their jagged edges,

Shrouded in a cloak of mystic woods and conifer hedges.
Of ancient spruce that tell nature's story unfolding,
Of beauty's triumph, God's glory beholding.
So deeply stirring, it's heaven on earth,
And to my soul, it has boundless worth."

"Have you swum in it?" I asked curiously.

Joseph shook his head. "This lake is always cold. I'm afraid the fish don't care much for swimming in it either."

"Why do you believe? I know why I believe, but why do you believe?"

"When I was coming home one day, I found a man pinned under his wagon in a ditch. Both legs trapped. After I pulled him free, I found tree branches to splint him until we could reach his home. We didn't have plaster or glue, so I had to tie his legs to splints with cotton rags which meant that he would not be moving for a long time. I left him in the best shape possible…was set to depart when he said 'thank God for you, thank God for you.' I believe God gave me a purpose to heal, and it makes me grateful and humbly blessed. I don't think your purpose in life is to break horses. I believe that's your passion. I believe your purpose is to be a peacemaker. I hear it in your words and see it in your actions. That is your purpose, and your strong faith will guide you in that path for the rest of your days."

I grinned with newfound hope as Joseph walked into the dull, grey morning.

He approached the barn and took in the sight of Sean in a red checkered shirt with sleeves rolled over bulky arms, tossing fresh hay into the stalls.

"You're looking more like a farmer everyday."

Sean dropped his pitchfork to wipe sweat from heavy brows. "How is he, Joseph?"

"Bring me my horse before he eats too much and wants a nap."

As they moved away from the barn, Joseph glanced up at the dimly lit sky while Sean kept eyes on the muddy ground, avoiding deep pools of water.

"Patrick's fine." Joseph added, "Physically."

Sean sighed in relief, feeling that maybe tonight would be a good night's sleep.

"He's in a sad state, though; and that can be worrisome."

"Hold on a minute. He's fine, could walk out of that house anytime, but isn't 'cause he's sad."

"It's not that simple," Joseph said as he continued to walk. "His spirit is weak and that's weakening everything else."

Sean stomped the direction of the bunkhouse until Joseph caught up and firmly swung him around.

"Leave him be."

"I'm merely gonna talk some sense into the kid!"

"Patrick, his name is Patrick; and if you walk into that house as you are now, you might as well bring a shovel."

Sean held a baffled look. "I'm the one who's been tending to him! Holding him! Going across this desolate land for medical supplies! Heck, I hunted every goose and duck this side of the border to make that feather tick and now you want me to leave him be!"

"Yes. Get Anne to give him plenty of liquids, sponge baths, and food, when he'll take it," Joseph continued, "and wait. Take the time to make your own spirit well."

Sean shook in deep indignation with a heavy foot to the house.

The door slammed and Anne looked up, rolling pin still in hand. "Patrick?"

"He's fine. Everything's fine."

"Well, it's going to get better. I'm making steak and kidney pies so don't disturb me. Go and milk me a cow. I'm trying to collect enough cream to make butter."

"We don't have a milking cow, Anne."

"Oh…..go and weed the fields. Then go find me a cow you can milk. I'm sure our neighbour, Pritchard, has one."

"That blond, brawny fellow with the mustache that curls around his thin mouth hasn't spoken to me since I stole his rooster. He has more muscles than a horse and walks around with a Smith and Wesson Schofield revolver holstered to his belt while he tends to his farm!"

"Well, if you're that afraid of him, Sean Thomas, just go weed the fields."

She knew it best to keep him busy when he was like this: all bent out of shape with his emotions.

"I'll return with that milk, Anne, even if I have to steal the whole cow!"

She disregarded his comment, wanting the pies prepared and cooked by suppertime.

And they were….

Sean walked in with a pail full of milk, eager to dig into one of the steaming, freshly baked meat pies that sat on the table.

Anne smiled blissfully. "I'm so happy Jim slaughtered a cow. We'll have meat for a while."

Sean pulled in his chair. "I'll have to help him with his fence."

"Wait for Patrick. You can do it together."

"He's never gonna use that leg to build a fence, again. Best he sticks to reading books," he said flatly. "Hell, he can't even get out of bed!"

"Give him time….just needs time. He's eating a lot more. Took him a pie and he eyed it ravenously. I think he's happy it isn't broth anymore. Strange though, he asked for a knife to cut into that pie like he was going to divvy it up and share it with someone."

"Did you give him a knife, Anne?"

"Of course! I think he can handle using a knife."

Sean squeaked his chair across the floor and slammed the door shut.

The bunkhouse door flew open. I jumped, the knife halfway through my cast, as Sean faced me full of wrath.

"Give me the goddamn knife."

I hesitated, but finally submitted after one last slice at the plaster before giving the blade away.

"I can't tell you how frustrated you make me feel!" his words sizzled. "Had an easier time on the run!"

"I just wanna go home," I groaned.

"You don't even have a goddamn horse! Gonna walk all the way with your gimpy leg!"

"Please don't use the Lord's name in vain anymore."

"Oh, does that offend you! But it's fine to take a knife to your cast. You take that cast off too soon the bones could snap and never be right again!"

Sean reddened with fury, hands firmly atop his hips, stance seething rage while his tirade continued, "Didn't know it'd be this hard to be a father. To think that Sullivan man took you in and you weren't even his kin!"

"Don't do this," I pleaded.

"Fine!" he growled, angrily grabbing the cast and thrusting the knife against its hard shell. My hands nervously clenched the sheets while sweat dripped into his furrowed brows. The firm bandage was finally freed and thrown against the far, emotionless wall.

"Now you can walk the hell out of this horrible place!"

He stormed out of the room but never hit me. He cut that cast away, but he never hurt me.

****

Sean re-entered the house with the knife, plaster still stuck to it, and sawed away at his pie.

Anne peered up, chewing, but was in too much rapture with her light and fluffy supper to interfere with his sulking mood. She smiled, ever thankful though, not to be blessed with any of his children.

Chapter 11

I was sitting on the bed, staring at the bottle of chloroform in my hand. There was a never-ending promise of sleep in that bottle; but it was not a choice, so I slammed it on the bedside table.

Reaching for my wooden cane, I held it at a bad angle and snapped it in two. I tossed it at the hearth and grabbed my head, shaking profusely as I tried to find Pa's reassuring voice through the suffering and angry voices of long ago and not so long ago.

The walls were taking giant steps toward me, eating the open spaces, crowding the furniture. Clearing my mind of everything, I prayed to God for guidance.

I heard a faint cry, not sure which horse; but it was enough to get me to slide on the moccasins and shuffle from the bed to the door.

A light rain was falling from the grey and empty sky as I walked to the barn. Once inside, I smelled the sweet hay, saw Taffy's empty stall, and my saddle sitting atop the unused gate. Moving a hand along the deep brown seat, I sank my weary head into it. Sean's horse nudged me with his wet, velvety nose.

"What do you want, horse?" Peering into the gentle eyes of the old creature, he whinnied, "Give me a name."

"Fine," I spoke soberly. "We start tomorrow. Just have to cut myself another walking stick first."

The chestnut horse nodded as I stroked his smooth head.

Sean came from the hayfield to find me on my porch.

Anne was just leaving her porch steps with a tray of food.

He quickly intercepted her and took the heavy tray.

As he approached, I was whittling a stick.

"I brought you some soup and biscuits," he offered.

My eyes didn't stray from stripping the coarse bark from the spruce branch.

He dropped the tray and walked briskly into the bunk-house, making my wary, until he returned and wrapped a blanket around my shoulders.

"You're not alone, Patrick," he whispered. "You're not alone."

****

The sun made its presence felt on a mid-June morning. While I was on my porch, dressed and ready to eat breakfast with Anne and Sean for the first time, he was coming down the steps with another tray of food.

I never saw the man move so fast, turning and scurrying back up the stairs, nearly loosing the tray and its contents as he stumbled through the door.

"Patrick's coming," he said quickly.

A place was hastily set for me with two full glasses of water.

Then they waited and waited.

"Are you sure you saw him?" Anne asked.

"I'm not delusional. I saw him hobbling along his porch with a cane…"

A faint rapping hit the door and it slowly creaked open.

"Patrick," Anne beamed. "Come and sit down."

"Patrick," Sean nodded.

"Morning," I said flatly, my cane thumping along the floorboards to a chair.

"I made pancakes. Would you like to try them or would you prefer oatmeal?"

"I'll try your pancakes, Anne," I replied, sitting stiffly in the wooden seat.

"You will want the molasses," Sean said in earnest, sliding over the small jug.

Anne glared his way before placing three of the pancakes, not thicker or wider that the lid on a jam sized jar, on my plate. Sean was right though, molasses was needed, because they were dry.

I didn't care. I was so hungry I could eat a horse even though I'd never do that. "Maybe I'll take that bowl of oatmeal, too."

"Of course, Patrick."

After emptying the first glass of water, I announced I would make breakfast tomorrow, pancakes, Montana style.

Anne smiled. She seemed pleased to see me up, though I sensed a sadness that lingered in her eyes. It was probably because I looked like a frail, old man. Heck, I felt like a frail, old man.

Sean stayed unusually quiet, appearing like he was in his own little world. I didn't know why, but it felt like I should be calling over Joseph for an uplifting talk.

"Well, I have work to do," I announced, slowly taking my dishes to the dry sink before limping out of the house.

"Where's he off to?" Anne asked curiously.

"I don't know, but I'm going to find out," Sean answered.

"Sit down!" she spoke firmly, though her hand lightly touched his.

"What's wrong with me checking on my son?"

"For one thing, that permanent scowl on your face. Looks like you're ready to tear a strip off someone. For two, you hover with your menacing past and over-powering presence."

Sean was set to tell Anne most indignantly that he did not do any of that as the scowl sat blatant on his face.

Anne folded her arms and continued, "When I worked in the hospital, I met men suffering from disease or injury, and all they wanted to know was that they still mattered. Patrick doesn't say much; his demeanor says it all. I see a man who feels like a speck of dirt on your shoe. He doesn't realize that you two are cut from the same cloth. Where you'd knowingly shoot a bullet to protect someone, he'd knowingly take a bullet to protect someone. Don't show him you're the better man. Show him you're a good man. Show me you're a good man by doing these dishes so I can wash the sheets."

Sean sighed. His Anne was a kind, intelligent woman; and it stirred him deep inside.

"Any chance we can soil those sheets one more time," he suggested with a huge grin forming across his face.

Anne leaned into the table. "I'll take that smile to bed with me anytime."

Sean wasted no time. He kicked the chair away and scooped up Anne in his strong arms. He knew he had to be quick otherwise they would both be sleeping in damp sheets by nightfall.

****

A bright and sunny morning brought some lightness into my step. Waddling into the main house with a bucket of water, I calmly asked Sean and Anne to move to the porch.

Anne left amicably, but Sean annoyingly stayed.

He wanted to bring out the pan and move the ingredients from the shelves to the table.

"Don't want your help!" I hollered, swatting him with my cane.

He didn't like being shooed out of the kitchen like a common house fly, and liked it even less when the door slammed in his face, narrowly missing the tip of his nose.

"That boy needs to learn some manners!"

"That young man is cooking me breakfast so leave him alone!" Anne yelled back with eyes never leaving a book as she rocked to and fro in a white-washed chair.

The door creaked open, and I handed Anne a cup of piping hot coffee before slamming it shut again.

Sean was still standing when I re-appeared and thrust a cup his direction, nearly spilling it over his hands.

"That should shut you up for a while!"

And the door slammed again.

"He's going to take the door off of its hinges!"

"Sit down," Anne growled.

Sean was ready to step into the kitchen when two Mounted police rode up to the front porch.

'Oh hell," he muttered. "Anne just keep reading your book. I'll tend to this nuisance."

"Watch your temper. They're wearing the guns."

Sean brazenly believed he could get his gun and cock and aim it before the officers could hoist theirs from holsters.

"Morning, Sean," Constable Paul Munroe grinned widely.

"Morning Munroe," he replied, raising a hand to shield eyes from the bright sun.

"I'd like you to meet our newest recruit fresh from the East, Thomas Livemore," Paul exclaimed.

"Actually, it's pronounced 'live' as in live bait," the young pock-marked officer with high-pitched voice corrected.

Paul nodded.

Sean smirked, nearly laughing his pants off. The man sounded like someone was crushing his scrotum. Sean disbelieved he could ever be protected by a man who obviously hadn't hit puberty yet.

"What you want, Munroe?" he asked, his patience wearing thin.

"We found O'Flaherty's body and would like to speak to Patrick Sullivan for a few moments."

"That's out of the question. Patrick's been ill for some time. He's very weak."

"I know. I've spoken to Doctor Andrews and.....well we just need a few minutes of his time."

Sean glanced at Anne, still engrossed in her book; so he approached the constable. "I'm gonna say this once and for all. Patrick's not well and will not be speaking to you today or any other day for that matter. Now get the hell off of this property before I pull you off your horse and show officer Livingnomore what it's like to get your ass whipped."

Paul's face went redder than his scarlet uniform.

The newest Mountie started to correct Sean about the pronunciation of his name again, but hastily stopped when Sean pointed an angry finger his way.

The door creaked open and Sean groaned, regretting that the door hinge wasn't greased a while ago.

I limped out with my cane and peered curiously at the uniformed men.

Sean kicked at the ground as I gingerly took the three steps before moving along level ground towards them.

"Patrick, this is Constable Paul Munroe and his…his newest recruit Livemore," he corrected, "Livemore."

Then he grumbled something incoherently.

I extended my hand to them, Munroe's face blaringly full of pity.

"Would you like to stay for breakfast?" I asked. "Made ample?"

"No, we're just here to see how you're faring," the constable said. "It's our duty to check in on victims of violent and malicious behaviour."

"I'm fine. Everything's fine," I reassured with a quick glance to Sean, who was biting his lower lip.

Paul muttered under his breath, "Peut-être que nous reviendrons un autre jour pour les questions."

"Avez-vous une autre question pour moi?" I asked.

Sean took a step back, his head taking a double turn.

Paul sat dumfounded while I shifted my weight, unknowingly grimacing in pain.

"No, Patrick, I think you've answered all of our questions," he answered kindly.

The Mounties tipped their white helmets and turned away.

I got an awkward stare from Sean.

"What is it?" I asked eyeing myself: white shirt half tucked in, gaping holes between my pants and slim waist.

"Nothing many meals and a little sun can't cure."

He approached me, his gentle hand on the small of my back as we moved to the porch. "So, let me get this straight. You had an Irish, catholic father who taught you

French and an Indian friend who taught you to speak Sioux."

"Actually my pa converted. He was protestant Irish. His ranch hand from Ottawa taught me French while his Indian friend, born Shoshone but raised Lakota Sioux, taught me the Siouan language."

"I'm still confused, but also impressed."

"It's nothing," I said. "In Helena, I was offered a job to teach French. Classes have been offered there for some time. I didn't take the job. Felt uncomfortable because," I rambled, "je croix que je ne connais pas tous les mots en Francais."

"Still don't understand what you're saying, Patrick."

"I said I didn't know enough words in French."

Just as we were entering the house, Anne snagged Sean's shirt.

"You were awfully rude to Paul. You know I quilt with his wife on Tuesdays."

"I'll apologize when I'm good and ready."

"You'll apologize if you ever want to sleep in my bed again."

"My pancake breakfast is getting cold!" I grumbled.

We sat down and the mood happily changed after their first few bites.

"I must say, these are the fluffiest pancakes I've ever tasted," Anne praised. "You'll have to share your recipe."

"Well, it's quite simple." I spewed out a half dozen ingredients. "An egg, one and half cups of flour, just a tablespoon of rising powder……"

Sean was so busy gorging his face, he never made any interruptions. Even when his plate was empty, he appeared peaceful.

"What can I do this morning?" I asked. "Feed the horses?"

Sean's peace faded. "Already been done."

"Clean the stalls?"

"Done."

"Plant any fallowed fields?" I asked desperately.

"Done."

I already felt utterly feckless when Sean casually mentioned that there was nothing for 'me' to do.

"Maybe, I just go for a walk around that new fence," I said, deflated.

"Patrick, our blacksmith has a wild mustang in his corral," he divulged. "Came in one day to the trough for water and Neilson fenced her in. She seems to be lifting her hind leg, though Neilson can't get near to take a look. I thought maybe next week when you're...."

I interrupted, "Need to go to the mercantile today to mail a letter to my Ma."

"You need a bit more time," he spoke assuredly. "You haven't walked far..."

"And I don't have a horse either," I admitted. "Anne, can I borrow your horse?"

She was completely caught off guard. "Yes, Patrick."

"I think it's too soon, son," Sean interjected.

I gave him a heated glare. "You want to tell me what to do? I had a father! Don't want another one! I'm going to saddle Maisy!"

After the door slammed, Sean turned to Anne. "What do you think of your Saint Patrick now?"

"I think he's human."

Sean added more pancakes to his plate while Anne peered at my half eaten breakfast with great worry.

"He'll be fine," he said, but couldn't ignore her gloomy face, forcing him to lose appetite. He huffed, taking his plate to the dry sink until movement from the window caught his eye.

"He's fine….already got your horse saddled."

With satchel flung over my shoulder, I clutched Maisy's reins and lifted my left foot into the stirrup, putting all my weight on that damaged leg.

"I'm pretty sure there was a shuck in that slew of words that just left his mouth," Sean remarked.

"Why didn't you give him your horse?" Anne whined. "Mine's at least sixteen hands?"

"Because he didn't ask for it."

After I climbed the wooden fence and painfully mounted Maisy, Sean ambled over.

"Patrick, hold up. I'll go with you. I also have a letter to mail."

Sweating profusely, I wiped my forehead with a quivering hand when Sean handed me a canteen.

"Can't go without water."

I clutched the water, wanting to crush its metal container. My leg and ankle throbbed in this position, but I remained silently steadfast in the saddle.

Sean leaned against the fence like he was in no hurry, talking about how important water was to a sweating body.

I yanked out the cork in a fury and drank from it.

He smiled and walked away from my blazing glare.

We didn't talk heading east. I was too busy clenching my teeth, but would rather die than admit that every step Maisy took hurt me.

The first words I spoke, high-pitched, in a shaky voice, after an agonizing dismount were, "That Maisy sure is tall."

I went directly to Sam and propped my arms on the lengthy counter. "I wish you had whisky, Sam. Even just a small drop in one of those fine teacups."

Sam shook his head, apologetically.

"Then give me four of those hard mint candies, please."

I took the letter from my satchel while Sean placed his letter on the counter with the name 'Holden' on the envelope.

"I just want them to know you're fine now."

I nodded.

"Patrick, I have a package for you. It's been here a while," Sam said, wiping dust from the lid of the box.

My eyes widened as I tore at it. I almost cried, touching the cowboy boots identical to the ones Pa bought me just before he died.

I don't recall how much time elapsed. Sam and Sean stayed quiet until a customer entered the store, the bell a loud reminder that I was not alone.

"Sam, can I play your piano?" I spoke softly.

"Anytime, Patrick."

"I'll take the boots," Sean offered.

My 'father' took a seat at one of the empty tables while I tried to relax shaking hands. After a few deep breaths, I brushed reticent fingers over the keys.

As I practiced simple scales, Sam walked over to Sean with a plateful of sandwiches and a pot of tea.

"I'm not hungry, Sam."

"You sit at my table, you eat," Sam said matter-of-factly.

"Really?" Sean slid open his jacket to reveal his just polished Colt forty-five. "People listen to me better when I'm armed."

Sam swallowed, "They're on the house this time. I'm imploring you to try them….and leave whatever you don't want to eat……..please."

Their conversation ended when my scales became quicker and quicker, eventually changing to songs.

I played parlour songs. Popular American tunes from Stephen Foster and some Irish tunes Ma had taught me.

After I played a string of six or seven songs, my eyes peered over to see Sean looking quite reminiscent. I asked if he had any requests.

"I can't remember the name. It was a classical song," he muttered.

"I think I know which one," I smiled confidently.

As Sean heard the familiar, somber tune from so long ago, he couldn't help but think of Mandy. She would never age in his mind, always playing her piano so intently, undisturbed, while dark wavy hair trailed down her slender back. He imagined sitting beside her, his cheek against her soft one, inhaling her.

While he held her, she whispered, "You have to let me go. You have to love the living."

He closed his eyes to keep the memory of her alive.

"That's exactly how I felt when Momma made me play that song over and over," I said barefacedly, "just wanted to fall asleep."

Sean opened eyes to my hovering. "You can continue your nap. I'm gonna see the mustang."

He snatched my arm. "Not until you eat some of these sandwiches. Don't be rude after Sam went through all this trouble."

My face was full of contempt, grabbing that sandwich and popping it in my mouth. I was still chewing when I grossly stuffed another one into my mouth.

"Sam, great sandwiches," I complimented, stuffing another into my mouth.

"Can we go now?" I said rather impatiently, my mouth jam-packed.

"Where are your manners? Were you raised in a barn?"

"No, I'm just getting very impatient with your attitude. Feel like leaving you in the dust, but I won't today because I can't; but I will get faster and you won't be able to catch me one day."

"Why don't we take it one day at a time and today you must be patient. Drink your tea," he mumbled.

"I don't want any tea."

"I said drink your tea!" he spoke impatiently.

Snatching the fragile handle, I downed the contents in one swallow, feeling the whisky burn into my stomach.

I smiled and said it was the best blend I'd ever tasted.

"Then drink mine, too."

Sean meanderingly rose from his chair, making it all too apparent he would not be rushed today.

I became obviously annoyed, so he offered some fatherly advice.

"Patrick, you have to have patience. Never rush your father," he warned calmly.

"Why, getting old?"

"Well, I've aged ten years since you've arrived, making me build the world's largest fence to protect my three horses, and working at a pace I find difficult to keep up with."

"Am I ever gonna live that one down? I tell you….you'll thank me once it's full of horses and cattle. You will appreciate me, then."

"I appreciate you, now. I just don't know it."

"That makes absolutely no sense."

After we walked our horses to the blacksmith, I watched the mustang in the corral with my arms across the top rail.

"Don't remember much of those first few weeks after I got hurt. I hope…hope I didn't embarrass myself," I said with great awkwardness.

"Patrick, take that out of your mind, son. Focus on this horse."

Turning my full attention to the mare, I noted that she wasn't an angry horse but did spook easily when I clapped my hands. The colour of buckskin, she was now patched fallow in rolled parts. Her contours and muscles made it appear like she'd be a comfortable, strong ride. A wide, dusty brushstroke ran from her forelocks to mouth.

I waited for her to resume drinking at the trough before grabbing my rope and hobbling into the small enclosure.

When she peered up, I outstretched my hand, saying, "Not gonna hurt you." Edging nearer, I could feel her warm breath and hard whiskers.

A booming voice came from Sean's direction.

She reared while I jumped back.

"Good morning, Sean!" Rudy Smith bellowed.

"Shut up, Rudy! You scared the horse!" he scowled.

The horse whinnied and reared again before tearing along the five foot rails at a loping pace.

I sighed, wiping grittiness from my eyes, knowing I'd have to rope her if I was gonna get anywhere near her now.

As my lasso whirled, I doubted whether I could catch her, and if so, whether I could even hold her.

My first attempt grasped air. I tried again, and again.

"Come on, Patrick, keep trying," Sean uttered silently.

"He just doesn't seem to have the will," Rudy observed.

"He has the will. He doesn't have the strength, but he'll never back down," Sean said with conviction.

"You packing, Sean?" Rudy asked timidly. "Didn't think I'd ever see that peacemaker again."

"How far away you think that horse is, Rudy?"

"Not far. Fifteen, maybe twenty yards at the outset of the corral."

"Perfect distance," Sean remarked.

I looked at my father and his confident demeanor gave me the strength to try again.

When the mare slowed and kicked out her hind hoof, I took advantage and swung my loop over her head, held high, before inching my way closer and closer 'til safely in front of her forelegs.

When we stopped, my fingers ran up her grainy head and down her tangled mane.

I called for more rope and Neilson's assistance.

After her front legs were tied to one hind leg, Neilson lifted the injured one to find a stone embedded in the cleft of her nail. He was quick to remove the stone and clean the affected area. Then he asked if I would come back to break the horse.

I accepted with a smile. As I walked away from the mustang, her name came quite easily.

"Faith," I whispered silently.

It was faith that guided me through my recent storms, and it would be faith to pull me through the rest of my tomorrows.

Chapter 12

On the early morning that I went fishing with my father, clouds lightly dusted the deep blue sky. When the sun poked through, the clear waters sparkled, and we felt warmth on our skin. We said very little as our lines dipped in the water.

It was Sean who finally broke the quietude.

"Anne is happy you're fishing with me. She doesn't like it when I fish alone. Her husband drowned while he was fishing a few years ago. The waters were high, and he must have lost his balance or had a heart attack. He was considerably older than Anne."

"Like your age?"

"No!" he snapped. "Older than me....by at least five.....ten years." Eager to change the subject of age, he inquired, "What do you believe is the most important sense?"

"Well, I know it's not common sense. Momma said I never had any of that."

Sean nodded in agreement.

I took a moment to ponder my answer.

"I was in the kitchen with my grandpa one morning, and he asked me to get him some coffee. I reached for the pot on the stove and would have burned more than just my fingertips if I didn't have my sense of touch. Grandpa said I'd never do that again, and he was right. I believe it is touch. Some animals need it to survive. I would touch the foals just after they were born to establish a strong relationship of trust and respect that would carry throughout their lives," I smiled warmly.

"You sure do love horses," Sean said, witnessing my huge grin.

I wasn't smiling because of horses. I was smiling because I truly believed it was Anne's soft and delicate touch that kept me alive. "Oh yes. I sure do love horses."

"I'm sorry I wasn't there to protect you from…"

"I'm not looking for sympathy. Sometimes a memory just comes, and I let it pass like fish flowing through the stream. And then I move forward. Except, I'm not letting this fish pass through." I pulled the trout from the crystal waters.

"I'm happy I found my father."

"And I'm happy you're not calling me old man."

"Momma's passion was poetry and music….writing songs in poetic tunes all the time. You have a passion?"

I hoped he wouldn't say killing people because that wouldn't sit well with me.

"I would say fishing, Patrick. You know, when I came up from Fort Benton one time, fifty cents lining my pocket, clothes tattered and dirty, I started fishing in nearby rivers and lakes. Caught so many, I decided to sell them in nearby towns. Made over sixty dollars!" Sean remarked. "I would say fishing. I did it with my father, am now doing it with my son; and we won't go hungry from it either."

We smiled, at ease with each other, while the soft river flowed.

Even though we each caught a trout that day, my father's was larger, of course. He cleaned and filleted it while I took a nap.

At supper, Anne mentioned that there was a dance in Mr. Pritchard's barn. She thought I might like to meet some of the young ladies, all five of them, living in the Highwood River area.

"I don't know….. I'm afraid my leg is very sore," I said, giving my best pained look.

"Maybe Patrick and I should stay here," Sean offered while shooting concerned eyes my way. "I wouldn't want to leave you alone. Besides, I'm not on speaking terms with Prichard at this point in time.

Anne frowned. "You are going, Mr. Thomas, whether I have to drag there or not."

Sensing another fight coming on, I said I'd love to meet the Highwood River folk, feigning a smile. With a population of twenty-five people, how bad could it be?

I rode in the wagon with Anne, who looked very pretty and smelled very sweet.

When we entered the barn, a wooden floor had been erected, and it was brimming with people. I growled at my father, saying, "This is more than twenty-five people!"

He gave me a devilish grin. "Math was never my strong suit. But to be forthright, Pritchard has lots of friends in Calgary. They look forward to this day more than the first of July parade."

"You mean the fourth of July," I corrected naively.

"No, here it's July first. The birth of this country called Dominion of Canada. It's like our fourth of July except there's no fireworks or circus. Actually, it's just a handful of people waving flags. How do I introduce you?"

I glanced at the crowd. "Speak the truth. Introduce me as your son, Patrick."

Inhaling deeply, I diffidently stepped to the first group of happy people.

"Patrick, this is Mr. and Mrs. Carver, their daughter Eloise, Mr. and Mrs. Charles...." And it went on and on.

I smiled and said my polite, "How do you do's." That is, until my throat was so parched everybody else got gentle nods. I escaped to the punch bowl, which was tainted with more than just fruit, and suddenly this dance wasn't so bad after all. My eyes roamed from the swarms of people to the fiddlers. There was a piano sitting empty, and suddenly, a choice had to be made. I could imbibe this punch until my mind went blurry, or I could play a tune. My decision was decided when four chatty women headed towards me.

Set to leave, my father was soon at my heels when Pritchard caught his arm.

"Tell me, Sean," I heard him say, "should I be doing an inventory of my livestock after you leave this barn?"

I laughed, walking towards the pasture. As I was lifting Maisy's head with a mouth full of grass, four Mounted Police Officers came into sight. Ensconced in darkness, their pistols and buckles gleamed in the moonlight. By the time I was at the gate, the Mounties had made a formidable wall.

"So Montana boy, you as tough as your father?"

I swallowed, wanting to say 'not since I've been shot and left for dead' but recollected the words my Pa taught me in times like these.

Number one: diffuse. I extended my hand with a smile to the big mouth of the group, saying, "I'm Patrick Sullivan." Pa always said it was harder to hate a friendly person.

Number two: respect. "You wear a uniform. You're men of honour. I have the utmost regard for those who protect the lives and property of others."

Number three: remind them they're doing their job. "What's your creed, your oath?"

The only Mountie who seemed to have a voice said, "Maintiens le droit."

I grinned. "Maintain the right. Does that mean I maintain the right to get out of this barn unharmed?"

They seemed very surprised. The big mouth went silent while two of them laughed.

Number four: get the heck out of there. "Well excuse me, gentlemen. This tired Montana boy got to get home," I said, slowly pushing my way through the gate while hiding my limp. "By the way, there's four ladies standing by the tainted punch just waiting to dance, and they have no interest in this sagebrush cowboy."

I hoped they would be gone when I returned. After spurring Maisy into a gallop, I let the memory in the pasture pass through my mind.

When I returned to the dance hall, I tossed back a glass of that punch, zigzagged my way to the stage, and began playing the piano alongside the band. The fiddler approached, whispering, "Have a song you'd like us to play?"

"Play what you were going to, and I'll just join in where I can," I whispered back.

The fiddler smiled and pointed to the sheet music. At some point, Sean and Anne glanced up from the dance floor, their faces full of surprise.

Slowly, the music re-started; and I played when and where I could, very eager not to make the same embarrassing mistakes made years ago in my small church. Galops were still quite popular, and I could play galops. When the last song was finished, the fiddler thanked everyone for coming out, including me.

I nodded in recognition but kept eyes fixed on the keys. As the band was leaving and the crowd dispersed, I took out the music to Momma's song, ready to play its entirety.

It was a song of happiness, mixed with sadness, longing and hopefulness. I played it with Momma's passion and felt the way she would have as she wrote it.

For Sean, it evoked the same emotions he felt the first time he met Mandy. He was amazed at how powerful one little song could be.

Anne's eyes watered. "Go get your son," she said, patting his arm before walking into the starry night.

I sat silent at the piano a moment, folding the sheet of notes into my jacket pocket. When I moved towards my father, I tried to discern his countenance.

It was…lightness in his face.

"It's a beautiful song, Patrick."

"I felt it was kind of sad. Don't want my song to be that sad. Am I that sad?" I waited for a response.

"No, I don't think you're that sad. I see a lot of cheerfulness in your face. I think if you were to write a song, it would be strong, powerful, inspiring, and full of hope, because that's what I see in you."

He put his hand on his my shoulder and slowly pulled me to him.

I was shocked at his affection and kind words. Heck, if I knew my playing could evoke such an emotion, I would have done it sooner. As my arms circled him, mixed up thoughts about his tough and angry ways subsided.

"I'm happy you found me, Patrick. Very happy you found me."

****

Over the next few weeks, my mornings were spent in Neilson's corral, taming Faith. By the afternoon, my leg ached and stiffened so much, I would gingerly limp over to Sam Tracey's mercantile to play the piano.

One particular afternoon, I asked, "Why do you have this piano if you don't know how to play?"

"Oh, I've always wanted to. Just don't have the time," Sam replied.

Looking around the stark and empty mercantile, I remarked, "Well you have time now if you want to learn."

So I started teaching Sam how to play while he supplied me with unlimited sandwiches and 'hot' tea.

One day, while we shared the bench, my father walked in.

"Fine Sam, let's try it again."

"Before we do, where is that middle 'c'?"

"It's right here, Sam. This is the sound of middle 'c', but you don't want that. You want a higher 'c', so let's begin."

Our singing filled the mercantile…..

"Oh, give me a home where the buffalo roam,
Where the deer and the antelope play.
Where seldom is heard…."

Sam stopped playing. "Patrick, your father's here."

"Thank goodness we weren't playing 'Beautiful Dreamer', or I'd never live that one down," I whispered.

"You forgot your dinner-pail, but I see you've already been fed," he said.

"That's very thoughtful of you….father."

"How's that horse coming along?"

"She's been saddled. I'll ride her tomorrow," I informed, patting Sam Tracey's back. "Keep practicing."

As we walked over to blacksmith's corral, the mustang appeared quite agitated and jumpy.

"You sure she's ready to be ridden?"

"We'll find out tomorrow," I answered, my eyes never leaving the skittish horse. "If she bucks, it'll be when I ride her for the first time. I've gotten her used to clatter….sacked her out to get the spook out of her."

My father held a confused look, so I elaborated that sacking her out was using a rope, or rein, or brown paper sack that Sam Tracey generously donated, to touch the sensitive areas of the horse.

"She's also been confined to this small corral for too long," I advised. "It's time to get her into a bigger pasture. You know where we can find such a pasture?" I smugly asked, leaning elbows onto the railing.

My father wagged his head. "Will you be content if we take this mustang home?"

"Not for long. Your pasture has to be filled with wild mustangs. You know what they say about a man and his horses?" I smiled. "Well, father, you just don't have enough."

****

Tomorrow came. As I swaggered into that corral, the whole community seemed to come out to see if I would fall embarrassingly on my bony posterior.

Securing my Wellington boot in the stirrup, I swiftly hoisted myself, gingerly swinging that tender leg over her slender frame.

From the walk, Faith was spurred into a lope, and this was when her head went down, preparing to buck.

Doing what I was taught, I stayed relaxed, my legs on, while taking that deep seat. I went for the ride and it felt incredible. Pa's voice played in my mind at first, but by the time Faith's rocking subsided, it was my voice guiding her into a smooth, forward ride.

I called out, "Open the gate!" And we escaped the suffocating corral, kicking up soft Canadian soil.

"Will he ever come back?" Neilson asked.

"When he's hungry," Sean replied plainly.

I felt I'd never go back. These were sweet moments as I tugged on the reins and slowed Faith to a walk along this vastly rugged land. I stroked her appreciatively while she munched on wild grasses, until I found myself getting hungry, remembering it was Sunday and had to be back for six o'clock. So I angled my reins back to the corral and practiced that gallop again.

As I struggled to get Faith through the gate, I heard Neilson mention to Sean, "That horse belongs to Patrick if he wants her. She needs room to roam. I've never met anyone like him, Patrick that is, and can't believe he's your son."

He walked away, vigorously tossing his head.

"Sometimes I can't believe he's my son either," Sean mumbled.

At supper, I could hardly contain my delight. I had one wild mustang in that pasture and wasn't having soup for supper. Sean was happy it wasn't goose for supper. Seems I missed a lot of goose suppers while I was convalescing.

The venison stew Anne cooked was the best I'd ever tasted, flavoured with onions and wild garlic that Joseph had discovered.

Sean was in heaven; At least, that's where I thought he was. Everything was wonderful until he opened his big, fat mouth.

"Why don't you cook like this every night? This is so tasty."

"Why don't you come in while I'm cooking it?" Anne retorted. "Add your own spice instead of just showing up with fork in hand and bottom in that chair, complaining the food has no taste."

"I was just trying to compliment you on this sumptuous meal."

I didn't want to see it end up on the wall, so I loudly interrupted, "I think it's time we went looking for wild mustangs."

"You're not ready for that," Sean patronized like I was still eight year's old.

I glared indignantly, "I'm ready! What do I have to do to show you I'm ready? Walk on water?"

"You can compliment me, Sean Thomas, by doing the dishes tonight by yourself," Anne urged.

"Patrick, if you can walk on water I'll gladly go searching for mustangs, and Anne, I'll put my hands in the soapy water to wash your dishes up after supper."

"My dishes!" she hollered.

"I may not be able to walk on water but I'm sure as heck ready to wrangle up some mustangs!" I advised heatedly.

"Joseph, what do you think? Is Patrick ready?" Sean asked.

Gently wiping his mouth with a napkin, he took his time while the three angry white people waited patiently for his response.

"Patrick, I like to believe that I know you just as well as anyone in this room. While I think you're much stronger, if you weren't, you wouldn't let anyone know. That being said, I can't stop a man from having a dream and wanting to fulfill it at all costs."

Joseph paused. "Two weeks. Take long walks hunting the forests and stretching that arm. Ride your horse everyday for at least an hour, eat everything Anne gives you, and yes, drink your water; and we'll go. Oh, and Sean," he eyed his friend casually, "just wash the bloody dishes."

"You mind if Joseph and I take our coffee outside?" I asked.

"Sure, go ahead," Sean replied while Anne gazed at him considerately before offering to dry.

Once alone on the porch, I gazed at the pale stars.

"What is it, Patrick?" Joseph asked.

"I'd like you to find out if a certain Sioux camp is still in Canada and where it might be."

"Why?"

I smiled demurely.

"What's her name?"

"Nawaji," I said softly, and her name floated away in the warm, night air. "I can't seem to forget her smile or her touch."

"I'll see what I can find out."

I turned to Joseph and held out the pouch of gold.

He shook the contents into his hands and the golden nuggets sparkled in the light of the half moon.

"Patrick, this is a lot of gold. I don't need this to help you."

"I want you to take it for all you've done for me and for all that you might be able to do for me. I want to help these people with supplies, whatever they need."

"If the Sioux camp is anywhere, it will be in the District of Assiniboia, southeast of here."

"Do you know this land well?"

"Land of the Metis, or at least it was the land of the Metis."

"Metis?"

Joseph peered up from his coffee. "My cousins, half-breeds."

"Why don't you live among them?"

"I prefer to live alone," he said dryly.

"I'm sorry. I don't understand."

"Do you really want to?"

"I may not be able to do anything about it, but I can hear your words, tell your story."

"The Canadian Government has ignored the Metis' requests for land or what white men like to call 'Treaties'. They do not have any rights, are being forced off their land, and starvation is slowly creeping in as the buffalo disappear. Why would I want to leave my cabin for that?"

"If they had a Treaty granting them land rights, everything would be fine?"

"Treaties not only promise land, but food and provisions," Joseph educated. "While the land remains in tact, the food and provisions quite often get rationed. The Nakoda would attest to this. They'll leave the reserve to hunt and trade when necessary."

"At least it's better than our record south of the border," I admitted. "Treaties have more value rolled up and placed in the outhouse where I come from."

"I anticipate more conflict in the near future," he believed. "A man named Louis Riel has already led the Metis into one rebellion. He now lives away from his people in Montana. Maybe he has finally realized what I have known for a while, that quite simply, there are too many of you and too few of us. Besides, I'm a healer, not a fighter, even though it disturbs me to see such torment and suffering."

A heavy pause lingered in the stillness of the night.

I unknowingly rubbed my aching shoulder.

"It will probably take us a good week to get to this land," Joseph advised. "Are you well enough to do this?"

I picked at a sliver in the wood of the railing. "I'm as well as I'll ever be. Can we find horses in this place?"

Joseph grinned. "It's the plains of Canada. That's where they'll likely be. When we do reach the Lakota, what do you intend to do? Whisk her away?"

"Your father whisked your mother away, so that's not entirely out of the realm. Besides, they like me. I'm wounded earth crusher," I smiled sadly.

"I'll see what I can do but this is too much gold," he said, trying to return the pouch.

"It's more yours than it is mine, and judging by what you've just said, it can be put to good use."

"Two weeks, Patrick, and don't hold out too much hope over this Indian girl. She may be back in the United States, or married, or..." His face went forlorn. "Just concentrate on getting stronger."

Joseph held out the pouch while I shook my defiant head, arms folded stiffly. "Not until you put that away."

We finally shook hands.

I walked out into the night air with much hope and anticipation over the next few weeks.

Chapter 13

The sun stung my eyes on this cloudless July morning. I had been up well before its brightness covered the damp earth, loading the wagon with supplies for the trip and the tribe. The horses were groomed, fed, and already hitched when my father appeared. I casually leaned against the covered wagon, hoping to shield its contents.

"Everything ready?" he asked, peering over my shoulder.

"Yep. I'll drive the wagon," I spoke eagerly.

"I'll get my horse," he said, walking away. "You know," he unexpectedly turned, "that wagon is packed like we're going for a month."

"Momma always said one should be prepared for anything, so I prepared for possible delays," I smiled coyly, scratching the back of my neck.

That seemed to satisfy his nosiness.

Heading east, we left the Taylor farm with Joseph on his faithfully slow steed.

Our route passed Jim Phillips's homestead and his wandering cows.

Waving from his porch, he called out, "Patrick, Sean, whenever you're ready!"

"What's that supposed to mean?" my father asked.

"I offered him a few pieces of wood and some nails. Just a small fence so his cows don't stray any more on cold, wintery nights."

"What a good idea," he complimented like it was the first good idea I ever had.

I soon discovered it was not a good idea to bring my father or Pepper on this journey. The painted horse moved slower than molasses in January. I offered to send him to greener pastures, but Joseph wouldn't have it until I had a replacement.

Sean sounded like a whiny four year old child, repeating "Are we there yet?" Or even better, "My run from lawmen was shorter than this!"

By the end of this seven day trek, my ears were throbbing, my leg was dreadfully stiff, and my patience had worn thin.

Upon arriving in Wood Mountain, we were soon surrounded by a terrain of flat land, fields of slender flowing grasses, and gentle rolling hills.

We made a hasty campfire meal of beans and pork with the last of the rock hard buttermilk biscuits made too long ago.

Sean and Joseph were arguing about whose turn it was to build the tents, so I slowly sauntered off with bow and arrows, hoping to catch something for supper.

Meandering along the riverbank, I was ensconced in the shade of tall poplars. The willowy trees towered as their tapered leaves twinkled in the breeze.

I contemplated catching one of the abundant fish that sparkled against the sun's rays as it jumped and dived with the current.

When I returned hours later, the two tents were set up; and Joseph had a fire blazing.

"I killed the rabbit. Who gets to clean it?" I asked in earnest.

"I just put up two tents so I guess that leaves you, Sean," Joseph said. "You can add all the spice you want to it. I want to show Patrick some of this land's natural beauty."

"Didn't he just see some natural beauty?"

His comment fell on deaf ears as we walked away.

Once clear of the sound of my father's booming voice, Joseph halted with hands atop his hips.

"Your Sioux camp's about twenty miles south," he divulged. "Sitting Bull's tribe has already returned to the United States. It may be a matter of days before this tribe leaves, too."

"Then we shall go tomorrow," I spoke definitively. "Maybe I don't have to tell my father. I thought we could just keep the liquor flowing in his tip cup so he'd sleep all morning."

"I think you should tell him the truth tonight," Joseph spoke wisely. "He's going to find out sooner or later if your plan is to have any future with…"

"Nawaji," I nodded. "Let's take our time heading back. By the way, how much of the Sioux language can you speak?"

"I speak it just fine. Why?"

"Well, could you tell me what Nawaji means?"

"Stands firm."

"Stands firm," I repeated. "Maybe you could teach me some more essential words."

By the time we returned, the rabbit was on a wooden spit roasting over hot ashen logs.

"About time," Sean snarled. "Have a pleasant stroll?"

"Took him to the river," Joseph replied. "He wants to go fishing if we're still here tomorrow afternoon."

"You get to clean it, Joseph," Sean added quickly.

I hauled out the fresh vegetables Anne had packed, as well as the hard tack I baked just like Ma did for our round-ups.

We ate ravenously, and the rabbit soon became a pile of bones.

I told my father he should cook more often.

"That's Anne job," he said, chewing unpleasantly on the hard tasteless cracker. "I wouldn't want to take that job away from her. She likes it too much."

Joseph and I exchanged glances at his absurdity.

When supper was finished, Sean uncorked a bottle of whisky. "How's your leg, Patrick?"

"It's fine!" I spoke too abruptly.

He smiled knowingly, passing me the first cup.

I pulled out three fat cigars.

"How much you pay for these?" Sean asked.

"One golden nugget," I replied smugly.

"At eighteen dollars an ounce, that's a lot of money," he grumbled, shaking his head in disapproval.

"The shopkeeper said they were from an Island called Cuba. I was so intrigued…just had to try them."

The men lit their cigars from the flames of the fire.

"Where'd you get the capote?" Joseph asked, pointing to the Hudson's Bay blanket around my father's shoulders.

"It's a long story," he replied. "I keep it as a reminder not to drink one hundred and eighty proof rum. It's was a good trade, though, after I brushed the stink out of it. Kept me warm and dry on many a good night when there wasn't a roof over my head."

I sniffed a little too loudly, figuring he should have scrubbed the fibres with some soap, too.

A scowl shot my way, so I anxiously spat out, "I've trained your horse to come either by whistle or name."

Pausing, I puffed on my extravagant purchase. "The whistle has four beats and goes like this." Licking my lips, I whistled in air for two beats, one up and one down, then whistled out air for two beats, one down and one up. "You try it."

He did.

"Now, call him by his name."

"I'll never call him Slowpoke."

"I didn't name him Slowpoke. Named him Lightening."

"How the hell's a horse go from Slowpoke to Lightening?"

"Well, I denied your horse his oats for a few days, and your horse loves his oats. Then I offered them oats to the fastest horse in the pasture, and your horse beat out Maisy in lightening speed," I lied, for the Morgan couldn't outrun a turtle.

"He's tied to a tree, Patrick," Sean replied gruffly.

"Call him anyway!" I cried impatiently.

"Fine….Lightening!" he bellowed, then whistled.

I grinned, sitting cool and calm as a cucumber.

My father puffed on his cigar with a look of rapture until something wet nuzzled his neck. "What the hell!"

"Say father, looks like you got a little lightening striking your neck there."

He swung around. "How'd you do that?"

"I learned it was safer if my horse could break free from his bindings should I need him in a hurry. Figured, it might come in handy for you as well."

"You never stop surprising me."

"Anyone have any good stories or jokes," I asked, and utter silence ensued. "Any great stories of spirits or Indian legend." My eyes fixed on Joseph.

"Let me get back to you," he replied, complacent to be making small smoke rings that evaporated in the damp night air.

"Well, I have a spirit story," I said. "Might be a bit corny, but I really enjoyed it when I was a kid."

"I grew up with spirit stories," Joseph affirmed. "The Sioux believe that every object….rocks, birds, trees, possess spirits; so you can imagine how many spirit stories I've heard."

"Well you know I was born on April fifteenth," I re-iterated. "The day our President Lincoln died. Do you know who President Lincoln was, Joseph?

"Despite my obvious Indian complexion, I am part white and do have a good grasp of the white man's history. I know Lincoln, Patrick. Man who brought one race out of slavery and ignored another one."

"How so?" I asked curiously.

"It all has to do with that precious resource, gold. Lincoln wanted access to it to fund the war and we all know whose land the gold would be found on. However, in truth the first time we lost our homelands, it was to another tribe called the Chippewa. We were a people living in the forests as hunters, or as fishermen on water in canoes."

I listened intently to Joseph's words on the history of the Sioux. The Sioux never had a written language, so their stories were told or drawn in pictures, but never written on paper.

"The Chippewa had guns and ammunition which made them a more powerful enemy," Joseph proclaimed. "Our tribes left the shallow lakes of wild rice, streams abundant with fish, and fields full of corn and beans, to go to the flat and dry High Plains. It was a big change for my people, but they persevered and settled for many years until the discovery of gold. Of course, my father and mother had already met before that time, and were living in Canada when the fighting over the wealthy land began."

"Lincoln was dead more than ten years before the fighting at Black Hills took place," I pointed out.

Joseph seemed harried, having to drudge up the difficult past of his and other Indian tribes; but my perplexed mind yearned for understanding.

"That is true, but he had a hand in earlier gold finds such as the one in Virginia City. He pushed for Montana to become a territory in, I believe it was 1864."

Sean and I nodded in agreement, all too aware of how meaningful that year was.

"When Montana became a territory, it claimed Indian lands but did not include Indian people. We had no protection for crimes committed against us, however white people were protected and we were punished for breaking laws that didn't even recognize us as a people. As you know, the treaties were no better, promising lands to us, then being disregarded as those lands became valuable to the white man. But I would still like to hear your spirit story."

I smiled awkwardly, thinking maybe I should chew on my foot instead. "My momma claimed that Lincoln's spirit visited her a few days after I was born."

My tin cup was drained before I resumed speaking. "She woke to find Lincoln at her bedside with me in his long and lanky arms. He kissed my forehead and said 'your son will be a great comfort and joy to you, full of love and laughter, wonder and curiosity. My wish for him and for all of mankind is that whatever struggle he encounters, because there will be struggles….that he is able to overcome and persist with his journey in life, learning and loving, in peace and harmony with the rest of God's wonderful creations'."

"That's a wonderful story," my father began to say.

"I'm not finished!" I interrupted. "He carried me to the cradle, saying 'it isn't what you see in the road ahead that will cause you harm, but what you don't see…the roads sudden twists and turns meant to throw you off course and threaten your very existence'."

I outstretched my hollow sounding cup to the bottle still cradled in my father's arms.

"Lincoln went to my momma, took her hand, and said 'your boy is strong, sensitive, and though he will stumble, he will face anything in his path with courage and determination, compassion and good-will. Rejoice in the fact that your son will make you proud'."

I smiled, eyeing my replenished drink, recollecting how those words gave me such a sense of importance and specialness during a time when I felt very sad and insignificant.

"That's a good spirit story, Patrick," Joseph affirmed. "Its good your mother told it to you."

I nodded. "She was a good mother. Under all circumstances, she was a great mother, and I miss her."

My father stared sullenly at the red and yellow flames.

"She loved to make me smile. I think it reminded her of you," I said, hoping he would feel appeased.

"That's not the only thing we have in common," he blurted out.

"Oh?" I asked with great interest.

He swallowed, "You have a birthmark on your inner thigh."

"How do you know that?"

"Ah…." He paused like the cat just got his tongue, his bumbling glare soon on Joseph, who was still making smoke rings.

Joseph wagged his head. "You're not pinning it on the Indian this time."

"I stand corrected," he said, "must have been Anne."

"You lie," I said hurtfully. "What else have you lied about? Did I embarrass myself?"

"No, you did not embarrass yourself!" Sean snapped. "You uncovered yourself. Joseph uncovered yourself. You were uncovered!"

"I'm going for a walk," I said forlornly, rising.

"No, you're not going for a walk!" he warned. "Sit down! I'm going for the walk. Resplendent nature walk in the pitch black of night!"

I sat back on the rotting tree trunk, peevishly eyeing my cigar, its embers turning slowly to ash.

"Patrick, you were very sick and your father rarely left you," Joseph disclosed calmly. "When he did, it was to get medical supplies or make that soft tick for your bed. The important thing to remember is that he was with you during most of it, and not that he saw you in your skins. He even helped me save your life when we took that piece of shirt from your shoulder," he sniggered. "He had a small….."

"Forgot my gun!" Sean called out from the dark abyss, "can't go walking without my gun. Could be a bear or wolf out there."

Leaning into Joseph's shoulder, Sean reached for the Colt and purposely spun and snapped closed the cylinder inches from his friend's ear.

"You were saying something, Joseph?"

"You wouldn't shoot an Indian, would you Sean?"

"I'm going for that walk. Don't wait up for me."

Chapter 14

I couldn't sleep. The dampness seeped into my bones, causing me to ache during every toss and turn against the hard and merciless ground.

Making soft steps away from the tent, I walked my horse even further away. When the peaked canvases were just a blur, I climbed Faith's bare back and dug in my heels under the watchful gaze of the moon's fullness.

Before the Indian camp came into sight, reverberated thumping filled my ears. The tribe was nestled amongst rolling hills and a cluster of poplar trees. Tipis were spread around a roaring fire.

There was so much movement, I wondered if they were doing a celebratory dance. Dismounting, I kneeled on my haunches and listened to the drums and chanting that filled the night air. I squinted to focus on a branchless tree in the centre of the festivities. But the haze of smoke and heat made it difficult to decipher what was transpiring. It appeared as if men by the angle of their bodies were somehow attached to the thin trunk.

Out of the corner of my eye, I saw them: mustangs dancing to the beat of their own music with shimmering backs reflecting white light. A smile swept across my face as I watched them until the stiffness in my leg screamed 'no more'!

Standing, I turned and my head exploded. The sudden blackness from a wet, searing swell left my body lifelessly crashing to the ground.

I woke and was being dragged, the tall blades of grass whipping at my face as the lights and sounds of the camp came closer. My eyes were obscured and watery, not from tears, but from blood.

Movement stopped.

Harshly, I was lifted by my arms and painfully hoisted by my groin over my horse. In sheer shock, tongue trapped in my mouth, arms dangling loosely over Faith's body, my mind kept screaming, *foolish Patrick, foolish Patrick.*

The sounds of the camp became more amplified before stopping altogether. Still blinded and seeming deaf, my trembling intensified as my horse stopped.

I was truculently thrown from Faith onto the warm ground, shaking and trying desperately to remember the Lakota word for peace.

"Wolakota, Wolakota," I croaked, my hands open to silent air.

My words ignored, angry voices charged at me as dirt pummeled my face. A cry pierced through the pugnacious rabble.

"Wounded Earth Charger!" she yelped. "Wounded Earth Charger!"

The rampant assault persisted until I howled "Nawaji!"

My shirt was hoisted and back exposed as blackness swallowed my senses again.

I awoke on a bear blanket with a cloth tightly tied around my head. Desperately struggling to see, a strong hand smacked mine away. I smacked back until Nawaji spoke harshly and hurriedly.

At the sound of her voice, I froze, not wanting to hurt the only person who might keep me alive. She spoke in a soothing voice, stroking my hands, repeating my Indian name.

I tried to speak, but she put fingers to my mouth. "Ssh….ssh."

Her breath warmed my face. Then crushing sounds filled the small space. The bandage was finally peeled away, and I opened my eyes to the dimly lit tipi and her blurry, yet smiling face.

I wasn't alone with her. An elderly man wrinkled with age and sun had a hand full of thick paste he began applying to my head. I complained, shaking in protest while Nawaji held me firmly. She blew warm air into my open mouth.

I understood: I had to relax my breathing.

After the old, withered man unbuttoned my shirt, he commenced his grinding and crushing again in an ancient mortar and pestle, forming another paste he smeared all over my chest. This one stunk like an angry skunk. I almost cried with the smell that wafted into my nose.

Soon after, he left the tent. I assumed he wanted to wash his hands.

Nawaji smiled and bit her lower lip when a scowling Indian man stormed in. He barked at Nawaji, and she barked back. He lifted the flap of the tipi, but not before growling lividly at me before stomping away.

"Mihinga," I stammered, hoping to pronounce the word for husband correctly.

She laughed, shaking her head adamantly. "Tiblo."

I assumed maybe a brother or cousin. "Mihinga?"

She smiled demurely, shaking her pretty head again.

I was very happy to know that she was unwed.

As her beautiful face came closer, delicate lips curiously grazed mine for brief seconds.

Her hand moved to my heart. "Wawate cante."

She repeated the words and they floated softly through my ears.

I had a heart, maybe strong, maybe kind; so I took advantage of her affection towards me.

Raising hands, I replied, "Šunkawakan...horses."

She looked at me blankly.

I said, "Taku kicic u Šunkawakan ….trade horses."

Raising ten digits, I pointed to a woolen blanket, my clothing, a dimly lit lamp.

A look of understanding lit up her face.

Her surly brother or cousin stomped in again with another surly man, and I instantly recognized them as the two men who dragged me along the wet grasses and lifted me unkindly to my horse, making me sound like a little girl.

Instinctively grabbing my manly parts, the two Indians I aptly named 'Rough' and 'Rougher' hovered over me.

Rough callously pushed Nawaji out of the way.

After I was appreciatively lifted by arms, rather than groin, out of the tipi and into the moonlit night, I was safely put on my horse.

Rough slapped Faith's haunches, jolting her into a lope away from the camp, but not before I shot a rushed glance at Nawaji, who held up ten blurry fingers, smiling.

I made it safely to our camp where a small fire raged and a large shadow loomed. It was Joseph who saw me firstly, his face no longer calm and at ease when he saw my bloodied shirt and head.

"Patrick, what happened?" he asked with alarm.

"I saw Nawaji," I grinned.

"She didn't seem too happy to see you," he replied, holding out an arm so I'd avoid eating more dirt.

My father came out of the tent, clothed, and ready to go on a rampage. "Where the hell have you been and what the hell happened to your head?"

"Sit down, Patrick," Joseph ordered. "Let me look at your wound."

Carefully removing the cloth, he determined that my cut would need stitches. "It's very deep."

My father showed less concern over my injured state, nostrils still flared, knuckles clenched.

"I went out for a ride and hit a tree," I lied unconvincingly.

"What the hell's all over it?" he asked. "And what's that smell!"

Joseph glared at me.

I glared at my father.

"Where'd you go?" he asked adamantly. "Oh hell, I'll find out for myself!"

"He needs stitches!" Joseph declared. "Stay with him while I go find a needle and thread. And put some water on to boil!"

"Father," I confessed. "I went to an Indian camp."

He halted his steps.

"They were doing some kind of dance. I think they were afraid that I was spying. Once they knew who I was, they helped me."

"They hurt you, and then they helped you."

I nodded fretfully, though too painfully, hoping it clarified the situation.

"Well, I'll go hurt them and then you can help them."

Sean reached his horse with me staggering behind.

"I forgive them, Father, and you have no right to touch them. This is not your fight. There is no fight. I forgave them."

"Go back to the fire!"

"No! You want to fight somebody, fight me 'cause I'm not getting out of your face."

Sean grabbed at air in frustration. "I can't just turn it off!"

"Yes, you can." I swallowed back the bitter taste of blood. "You can turn the other cheek. Now's the time to turn the other cheek. I'm begging you."

The ground shook, my legs faltered, and I felt queasy.

Sean caught me and suddenly we were at the fire.

"Lie him down on the blanket and keep him still," Joseph commanded.

"Sure thing," Sean obliged, his gaze transfixed while he harshly tied me in his foul smelling striped capote.

As I squirmed against the itchy fabric, he mumbled that it might remind me never to go Indian spying again.

"Tell me something?" he asked, "you forgive me?"

I took a moment to answer, my head still spinning like a wooden top.

"There's nothing to forgive. I understand why you did it."

Sean sat heavily on a wooden log. "That's bullshit. Me leaving was the first of your...your dominoes to fall to the ground."

I eyed my father carefully.

"You don't have to forgive me," he said. "You can hate me for the rest of your life."

"If you think that, you don't know me at all! You don't know why I'm here!"

"You're here to fulfill a dying wish."

I shook my head delicately because that wasn't my truth. "I'm here to help you climb up from your well. To help you ask for forgiveness, not from me, but from God. To free your heart from anger and regret.....to free your spirit."

"You want to hear my story?"

I nodded, staring at ebony sky.

"I was seventeen years in the saddle, no home, no peace. When I left Virginia City, I moved in and out of clusters of trees expecting a posse to be on my heels. I arrived in Helena to find that the lawmen were already there, stalking the town, putting up posters, disturbing merchants and townspeople."

I continued to stare as the moon blurred and came into focus, then blurred again.

Sean continued, "I quickly moved into the shadows of the forest along the mountains and remained there until they found me. I was chased, the bullets like giant clusters of mosquitoes whizzing past my ears while limbs of trees beat at my head and arms. I jumped from my horse into a thicket of green brush and waded on my knees as the lawmen scratched their heads, searching for me. I had a choice to make. Start shooting, or lay low and pray they wouldn't find me. Got too impatient, so I started shooting. I aimed for limbs, just wanting to wound them so they'd go back to town for medical treatment. Well, I tried my best to wound them. One may have moved too swiftly and I may have shot him accidently."

I remained hushed except for the slight nod of my swollen head.

"Darkness continued to fall, so I went deeper into that cluster of bushes and the lawmen finally retreated. It took me all night to find my horse. I found a hollow in a giant cottonwood tree and wedged myself in that space for too long. My bones felt like they'd fused to that trunk and, I had a devil of a time breaking free. My shirt was like a second skin to me; the dirt and dust caked so heavily onto my clothes ….made them an entirely different colour."

Sean reached for a log and thrust it into the frail, grey remnants lining the campfire pit.

"Moved into the town quietly and got swept into crowds of carriages and people, however every sound…a dog barking, or a child crying, made me jump too suspiciously. I retreated to the conifers amongst a soft ground of dried needles and a sky of pointy treetops and tiny stars. Slept too long and the dawn made me vulnerable. I sat up searching for bullet holes and decided I had to become…to become a 'dead man walking' because a dead man walking doesn't fear getting shot, doesn't fear pain, doesn't have human emotions that jeopardize his sanity, doesn't harbour doubt and regret in every crevice of his body. He lives in the moment for the moment."

My father paused, trying to sort his memories like pictures for an album.

"Last time I was in Fort Benton, I met up with a man who could play poker just as well as I could. We both walked out with the bulk of the money that night. As we walked along the gloomy street, I saw something shining in the dirt from the light of the moon. Reaching down to pick up the golden nugget, a bittersweet memory of long ago with my father passed through my mind. I smiled at the recollection but was distracted by something mottling the ground, looking like black rain. I stood to find the man had a dark hole in his head, blood streaming down his shocked face. I mustn't have heard the gunshot. He fell into my arms and the shooter emptied the rest of his chambers into his back. My fierce cries filled the silent street as I lifted my gun, releasing five bullets into his chest. I'm positive he was casualty number six. Later, I found out the man in my arms was also an outlaw, his name I can't rightly recall."

Sean looked reflectively at the fire, its bright flames accentuating his heavy, wearisome face.

"Every time I thought I'd be paying my dues, someone else was there to save me. Don't go after my lawmen, anymore. It's time for me to pay my own dues."

I unknowingly winced in pain while picturing my father and the life he was confessing himself to with as much clarity and sobriety a man with a head wound could do.

His voice went soft. "I lived in the saddle for seventeen years, and that's a lot of saddle sores. If my cheeks were limbs, they'd have fallen off."

I laughed gently. "I know about saddle sores."

"Is that right?"

"We have this ranch hand…name's Jimmy. He gets them something terrible. He wanted Ma to put the jelly on them, and he was already smitten with her, so I bucked up, offering to do it. I didn't want Ma touching any part of Jimmy, so I go to putting the jelly all over those red marks on his fat backside, and I couldn't resist smacking it. Never saw an Irishman jump so fast, faster than a soaring arrow." I chuckled too loudly and my head complained.

"That would be pretty painful, Patrick."

"Like I don't know pain!" I groaned. "Hell, I've had every kind of sore known to man. Jimmy deserved my smack. He was a kind and jovial man, but he was overweight and lazy. If he could move as fast as he could chat it up with Ma, he'd have been in great shape."

"Where the hell did Joseph go? Back to Highwood River for that needle?" Sean glowered as he added another log to the burning embers.

"Patrick, the worst part about being an outlaw is running out of bullets. One time, I came from an alley, peered up, and found O'Flaherty and his posse coming my way. I dipped back into that alley behind a barrel and found two bullets in my gun. Not good odds when four lawmen are coming your way."

He sighed. "I uncorked my whisky and shook it all over me, then clutched handfuls of dirt and….horse turds, coating myself in it. Tucked my hat over my head and waited. They come through, pace slowed, one of them saying 'men like me should be thrown in jail for stinking up the town' but kept walking."

I figured 'that clinched it.' I knew right then and there that my father undoubtedly had odour issues.

"Soon after, I walked into a mercantile and had to decide, while the clerk was holding his nose, whether to buy more bullets or food with the last of my money. I chose the bullets and retreated to my woodland home."

"Joseph must be looking for that needle in a haystack," I said despairingly while sensing my father's attention keenly on me again.

"He should be looking in my sewing kit," he sighed. "Oh hell, Joseph!" he shouted, "got one in my satchel!"

"You have a sewing kit?" I asked.

"It wasn't as if I had a seamstress at my beck and call in the wild. Clothes got threadbare and needed to be patched!" he grumbled. "Now, where was I?"

"Buying bullets instead of food or clothing."

"Flash to two days ago, Patrick. I wake up in a warm, comfortable bed with a beautiful woman by my side. Walk into the kitchen to find you making your fluffy pancakes. You turn from the stove and smile. That smile fills me with…it fills me with hope, for you are my legacy, a legacy of peace, kindness and….love. I can't tell you how much it hurts when I think that legacy may die before I do. Seventeen years in the saddle, no home, no peace."

"Hold up a second," I said in disbelief. "You mean to tell me you couldn't get your horse to come to you during all those seventeen years. You had to go running through the forest saying 'horse…horse' and he wouldn't come?"

I chuckled too hard, making my head feel like a ripe melon being split in half.

"Hurt much, Patrick?" he asked, shaking his head, surely fearing the worst…fearing brain damage.

Joseph returned, looking quite concerned as I lay grimacing on the ground while my father glowered over me with a sadistic grin.

"I found a needle in your satchel," Joseph said nervously, "and will use horsehair to stitch, but you didn't boil any water, Sean."

I piped in, "Just pour whisky over it! Just do it!"

"Just do it," Sean agreed.

Joseph passed the chloroform filled cloth to Sean.

"Just pour it over my head, Joseph. I'm ready," I pleaded. "After you patch me up, we can go back to the Lakota camp. They have horses for me. So patch me up quickly."

"Sure thing, Patrick," Joseph spoke unbelievably while uncorking the whisky. "You ready, Sean?"

He nodded. "Just pour it over his head."

Joseph tilted the whisky at a steady pour into the swollen crevasse and out through my hair.

I screamed, but the word muffled when the rag was stuffed into my mouth and nose.

My father leaned harshly into me until he and the rest of the world went blurry and black, my body sagging like a heavy stone.

Sean sauntered away.

"Where you going?" Joseph hollered.

"I'm gonna get some rope and stakes. Gonna tie Patrick so tightly to the ground he won't be able to scratch himself."

And he did.

However, some time in the night he woke to my moans and struggles as I fought against the ropes. He must have taken pity on me for a cold cloth soothed my hot and swollen forehead.

I didn't hear any snoring: just uncontrollable moans and cries as I struggled to ease the pain in and out of my head. And to make matters worse, I kept trying to move away from the smell that emitted from my chest.

At one point, I heard Sean say he was thankful he had only one child.

It wasn't until dawn was beginning to break when I finally slept in a motionless peace.

"Patrick?" he called, gently slapping my face. "Wakey, wakey."

"I don't want anything. Leave me alone," I said grumpily.

"It's time to get up. It's almost noon."

I looked wearily through watery eyes, seeing three of his faces staring at me.

"There's too many of you," I shook my head, closing eyes again.

His slapping continued until I couldn't take any more. "If you hit me one more time, I'll pull your arm out of your socket!" I snapped.

"Not likely," he replied. "Made you something to eat."

I stumbled out to the campfire, my head the weight of giant squash.

He handed me a plateful of scrambled eggs and toast, and I felt regretful.

"I'm sorry I took off last night. It was very irresponsible of me. Went looking for a girl…a woman, and I guess I was a little impetuous," my voice spoke thick with remorse.

"Women can do that to you," he replied quite calmly.

"I really like…love her. She has a sweet smile, gentle eyes, and is quiet most of the time."

Sean chuckled. "They don't stay that way. Once you live with them, they never shut up."

"Momma wasn't like that. She wasn't a big talker. We used to walk to the creek and say very little to each other. She would say people talked too much, listened too little. She would tell me to close my eyes, pick out every sound of nature's voice, from the cricket climbing a blade of grass, to the bee searching for nectar in a flower. We could pick out every finite sound at Willowtree Creek."

My father nodded. If he was letting good memories of Mandy flow through his mind, he was not sharing them with me.

"Do you have any fatherly advice you can give me about women?"

"Once you find the right one, never let her go."

I agreed, rubbing my sore head.

"I have one of those words for you, Patrick."

I glanced up, confused. "Portmanteau?"

"Yep….splendiferous," he smiled smugly.

"Splendiferous?"

He leaned against a rotted log, looking much at peace with himself.

"Well, its splendid and ah…amourous, no….that's not it….coniferous?" I pondered. "No, that doesn't make any sense."

My father displayed dimpled cheeks again. He must have been recognizing the similarity in intelligence, that is, until he said, "You do take after you mother."

Despite that comment, I mumbled, "I forgive you."

He gazed at me with eyes of gratitude.

"Father, is my head pounding or is that the sound of horses approaching?"

"Those would be horses, Patrick."

I dropped my plate and walked toward the mirage of ten horses. Alongside the mustangs were Nawaji, her lousy brothers, Rough and Rougher, and Joseph, driving the wagon.

Nawaji dismounted and moved swiftly to me.

"Patrick," she smiled softly.

Joseph approached Sean. "They were doing a Sun dance that is prohibited....didn't mean harm. They were just protecting themselves and are deeply sorry. They offer these horses to Patrick."

Nawaji and I were being studied as we used sign language to communicate. It was the wild horses that interrupted everyone when they started to whinny.

Joseph introduced Nawaji's brothers, 'Two fists' and 'Howling Wolf'.

Sean feigned the biggest smile he could, but through clenched teeth muttered, "You harm my son again and I'll put a bullet through your skulls."

Joseph maintained his calmness. If he heard Sean's comment, he certainly didn't react to it.

As I watched Nawaji ride away with her brothers, I silently promised I'd go back to see her as soon as earthly possible.

Not long after, we began our own ride home. I was contented, feeling that despite the minor headache and stained white shirt, that this was a fruitful journey.

Sean glanced my way. "What are you thinking?"

"I'm wondering what it would be like to have a woman in that little house with me."

"Have you ever spent time with a woman?"

"Does one night in Fort Benton's finest…." I bit my tongue, cheeks feeling rosy.

"No, one night doesn't count, and besides, you said you were in Fort Benton for candy."

"Well I was….but was also introduced to a woman named Katherine, who said she had something even sweeter than candy. I curiously followed, and she sure did have someone sweeter than candy."

"What was her name?"

"Who, the sweet lady? Oh, her name was Dhalila. No, that's not it. It was a name from one of Shakespeare's plays."

"Ophelia," Sean said knowingly.

"Yup, Ophelia. She was very complimentary in many ways. Said my birth day was prodigious."

"That's probably because she was a virgin…," Sean mumbled while madly swatting flies, swarming his capote.

"Well that would explain why I didn't know her in the biblical sense. What'd she do for you?"

"Pardon?"

"If she was a virgin, what'd she do for you?"

"A virgin in a whorehouse!" he scoffed. "Not likely! She was a Virginian from Virginia," he clarified succinctly. "Lost everything during the civil war. Like her, many southerners saw Lincoln's death as prodigiously wonderful."

"Oh," I said, somewhat deflated. "Well, she couldn't keep her eyes off…me."

"I know son….that runs in the family, too," Sean boasted, still swatting flies, "except, I'm circumvented."

Joseph and I traded quizzical glances.

"No, that's not it. It's circum….."

"Circumcised?" I asked.

"Yes. I was a child. Had a minor irritation, but it was felt prudent to avoid further complications. It's a simple procedure. There's word of it in the Bible, too."

"You've read the Bible?"

"Hell, yes! Psalms, Corinthians, Commandments. 'Though shalt not covet thy neighbour's chickens' is permanently embedded on my hide. Joseph could perform the minor surgery if you want to have the same, uh…appearance."

"I think we have enough similarities," I shuddered.

"Yes," Joseph said, straight-faced. "That nervous scratching at the back of your necks like gophers digging new holes is more than enough similarity, besides I must return to my table of leaves and roots."

"Can't," Sean said. "We need your help in translating Patrick's intent towards his true love."

"As long as I don't have to translate your intent towards them," Joseph retorted.

"Can I help it? They growled at me like savage wolves."

"Nawaji's brothers have quite the tempers," I admitted. "Though, I believe they can change. Anybody can change. Just takes patience and time. Look how far you've come."

He doubtfully shook his head.

I intuitively replied, "Feelings of anger and hatred never end. It's how you deal with those feelings. How you play your cards, and you have the power to play those cards any way you choose."

My father seemed to be in a contemplative way, until a glimpse my direction denoted pride. If I could hear his thoughts, I would hear him say that I'd been through my own struggles and come out a good man.

Chapter 15

Over the next few months, I split my time between baling hay, visiting Nawaji, and taming mustangs with my father's help.

It was one of those days while I was in the corral lunging a painted horse named Rusty, on account of his brown spots looking like rusty nail heads, when a wagon pulled up and a small woman jumped down from her seat.

Taking fast strides, she unchained the tailgate and proceeded to pick up a fifty pound bag of potatoes.

I darted over to extend a hand.

"Ma'am, let me help you with that," I offered.

"No," she replied tartly. "Just get the door, sonny."

I pulled ahead of the spry woman so she could march right into the kitchen.

"Why, Rose," Anne remarked, turning from the dry sink. "What have you there?"

"I just thought I'd bring the first crop of potatoes to you for all your help delivering my breach baby!"

"Why, thank you Rose. That's very thoughtful. Patrick, this is Rose Winterborn. Rose, this is Patrick."

"Ma'am," I said, tipping my hat.

"It's good to see you looking so healthy. I heard about your bad stroke of luck and was praying for a speedy recovery every night."

"I appreciate it," I replied.

"Patrick, would you milk the cow so Rose can have some to take home to her baby?"

"Sure thing, Anne. Is it a girl or boy, Mrs. Winterborn?"

"It's a girl and please call me Rose. The only one calls me Mrs. Winterborn is Mr. Winterborn. I am mighty pleased Anne could help me with my Beth. It sure wasn't the way I came into this world. I was born on a sod floor in Red River, Manitoba."

"I'll be back with the milk soon," I said with a smile.

"My, my," Rose grinned. "You have one fine young man tending to your property. It looks entirely different with the herd of horses, cows and calf. Did you let the other man go?"

"No, Rose. I'm afraid I haven't told you that Patrick is Sean's son."

"You're joking," she replied, dumbfounded.

"No, they are definitely father and son. Come for supper one night and you'll see that they are undoubtedly kin to one another. Let me get you some coffee while we wait for the milk."

"I notice he's still limping."

"That may never change."

"And his affliction?"

"As long as it doesn't get too cold, he'll be fine."

"According to the Almanac, it's going to be another harsh winter so keep him near the farm."

"That will be hard to do," Anne divulged. "He's met someone in Wood Mountain and intends to go there every chance he gets."

"Only ones I know of living there are Indians."

"She is Lakota Sioux."

"Oh," Rose said morosely. "I thought they'd be gone by now. Figured the Mounties sent them packing to where they belong months ago."

"Not all of them."

"Keep Patrick home as much as possible or he'll be needing more than just your healing touch. By the way, where did you get your nursing experience?"

"In Toronto," Anne replied. "We were given instruction from a book written by an English nurse. Her name was Florence Nightingale. She's a pioneer in the world of nursing. As a child when I was sick, which was quite often, I had the meanest nurses and doctors. And when you're suffering, there's nothing worse than someone poking at you like they were using a stick," her voice spoke with dreary recollection. "Thrusting horrible tasting medicine at me so fast, it made me gag. You'd almost want to die just so they wouldn't hurt you anymore."

"But you're not like that, Anne."

"Florence Nightingale nursed compassionately, tirelessly. She brought better sanitary conditions to her hospitals. And even when there was nothing but death ahead of so many of the patients under her care, she gave them relief and dignity. And that's what I strive to do, even in this small community."

"That young man and his father are so fortunate to have you," Rose said, clutching Anne's caring hands.

I entered with two pails of milk, and the room went quiet.

"Why, that'd be plenty of milk for my Beth. I could also make butter, and maybe even a cake with sweet icing. Thank you, Patrick."

"Let me get some bottles, Rose, so you don't lose it on the bumpy way home," Anne offered, moving to the keeping room.

"Patrick, be careful going off to them Indians. They don't have many friends."

"I intend to change that, Rose. I intend to make them my friends."

"Well, you're a brave soul. God bless you on your travels. And make sure you're packing a rifle. Other tribes get wind of what you're doing," she paused, "they're liable to skin you alive."

I glanced down on the feisty woman as she gave the firmest handshake I'd ever experienced.

"We're made hearty in these parts," she intoned with gumption. "No softness in these hands any more: just a lot of dirt and muscle."

"Anytime you want to give those hands a rest, call on me, Rose."

I hauled the carton of milk bottles to Rose's wagon despite that she shot me a querulous scowl for doing so.

Anne approached me as the wagon wheeled away, bottles rattling.

"Rose has a point, Patrick. You should be carrying a rifle when you go to the Lakota camp."

"I might consider that if I ever do go alone. As long as I have Father shadowing my every move away from this ranch, I'll stick with my arrows."

Despite that my journeys to Wood Mountain began alone, he always caught up, sometimes breathless, sometimes donning that unforgettable grimace that is so reminiscently my father's face.

Most times, I didn't mind and neither did the Lakota. I told him that the greatest gifts he could give were bullets so that they could hunt.

He vowed that he would never do that for he did not trust that we would not be the hunted ones. So he offered food and blankets instead.

It was in late autumn, when the poplars looked emaciated with long white limbs devoid of flickering yellow leaves, that I would ask Chief White Bear for permission to wed Nawaji. I just had to wait patiently for the four legged animals, or birds, to give Joseph a sign that the timing was right.

After we made camp on that first night, erecting our tents about a mile from the Lakota, I looked out at the blackened lodges against an orange sky, scattered along the flat prairie, with leaders like Hunkpapa No Neck and a Brule named Black Bull; however, I was only interested in the one led by Minnecoujou White Bear.

At one point, there were a hundred and forty lodges covering this vast prairie, but after several years of struggling for survival, most of the exiled Lakota, including Sitting Bull, crossed the border in July of 1881 and surrendered to the Cavalry.

We entered the Minnecoujou camp at dawn's first light and were quickly greeted by the women and children. Even the youngest waddled over on unstable feet. They knew I doled out the sweetest goods: mint sticks compliments of Sam Tracey.

As I searched for the woman who stole my heart, Nawaji's aunt, Ehawee, stood out among the crowd. However she wasn't gazing at me; she was batting amorous eyes at my father.

Ehawee was a plump, widowed woman with rotund, ruddy cheeks and a big laugh that revealed widely gapped front teeth.

When she found Sean, she tugged him away.

Despite that he had just been fed a hungry man's breakfast of three eggs, a quarter pound of bacon and a stack of toasted bread, he'd be given more food while she stripped off his capote and rubbed his back.

He didn't do enough to discourage her, and one night I woke up to find her spooning him. It was quite cozy: me on one side, Sean on the other, and Ehawee, becoming a great wall that muffled out his pig sounds, even changing them to moaning sounds the odd time.

I didn't complain for I got to be alone with Nawaji.

We would walk to a treed coulee, holding hands, but nothing more. An unmarried Sioux woman wasn't allowed to show any desire or affection for a man. Even raising her eyes to me could be seen as a promiscuous sign.

The only time she offered soft smiles and girlish giggles was when my hands filled her arms with wood. I would test the limits of her carrying abilities, just so I could see her lips curve so rapturously.

One day, a dog distracted our happy moment. I frowned at the barking intrusion, eagerly wagging his tail.

Nawaji got on her knees and stroked his head vigorously. "Sunka," she said.

Glaring at the mangy mutt, I replied, "Dog."

"Dog," she repeated, resuming her petting.

Sunka was at our heels when we entered the camp and passed a Lakota man cleaning his rifle. Sunka growled, her saliva splotching the ground.

The brawny man, unfamiliar to my eyes, growled back.

While the dog scampered away, my curious eyes remained fixed on the man's peeved face, until I stumbled into Nawaji, my load of wood falling in a heap on my toes.

Wanting to know more about the fellow who gave me an unsettling feeling, I searched for Joseph, however he was hours in the lodge of the Chief's wife, who was ailing from a scourge that was difficult to treat.

It was three days into our visit, as Nawaji was stacking logs into my arms, when Joseph appeared with urgency.

Chief White Bear was ready to see me.

Rushing back, we collected my father, who was getting his feet washed. Then we rushed to White Bear's tent, dog still at our heels.

"What's the hurry?" he complained with eyes on the dog.

"Chief wants to see me!" I blurted out nervously. "Do you have our offering?"

"Yes," he uttered resignedly. "Can I put my boots back on? My feet are getting dirty."

"Hurry up!" I blasted. "Don't want to keep the Chief waiting!"

I watched him struggle to shove his foot in the boot against the tightness of his striped coat.

"Why don't you get Ehawee to wash that thing?" I griped, pointing.

"If she washes it, I may never fit in it again! This thing repels the mosquitoes. I haven't been bitten once!"

"I can think of at least two people it repels, as well!"

"Gentlemen!" Joseph bellowed. "Let's not keep the Chief waiting!" He squinted into sky.

"Come on," I said, snatching my father's arm. "Let's not wait for any more signs."

No sooner had the words left my mouth when Sunka started barking. I glanced over and the aloof, fierce eyed Minnecoujou man was approaching, his hands in reach, when the dog bolted away, sending dirt flying in the air.

My mouth was poised for inquiries when my father interjected lightly, "Was that a sign to stop proceeding?"

Lifting the flap of the Elkskin tipi, I let it smack his face, hoping that was sign enough for him to stop wagging his tongue.

My face must have fallen into sagging shoulders when I took in White Bear with Nawaji's two brothers, sitting, arms crossed with sullen faces.

If they had any say in this matter, I'd probably be tossed out of the camp.

Since our arrival days ago, I rarely saw her kin. They were doing a bang-up job of avoiding me, hunting most of the day.

I sat across from the Chief, his impassive and weathered face shadowed by an impressive eagle-feathered war bonnet.

Through Joseph, he spoke of being in the Land of the Great White Mother for many moons, safe from the army to the south, but also hungry. Many buffalo would graze these hills until the Cavalry caused great fires to prevent them from coming north.

He continued after reflection, "Our children were crying with swollen and empty bellies when a trader named Legare provided food."

White Bear spoke of how the Red Coats, led by a man named Walsh, boldly entered the camps, offering protection if the Lakota obeyed the Great White Mother's laws, but granting no provisions and no land under treaty.

When Legare's supplies ran out, Sitting Bull and most of the Sioux tribes surrendered. Nodding, he said, "The buffalo have slowly returned, but in fewer numbers."

I watched as the beads that embellished his headdress shimmered brightly against a pale, sluggish face. His eyes turned forlorn as he spoke of his ailing wife and how he would not leave until she could survive the journey.

White Bear continued softly, "I understand you wish to make union with Nawaji. I must tell you truth of Nawaji."

His words sounded so ominous, my mind wandered to a possible deformity.

"Nawaji no cook," he spoke with a slight sway of his head. "Her sewing…not good. She does not make peaceful home. But," he said, raising a finger, "she quick with rifle."

My father couldn't resist.

"Sounds like a match made in heaven."

I elbowed him.

White Bear turned to Nawaji's brothers before speaking again. "She has other man wish to make union with her. A red coat. He offer blankets," he mumbled, pointing to my father's capote.

"Ahem," I said.

My father unwillingly dug into his shirt pocket and pulled out boxes of bullets, placing them on the bear blanket.

The Chief raised eyebrows. "Red coat offer horse."

I peered at my father.

"Don't look at me," he grumbled. "How am I gonna drive the wagon without them?"

I peered at Joseph.

"I just got that horse used to my bridle!" he whined.

"Please, Joseph? I'll give you another horse when we get home!"

He translated that we would offer two horses.

White Bear nodded grimly.

Nawaji's brothers stared oddly at the bullets before glaring icily at me.

We were ready to rise when White Bear raised his crooked finger again. "You must be warrior or hunter."

"What," I asked, staring confoundedly at Joseph.

"White Bear wants you to hunt or become a warrior. If you want to become a warrior, Nawaji's brothers will test you, or, well, you should just choose to hunt."

"I'll hunt," I said decisively. "Hunt what? Deer, turkey?"

"Buffalo," he advised. "You will bring back buffalo."

My feet were two steps out of the tipi, when I asked, "Where am I gonna find buffalo?"

"I've seen buffalo, Patrick, to the north, just behind those rolling hills," Joseph replied.

"The more important question is, how are you gonna kill one?" Sean asked.

As we walked towards our horses, I simply suggested, "I'm gonna shoot my arrows into them, just like I would the deer or the elk."

Sean turned to Joseph. "How fast those things move on the open prairie?"

"Very fast," Joseph answered.

"How far do those arrows travel at top speed?" Sean asked.

"Maybe a hundred yards," I replied.

"Well, son," with eyebrows raised, "now's our chance to see what's better, arrow or rifle. We'll see you back in time for supper with that buffalo, Joseph."

"Stay by your father's side, Patrick!" he cautioned.

As we rode out to the buffalo, I reminded him that I was supposed to slay the big, tawny beast, and drag it back to the camp.

When we found them, they were scattered two to three hundred yards away and unsheltered by trees. I could see his point about the effectiveness of my arrows.

"I'll just have to chase after them with soaring arrows."

"You ever do that, Patrick? Gallop on your horse, full speed, both hands on your weapon, bouncing up and down, with perfect aim?"

"I've roped horses, full speed, perfect aim."

"The way I see it," Sean contemplated, "you've got one shot at this, and that would be my shot," he boasted. "Perfect aim, right here, from this hill, with my Sharp's rifle."

"I don't know. What if they're watching?"

"Fine. This is what we'll do," he spoke excitedly. "I'll wound one. As soon as I let off a shot, you tear across the prairie and shoot your arrows into it."

When we returned with the buffalo, pierced by half a dozen arrows, there were cries of joy as the woman went to work, cutting away at the hide. I was smiling, too, as Nawaji peered at me proudly. My father was still wiping the bloody bullet against his pant leg when Nawaji's brothers approached.

They were pointing and shouting until Nawaji pushed them away.

Joseph quickly appeared and translated that I had to hunt with her brothers. That was the ritual, or at least it was the ritual for me.

Of course, my father was on my heels, ready to go, when the Rough brothers shook their sullen heads.

Just minutes out of the camp, horse hooves approached. I shook my weary head, figuring it was my father catching up. Spinning, the wind stole my breath as I stared into the embittered face of the Lakota man I aptly named 'Growls at dog'. It turns out that he would be a part of this ritual, too.

He wheeled us away from the rolling hills into a forest of poplars. We left our horses on the outskirts and maneuvered on foot around the lanky white poles when an elk came into view.

Growls at dog smacked me in the back which was my not so obvious cue to shoot.

About fifty yards from the elk, I lined up an arrow, feathers grazing my cheek, when Growls at dog leaned into me, his knife pressed against my throat. My head was thrust back, forcing eyes to gaze at a sun torn apart by wavy thin branches, as I stammered the word, "Wolakota."

I felt his breath before he uttered the word, "Momma."

With the knife removed, his knee into my back sent me hobbling to the ground.

I turned to see a pernicious grin before his sinister laugh filled the quiet forest.

Growls at dog walked away, leaving me bewildered, then enraged.

My father found me slumped by the tent, staring into the ashes of our last campfire.

"Aren't you supposed to be hunting, Patrick?"

My burning glare stayed on the ashes, willing them hot again.

"If that ain't a look of vengeance," he observed. "Things not go so well with Nawaji's brothers?"

He sat down and peered at the Lakota camp.

"We can ride out of here right now if that would make you feel better. But we're not going to fight these people. I can't abide by that," he said to my surprise. "They're barely alive, Patrick: their faces sullen and hollow, all except one, well maybe two of them. That's why I offered the bullets. Hell, if I thought that they were any threat, I'd never…."

"You don't understand?"

"I understand that if you go in there and cause any trouble, you may never see that woman again. And you are all that woman has right now."

He walked away to leave me pondering whether I should deal with the threat of my past or walk into the unknown of my future.

As we departed Wood Mountain, I sat in the back of the wagon, my body jiggling from side to side and legs dangling over the open tailgate, watching Nawaji get smaller and smaller.

I would have time to ponder my decision. The union would not take place until the following spring.

"What did you find out about Patrick's future family?" Sean asked Joseph as he peered over his shoulder.

Joseph glanced out over the shrinking lodges, feeling it safe to speak against the Minnecoujou as Sean's Colt forty-five sat safely holstered just inches from Joseph's fingers.

"Nawaji's brothers and cousin, Canowicakte, were at the Battle of Big Horn. For a while afterwards, the one called Canowicakte wore a shirt of scalps. Ehawee calls him a great warrior. He earned that name after defending his cousins from a gun attack with the white man in the woods. The way I see it, Patrick's just too white for Nawaji."

"Would they hurt him, Joseph?"

"It would be wise to change Patrick's mind. If the Chief dies, this Canowicakte will lead these people back to the United States. Besides, I promised Ehawee that you'd consider a union with her."

"Why'd you do that?" Sean griped.

"So she would talk faster."

"You see the way Patrick looks at Nawaji?" Sean asked, rhetorically. "He won't giver her up."

"Maybe he won't have to. The Chief's wife will not survive the winter…and," Joseph said, turning, "he's not well. His tribe may not be here in the Spring."

Chapter 16

The long winter days put me into doldrums. I knew Anne's books so well I was reciting Shakespeare's words to a horse's skull I found in the mountains, now sitting perched on my mantle over the hearth.

When I got bored of that, I turned to the Bible, and read it from cover to cover until it played in my mind to the sound of Pa's voice. Upon my return to the Minnecoujou camp in the spring, I would know how to deal with this threat from my past, fearlessly.

I got so antsy I set a plan in motion to leave in the dead of night while my father rocked Anne's bed with his abhorrent breathing.

My dresser drawers were so stuffed with apples, potatoes, beef jerky, and mint sticks, I could barely close them.

The night I planned to leave, I was at the supper table eyeing the basket of biscuits that would fill my stomach on the journey.

I saw my opportunity when Anne and my father had eyes on their full plates.

"So, Patrick, why don't we play some cards to-night?" Sean enticed. "Poker. We can bet quarters?"

"Well," I said, jamming a biscuit in my pant pocket. "I'm kind of tired, tonight. Maybe tomorrow. I'm sure my calendar's clear for the next fifty nights."

Anne smiled. "I guess that means you're doing the dishes with me, Sean."

"I guess so," Sean scowled. "You know, Patrick, I found a satchel full of oats in the corner of the barn and can't fathom which horse would have done that?"

"I may have done that a while ago and just forgotten about it. Ah….where did you put it?"

"I fed them evenly to the herd."

"Thanks, Father," I said dryly. "I love it when you chip in and do chores."

"Patrick, you should join us in the keeping room tonight," his nagging persisted. "You seem a little lonely."

I yawned. "Only if you promise to carry me back to my house when I fall asleep, 'cause I won't be sharing the bed with Anne and you. I know how much you like a good spooning."

"That's enough, Patrick!" he snapped. "Good night!"

"Night, Anne," I said, covering my pants.

I wasn't out of the room before Anne turned to Sean asking, "What's he mean by a good spooning?"

With the door closed, Sean glared at Anne.

"We have bigger problems than his muddled words. Did you see how his pants grew fat after supper? I know I've been bloated once or twice after a good meal, but he's stuffed his pockets. There's something up his sleeve, literally, and I have to put a stop to it. Sorry, Anne. You'll have to do the dishes alone."

Sean grabbed the whisky and two glasses but left a peck on Anne's cheek. "A man's got to do what a man's got to do."

Anne took the empty biscuit basket and scattered the remaining few crumbs on her plate. "As long as it keeps Patrick safe," she said to an empty kitchen.

I was stuffing clothes in my saddlebag when a quick knock and the twist of the door handle sent me shoving the whole kit and caboodle under my sheets.

"Evening, Patrick," Sean scanned the room, his eyes lingering on my open dresser drawer. "Why, I say you've got enough in there for a midnight snack."

The drawer was hastily rammed closed. "What do you want?"

"Thought we could have a drink together," he offered, sloshing the whisky in its jug. Help you sleep. Your mattress getting too lumpy?" he asked, about ready to tug at the sheets.

"Sit!" I ordered loudly, scraping a chair across the room.

"You know, it's expected to drop well below thirty-two degrees tonight, with at least three feet of snow," he enlightened while pouring.

"I never knew you had the ability to forecast the weather," I mocked. "You have endless talents, Father."

"I predict other things, as well. I'm very perceptive."

"You're also very protective," I said, swallowing back the whisky in one shot. "Don't know if I'll ever get used to that," my voice ranted out hoarsely.

"You're very important to me, and you've already admitted that you have no common sense."

"I meant the whisky! I don't think I'll ever get used to it scorching my throat."

More alcohol glugged into my glass.

"Try again," he taunted.

"Bet I could drink you under the table," I boasted, downing my drink until his distorted face appeared through the flat-bottomed tumbler. "My liver's not as saturated."

"Oh, Patrick, that may be so," he poured, "but only one way to find out."

We clinked glasses.

He squinted at the bones atop my hearth, saying, "What the hell is that?"

Lifting my tipsy hand, amber liquid sloshing over the rim, I said….

> "Alas, poor Yorick! I knew him,
> Horatio, a fellow of infinite jest,
> Of most excellent fancy.
> He hath borne me on his back a thousand times…."

"That's enough!" my father interjected.

When the last few drops dribbled into my glass, I peered at my father, slouched on the table, eyes half shut.

"You want…you want me tuck you in, Father."

"In that lumpy bed?" he grumbled. "You might be spooning me."

I snorted.

"Do you think…" I said, pointing to him so he wouldn't think I was talking to the skull, "do you think I could put out the fire at this proximity?"

"With the amount of liquor in your pee, you could set this house aglow," he chortled.

So did I.

"Well, let me get little closer to it," I slurred.

Standing was a bad idea, and I didn't do it for very long.

Sean sat smugly in his chair. "The lengths I'll go to keep you safe." Reaching into his jacket pocket, he grasped the small bottle of chloroform. Then he stood, staggered, and dragged me to bed before passing out.

Anne peaked in sometime later even though she didn't have to. The rumbling from our heavy breathing was so vociferous it could be heard from the porch.

When the door creaked open, she got a good picture of what spooning was about. It was the closest the two of us had ever been together. Stepping off the porch, her laughter filled the quiet pasture.

When morning came, a heavy arm was dangling over my shoulder, sour breath tickling my ear. Straddling my satchel, eyelids glued shut, the best part about this whisky overindulgence was the pain in my head. Clutching it tightly, I hoped it wouldn't fall to pieces as I stumbled to the door. Opening it, a mound of snow rushed at my feet.

"Shuck," I groaned, glaring out at three feet of white powder. I slammed the door which rocked my brain against a throbbing skull.

I didn't try another night time wintery escape. My father watched me like a hawk, the chloroform on the table indicating that he would go to any lengths to keep my from leaving; and I didn't want another liquored overdose anytime soon.

Itching to keep me busy until spring, he managed to coax Pritchard into loaning us his piano. After we trudged it through the snow and practically broke our backs getting it up the porch steps, it filled up half of Anne's keeping room.

My father got me to write down how I tamed my horses. I got him to write down his outlaw days and encounters with the men he….shot. Let's just say that he was a little off on the body count.

Every night, he took his outlaw diary and shoved it under the mattress. Like no one's ever hidden anything under their mattress before.

Just before Christmas, my father was entering the house with more than just an armful of logs for burning. Dragging in a pine top, the four foot conifer was stood in the corner with a proud smile and proclaimed 'our festive tree'. It was sparse in places, so we decided to add ornaments. Anne made lace ones. I made hard and un-breakable cookies in the shape of bells and balls, glazed with powdered sugar and water. Father brought forward a deerskin pouch containing dried corn.

As we were popping it to make a garland, I kept taking samples.

"Patrick, you keep eating these kernels and we'll have a pathetic garland," Sean griped.

"It'll go quite nicely with this pathetic tree," I replied.

"Maybe you could get some more corn," Anne suggested while inspecting the pouch embroidered in beads. "Where did you get it?"

"From the Lakota," Sean admitted candidly. "There's a woman who likes to give me gifts in exchange for my gifts."

"And what gifts have you given her? Did you spoon her?" Anne blurted out jokingly.

The corn popped right out of my mouth into the fire. I stared at my father and couldn't resist. "Speak the truth, 'cause we know how much you hate liars."

Sly as ever, his response, "Patrick's slept with her, too."

"Only in the sleeping sense!" I replied.

"That goes for me, too!" Sean piped in.

Anne seemed upset. "I'm going to bed. Thread your own garland!" she cried, sticking the pin in Sean's shoulder.

When the bedroom door closed, I plucked the needle from his shirt. "You need to marry her. You need to make it right."

The next day, a man blew onto the property with the drifting snow. When Sean answered the door, napkin in hand, the burly fellow stepped in, covered in flakes, many stuck to his beard. The child in me thought he was Father Christmas.

"Afternoon," he spoke deeply. "My name is Lewis Snow. Somebody call for a preacher?"

Both Anne and I looked up from our plates, waiting for a response from Sean.

"Why, I don't believe that is so?" he said warily.

"Is this not Calgary?" the Preacher asked as the snow began to melt away.

"No, you're about thirty miles shy of Calgary," he answered. "But you're welcome to stay for some food."

"Mighty obliged, Mr.?"

Sean wiped his hand before offering it. "Sean Thomas, and this here is....this here is Anne Taylor. This is her farm, and that is my son, Patrick."

Lewis tipped his hat to Anne, and the water from the rim gushed over Sean's foot. "Sorry, I'm afraid I'm a tad bit wet."

"Please give me your coat and hat," Sean said after taking a few steps back.

Anne grabbed a plate and spooned out stew.

"Awfully poor weather to be travelling to Calgary," Sean surmised.

"It's been a slow journey," the pious man replied. "The Preacher in Calgary died a few months ago. Townsfolk wanted a new one by Christmas, so I left with two horses; however, one went lame just before I crossed the border. Made it to Fort McLeod but met up with a number of Mounties who required my assistance. Stayed a bit longer than expected, and now I'm late," he replied with curled lips blazing red around a white beard.

"What can I get you to drink?" Sean asked. "Would whisky be acceptable?"

"Whisky'd be fine."

"A man of the cloth who drinks."

"This one does, yes."

"It is terribly cold out there, Reverend Snow," Anne stated. "Would you like to spend the night?"

"That would be greatly appreciated, and call me Lewis. I pray the people of Calgary aren't too upset that I will not be arriving by Christmas Eve, but I don't believe my horse has anything left in him to carry on."

"I'll tend to your horse, Reverend Lewis," I offered. "Try my best to squeeze him in the warm barn."

"Don't be too long out there, Patrick," Sean voiced with concern.

"Yes, Sir," I replied crisply.

"Reverend," Sean said, raising his glass. "Your presence is already making a difference in this house."

The Reverend's eyes scanned the room and fixated on the Christmas tree sitting empty of gifts.

When I returned, Anne was adding blankets and pillows to the crammed keeping room.

I offered my feather tick for a mattress, ready to rush away from my father's glare. Looking at the small room and the big man, I figured I'd do better fitting into that small space.

"Reverend Lewis, you're welcome to use my room for the evening."

"That's mighty generous of you, Patrick, but this room will do fine."

I brought over the feather tick and wished the three of them a cozy goodnight.

****

On Christmas morning, the sun was shimmering over mounds of snow. Scooping up a fluffy handful, I crafted a firm ball and pitched it at the barn door when it opened. I got the Reverend centre of his face.

"Sorry, Reverend," I cringed, running over. "Forgive me for being so foolish and on Christmas day, too."

I offered my handkerchief.

"No need to forgive," he replied, wiping his face. "I've been known to throw a powerful blast of snow at least once or twice in my life."

He concentrated eyes on the embroidery of the lace cloth. "My wife, Bernice, used to sew her flowers the same way. She died a few years back," he said in a deep baritone voice.

"It was my mother's," I informed lightly. "She's gone, too. Anne's probably got food on the table. She's prompt about morning breakfast."

"Well, we best be going then," he replied, returning the damp cloth.

We opened the door to a table full of pancakes, sausage, fried potato wedges, and dried fruit. I was about ready to dig in when a stocking hanging from the mantle caught my eye.

"I think it's for you, Patrick."

Set to grumble about being two old for stockings, I had a change of heart. Anne and Sean seemed very pleased as I reached my hand into it. I pulled out an orange, a handful of red and white candies, and two quarters.

"Where did anybody ever find an orange in this country?" Sean asked.

"Don't look at me," Anne replied. "I supplied the candies."

Passing it to my father, he fondled it like a golden nugget.

"There are packages under the tree, Patrick," Anne remarked. "See who they're for."

I picked up the first one, wrapped in brown paper. "This is for you, Anne."

She peeled away at the twine and gingerly unfolded the wrapping.

Lifting the lid of the tin, she smelled, "Why, it's cedar mint tea. How delightful," she cried.

Sean was given the next parcel. He tore it open and glanced at the cover of the book. "It's a Bible. I wonder who this could be from?"

Our eyes focused on the Reverend, who had a red welt forming over his nose. "Everybody needs a good book to read."

I lifted the last package meant for me. It shook when I rattled it. "I doubt this is a Bible." With paper torn away, I lifted the lid of the wooden box to reveal carved wooden horses, ten of them.

"When did you make these?"

"Most of them were made a long time ago when I was searching for you. One for every year you were apart from me. I always hoped I'd find you, and give 'em to you; and well, that's that."

I was speechless for too long.

"Why don't we eat," Anne offered. "Food's getting cold."

The somber sadness that had filled the room slowly dissipated. My thoughts were still on Momma as I smothered the hotcakes with molasses. While my father may have been searching for me, how could he have been searching for Momma if he was renowned for visiting a Fort Benton brothel?

"Your awfully quiet, Patrick," he said.

"Your gift took me back aways," I said, most humbly. "Forgiveness is the key," I mumbled.

"Pardon?" he asked.

"He said 'forgiveness is the key'," Lewis spoke pastorally.

"Tell me, Reverend, will the Lord forgive a man who has killed over half a dozen men?" Sean spoke with incredulity.

"The Lord forgives all kinds of sin."

"Is that what it's gonna take, Patrick? Is that all it's gonna to take?"

He besieged me to answer but I couldn't. My memories were trapped on a Christmas morning at the Wilkes ranch, my grandpa tossing stockings out the front door, burning gifts before my little eyes, because Christmas was a waste of money.

'I didn't have anything when I was a child!" my grandpa would bellow. "Nothing!'

Sometimes those memories came rushing in, and I felt totally helpless in stopping them.

"Well, it would be best if I make tracks for Calgary while there is still light in the sky," Lewis informed.

"Could you stay another day, or two, if...." Sean turned to Anne, "I was going to give this to you tonight, but maybe now would be more appropriate."

He reached into his shirt pocket and dug out a gold ring. "I thought maybe, if you were willing, we could get married."

Anne gawked at the ring, speechless.

I smiled because my bad memories were replaced by this good one.

"I suppose, I could stay if the lady of the house is willing," Lewis smiled.

"Yes," Anne whispered, "yes," she nodded as Sean showed her the ring.

The Reverend fashioned a makeshift church out of the empty building beside Sam Tracey's Mercantile. We used empty crates for chairs, hung popcorn garland and lace snowflakes for decorations. The place was lit aglow with soft candlelight. Any of the twenty-five townfolk who would brave the snow and cold were invited to attend. Rudy Smith rolled over the piano while Sam Tracey carted in sandwiches, mostly made of ham and turkey. I made a cake with a sweet buttercream icing. Rose attended with Mr. Winterborn, hauling in a pot of hot apple cider.

My father wore his best black suit, all threadbare spots nicely sewed shut. Anne took the shears to her old wedding dress and transformed it with wool and lace.

When my father stood and waited for Anne to walk down the aisle he seemed ready to bolt, shuffling his feet from one side to the next, so I quickly approached and wound my arm around him. I might have sounded a little condescending when I whispered, "You're safe here,

Father. Nobody's gonna hurt you in this house of the Lord. While you're here, you could ask for forgiveness?"

"One step at a time," he grumbled.

I was about to sit down when he snatched my arm, still tender from the bullet wound, his teeth clenched, mumbling, "Stay here."

The man had stared death in the face countless times, filled men full of bullets, but was sweating like a horse watching Anne walk up the aisle.

I stayed until my father repeated his vows and placed the ring on Anne's finger, if only for the sake of Anne, who looked stunning. If I wasn't so besotted with Nawaji I would have scooped her up and made her my own.

My father must have caught me ogling his bride for too long. "Back off," he growled.

I quietly headed over to the warm apple cider.

The Reverend quickly followed. "You know, Patrick, I may be inclined to stay here."

His nose was running as he scrambled through pockets for a handkerchief.

"Reverend Snow, take mine," I offered. "Welcome to Highwood River."

We shook hands until I was summoned to play a few tunes. There would be no Beethoven on this day, though I did try my hand at a little Chopin.

Chapter 17

Spring's tears were streaming down my porch while I penned a letter to Ma, humming the rhyme,

'Rain, rain, go away,
come again another day.'

It didn't.

My father wouldn't leave the ranch while the roads were muddy trenches, so I spent my time lunging horses and getting messier than pigs do in a sty. Under a drizzle, I watched my most docile horse, named Joseph, go from buckskin to brown skin when an idea sprung to mind. I would give this horse to Chief White Bear.

"Patrick," my father hollered, "that horse is getting filthy."

"Oh," I replied with a sullen stare. "That's fine! It'll come down in buckets soon!" Outstretching my hand, I dared God to saturate it in wetness.

He did.

The next day, I was in the corral with that mustang again. The horse turned brown, I was a muddy pig, cocky smile across my face, when...the sun shined down. I looked the fool, filling bucket after bucket of water to get that horse the colour of buckskin again.

Anne would be accompanying us on our journey east. She would also be the one to make it an even longer one, becoming wagon sick, though Joseph wondered if she was with child, sick. Just the sight of food turned her white skin a pale shade of green, her diet consisting of dried bread and cupfuls of that cedar mint tea.

Her health improved when we arrived in Wood Mountain. She took curious steps, roaming the Minnecoujou camp, fascinated by the tasks the Indian women performed daily.

Often, she would be found with head down, embroidering beads onto dresses or sewing moccasins for little feet.

It was I who held the enthrallment of the children, though. They were in awe as this white man wielded his arrows at prairie chickens and rabbits. They were very appreciative when I whittled spears meant for fishing, their mothers very unappreciative when they became used for sword play. Joseph and my father approached as I was breaking up a tussle, one child testing the point against the other's ribcage.

"No, no, no," I scolded, "for fishing only!" Flapping one hand around, the other pinched my nose.

The children giggled.

"Hoghan," Joseph said to the children with a smile.

"Hoghan," I repeated. "Now, go catch some hoghan for your mothers," I urged, shooing them away.

"Patrick, I need to know where you want your elkskin lodge to be built?" Joseph asked.

Walking back to the camp, I stopped directly across from Growls at dog's lodge.

"Are you sure about this, Patrick?" my father asked.

"Keep your friends close. Keep your enemies closer," I replied unwaveringly. "Who owns that horse?" I asked, peering at the finely poised mare being smothered in curious small hands.

Joseph turned. "That's the Mountie's horse. He's speaking with White Bear."

"Now, that is a Morgan," my eyes admired, "a young Morgan!"

I approached the horse and leaned over two small children. Cowering in fear, they ran from my shadow despite that I was the candy man and a big kid at heart.

"Sorry," I hollered, too sadly aware that the white man was more enemy than friend to them.

My hand stroked the chestnut mare with the two white socks when the Mountie approached.

"Tom Aspdin," he announced, offering a handshake.

"Patrick Sullivan," I replied.

"I know," he said with a grin. "We have something in common."

"A good horse," I answered.

"That may be so. The police mounts are normally thoroughbreds; however, I couldn't leave home without my Morgan."

"She's eight or nine years old?"

"You're correct, Patrick. Two socks is eight. It's not about the horse, though. We're both smitten with Lakota women."

"Is that so? Where is she?"

"She's not in this camp. She's Black Moon's daughter. His camp is near Willow Branch," he divulged, pointing away. "Her name is Mary."

"Do you have to ask Chief White Bear for permission, as well?"

"No, I'm here on official business. Maybe you can help me with it. I have to convince White Bear and his tribe to return to the United States."

"Why's that?" I asked, perturbed. "The way I understand it, the tribe will have to surrender to the Cavalry at Fort Buford just like Sitting Bull did."

"That's true," he replied undeniably, "but there's nothing here for them, Patrick: no food, and no land. They will be escorted to the Standing Rock Agency in Dakota Territory and be given provisions, whatever necessary."

"Are you putting the same kind of persuasion on Chief Black Moon?"

"Yes, Patrick. He must return, too."

"I'll try my best. But I'm not in good favour with my intended's kin, so I don't want to jeopardize my union with Nawaji. After we are wed, I will speak to White Bear."

"Thank you. You're a good man, Patrick. My best to you and your future wife."

The ceremony was quick: my vows simple, though heartfelt, and Nawaji's smile unforgettable.

We dashed to our lodge amongst the sorrowful cries of women and rosy-cheeked giggles from children.

My eyes were distracted as small hands rapped against the tipi until Nawaji grabbed at my shirttails, nimbly hoisting until I was bare-chested.

As her fingers mapped a journey to my heart, mine traced the contours to her moist mouth.

"Lips," I whispered.

It was all too apparent that she didn't want a language lesson, pushing me with unbridled hands onto the bear-skin rug.

Tugging away at her dress, there were no corsets or petticoats to fiddle with.

I released her silky hair from its braid, the raven weaves flowing over firm breasts.

Placing soft kisses on my forehead, cheeks, and chin, she slid my pants away, her fingers firing the skin of my thighs all too much.

"Sorry," I whispered.

"Iha," she said, touching my lips. "Pahte," she exhaled against my forehead. "Nakpa," she cried, biting my ear. "Cante," she trembled, fisting her heart. "Aze, she moaned, placing my hand on her breast.

Every body part was labeled, explored, admired, tasted, until my arms draped her sensual frame, her legs clinging to me tightly.

"Nawaji," I groaned, my movements slow and tender, until she pulled me closer, deeper. Our muscles tightened, bones grinding; an unending and breathless heart-pounding rhythm that ended in blissful, shuddering release.

My mouth searched for air in the scorching heat of the tent.

"Patrick," her sweet voice oozed with concern.

"I'm fine," I panted. "Just give me a minute and we'll do it all over again."

When her face remained worried, I laughed reassuringly, never wanting these moments to end.

When we emerged from the tent, hungry, languid and light-headed, the aroma of buffalo roasting over an open fire filled the air.

As we feasted on meat, rice, cornbread, and dried berries, the women performed a dance around the blazing flames.

When Nawaji was nestled in my arms, fingers weaving through mine, I glanced across the haze of heat to find my father sitting with Anne, though his eyes focused on Ehawee, who was shedding a torrent of tears.

Anne was watching her, too.

Ehawee moved away from the fire with my father just steps from her fleeing moccasins.

But it was Anne's pang of anguish knotting in an ailing constitution that brought me great fury.

I found my father embracing Ehawee, her shuddering face in the folds of his jacket.

"What are you doing?" I cried.

"What does it look like I'm doing!" he bellowed.

Ehawee gasped and fluttered away.

"Anne looks like she's being torn in two!"

"Anne's fine! She's got a warm home, food on the table, and land of her own!"

"And you!" I glowered.

"Patrick," he said, approaching. "I care deeply for Anne. She's just not your mother. Nobody will ever replace your mother. She had a radiance that I just can't forget."

"Did she have that radiance when you were bedding Ophelia?"

His slap stung my cheek and tore at my already swollen lip.

"Patrick, I…" he spoke with remorse.

I interrupted, "Don't worry, father, rest easy! I can take a good hit!"

When I returned to the fire, Joseph was holding Anne's hand, showing great concern, until he squinted at me through the blur of flame's heat, being pointlessly questioned by Nawaji's foreign tongue, blood dripping down my chin.

That's the last I saw of my father, Anne, and Joseph on my wedding night.

I went to bed thinking that this lodge on this prairie with these Native people might just be my new home.

I should have been able to sleep through the night, but the unfamiliarity of the hard ground and the nearness of animals howling and shuffling around the camp, had me wide awake staring into darkness.

It was the sound of footsteps that encouraged mine right out of the lodge and into a damp, dewy air. The moon cast a silver sheen over the camp as I peered at the quiet lodgings. My eyes focused on Growls at dog's tipi. Gingerly lifting the flap, his wife, Crooked Nose, was sleeping alone.

Moving stealthily around the conical tents, the night was filled with snoring, mumbling, and moaning. I stopped at the lodge of muffled groans and soft cries but didn't have to lift the flap to know it was Ehawee's adobe. Thoughts ashamedly went to my father, but were inconceivably shaken from my weary head.

Returning to my lodge, I slid under the warm blankets and snuggled closely with Nawaji, her skin pungent of smoke and sweat. I was so tired, my lids closed heavy over eyes to a mind that wouldn't stop thinking. At one point, I heard the dog barking and imagined my hands full of wood with Nawaji leading the way.

Smoke filled my nose and it seemed so real, I began to cough and wheeze. My eyes opened to a grey fog. I pulled Nawaji from the lodge, gasping, gagging, and choking out powdery ash.

Looking up, the camp was ablaze in places. In others, the moon's lightness continued to loom. Indians were crawling out of their homes in drunken stupor, dazed. I squinted at a figure cloaked in red on horseback, its two socks flashing whitely, galloping away.

Ehawee was screaming wildly as her home burned brightly. I grabbed my blankets and lunged at the fire, but it raged back.

Joseph appeared, carrying buckets heavy with water sloshing over the rims. The fire sizzled but still roared as I swatted with the blackening blankets.

When the flames were extinguished and smoke swirled from charred poles, I turned to my lodge relegated to nothing more than a large campfire.

"Patrick!" my father howled at the top of his lungs. "Patrick!"

Panic filled his face at the sight of my tipi. Nawaji ran to him, tossing her head, telling him that we were fine. But the fear never left his face until his found mine.

The words he spoke when he reached me were incoherent, but the embrace would never be forgotten. I knew it wasn't just for me.

"I can't lose you, Patrick," he mumbled. "I can't lose you, too."

In the distance, I saw Growls at dog working vigorously to save the Chief's burning tipi.

The last of the flames died with the break of dawn. About a quarter mile from the camp, the children found the dog, their anguished screams sending most of us charging the scene.

Turning my gaze from the dead animal to the camp, an eerie shiver ran down my spine, for it appeared that the red coat was choosy in the lodges he wanted to turn to dust.

My footsteps were marching back to the destruction when a little boy named Bend in Knees tugged at my shirt and pointed to the treed coulee.

He led me to a Red Coat dangling from the limb of a poplar, the older boys spearing great holes into it.

"Go," I cried, shooing them away.

Inspecting the torn coat, I found small holes in a sleeve coated with dried blood.

Joseph was shaking water beads from his face when I approached him. His shirt was hanging loosely over a sooty chest, his pants still unbuttoned, bare feet muddy.

With the coat draped over my arm, my tongue was poised to mention the oddity of the burnings when Ehawee stomped over and clutched Joseph tightly, her Lakota tongue coming out loud and clear to his nodding head. I figured she was grateful for his fire fighting skills until she grabbed his bottom cheeks, her kiss full-mouthed. It got even less explanatory when he hugged her warmly.

"Ahem," I said.

They seemed surprised by my intrusion.

"Forgive me, but may I have a moment with you alone?" I asked.

Joseph gave me a stupefied look. "She can't understand a word you say, Patrick."

I paused, acting like I didn't understand a word he was saying.

He asked Ehawee to leave us.

She obeyed with a pout.

"Go ahead, Patrick. Fire away."

"Were you, hmm…..." I was still clearing soot from my lungs, "sleeping with Ehawee last night?"

"Yes."

"Do you like Ehawee?"

"Yes."

"For how long?"

"For a while, now. She is quite voluptuous," he re-marked, exuding desire. "She also happens to be the daughter of the Medicine Man."

"Good," I replied with great relief, figuring less distraction for my father.

"We entered into a quiet union yesterday," he spoke as if justifying an improper tryst.

"And your tipi is a pile of ash just like mine."

"And the Chief's. He's very upset."

"I saw the shadow of a man leaving the camp," I divulged, eyeing the red coat. "I just don't know if I believe what I saw."

"I don't believe it matters now," Joseph said oddly with a shake of his head. "The Chief is leaving with his tribe."

We paused as Growls at dog walked by, his callous stare hard to ignore, and neither was his arm, tightly covered in a sooty cloth speckled with blood.

"I want to speak with the Chief."

"He doesn't want to speak with anyone," Joseph spoke crisply. "Whatever you have to say won't change things. The Chief wants to leave with his people."

"That man tried to kill him," I pointed.

"That man is Canowicakte. He's Great Bear's last living son."

"He just tried to kill me.....Nawaji!" my voice crackled.

"Canowicakte wanted to change his father's mind. Anger fills his heart, Patrick. His hands seek vengeance. Let him seek this vengeance with those who have sparked it. Let him return to his land."

****

After the travois were filled with their meager possessions, I watched the Minnecoujou band move south in a slow line with Chief White Bear on the buckskin horse I had offered just days ago.

Joseph was quick to stand by my side as Nawaji cried into my shoulder.

"Is that your favourite horse taking White Bear home?"

"When I gave it to him, I said peace 'wolakota' and he looked at me with such strangeness."

My hands were still outstretched, palms upwards as I stared peculiarly, when Joseph said, "It is kind of you, Patrick, but there's no Sioux word for peace. I've never heard of wolakota. Is that how you spoke it?" he asked, glaring at my hands.

"Yes. A Shoshone man taught it to me, though I believed he was speaking in Lakota."

"Well, Patrick, the last word the Chief spoke to me was wolakota and he stretched his hands like yours. I would say it is now the word for peace in Lakota, and I will say it for peace in Dakota."

Squeezing Nawaji with a sigh of relief, I watched my threat move away from my future to surrender to the United States Cavalry; but I also felt a pang of melancholy at the Chief leaving this land of the great White Mother, never to return again.

Canowicakte gave one final nefarious glare but through a face now black and blue.

"It looks like he ran into a wall of rocks."

"There are no rocks out her, Patrick: just rolling hills and treed coulees."

"Where's my father?" I asked apprehensively.

"Last I saw of him, he was taking an armful of logs to his camp.

"Wolakota," I said with eyes still on Canowicakte.

"Patrick," Joseph uttered softly. "Anne is ill. You need to keep an eye on her, and if she becomes bedridden, send for me or the doctor right away."

Sean was leaning over the campfire watching the bloody log burn when Anne appeared and put a hand to his shoulder.

"I thought you'd be saying good bye to your Lakota friend."

"No, she's keeping better company these days; and I'd just as soon stay away from that band."

"You didn't do something you're going to regret?"

"I hope not, Anne. I hope not."

****

We moved in a solemn silence. My mind was heavy with worry for Anne, who sat still as a stone for most of the journey home. Though she appeared to be fine, her face was colourless; and she ate like a bird while her fingers trembled.

One night, I lit up one of my thin smokes and got her to inhale from its soothing leaves. My father said it was her best night's sleep in weeks.

When the horses' hooves clopped onto the Taylor ranch, I scooped Nawaji from her pony to my small cabin. Tossing her on the bed, the quilt puffed from the weight of her slender frame. When my impetuous self went to kiss her, she pushed me away and bolted from the mattress to examine every inch of the room.

She blew away dust that was coating the mantle.

"Sorry, I didn't have time to clean."

Nawaji's eyes floated across the furniture, her fingers feeling the smoothness of the tables and chairs, her cheeks brushing against the curtains, her nose smelling my clothes.

Reaching for the skull on the mantle, she said hesitantly, "Horse."

"Bed," I replied, pointing to the mattress.

She giggled.

I kicked the door closed and hoisted her onto the bed again. Gentler now, I played soft kisses on her neck and shoulders while she rubbed her cheek against the smoothness of the quilt.

Meanwhile, Sean and Anne were just entering their house.

Anne clutched at the table and swallowed back swells of nausea.

"I'm going to bed," she spoke weakly.

"Well, I'll just tend to the horses and unpack," Sean muttered to the empty kitchen.

When he returned, the house was in darkness. Too tired to light the room, he kicked at a kitchen chair and grumbled the rest of his way to bed. After he peeled off boots and pants, his fingers rubbed at throbbing temples.

Anne moaned oddly.

Reaching for a curly blond strand, his hand brushed against her warm forehead.

She mumbled incoherently.

His body relaxed with the familiarity of the house: the creak in the far window and the shadows of light that emerged beyond the dark curtains while his mind contemplated the changes to his life in the past two years.

Anne deserved so much more but asked for nothing in return. His thoughts dwelled on loving her more, kissing her more, until darkness seeped into his mind.

It was the moaning that awakened him. Stretching his arm, he found nothing but empty space. "Anne?"

A thin light exposed her standing hunched over the chamber pot, crying.

He stumbled out of bed and stubbed a toe against the bed frame. "Anne?"

"No, no, no," she cried as his arms enveloped her.

"Let me get you back to bed," his voice quivered.

She crumbled in his arms, crying and breathless. "I'm sorry. I'm so sorry."

"Are you sick, Anne? Should I fetch the doctor?"

"No," she trembled. "It's fine now," her watery eyes glanced up. "I'm just tired."

Leaning into strong arms, she was eased onto the bed, sheets ready to be floated over her when he saw blood staining her nightgown.

"I'm fine, now," she moaned.

"You're not fine. You need a doctor!"

"No," she replied with a sudden composure. "It's normal to have some bleeding after this. There's nothing a doctor can do for me. Come to bed. Keep me warm," she pleaded.

Sean covered her trembling form gently, his head leaning into the silkiness of her hair.

"I love you, Anne," he said hoarsely.

****

I awoke alone, and for a moment, thought it was all a dream, until I tripped on Nawaji's dress and moccasins.

"We'll have to do something about that," I said, opening the door with a stretch. My eyes searched for her, figuring she couldn't have gone far in bare feet.

She emerged from the barn in my plaid shirt, chewing on a wisp of hay. Figuring her hungry for food, I quelled my appetite for her and headed to the house.

I assumed a big breakfast would be waiting, ashamedly forgetting that Anne was not well.

Sean emerged, his hand bloodied. "She says she's fine but there's a lot of blood."

Nawaji rushed to Anne's room and then rushed out. "Mni!" she cried. "Mni!" Her fingers flittered to the ground.

"I'll get water," I stammered.

"No," my father said. "I'll get the water. You make some food."

Breakfast was being put on the table when Nawaji entered with soiled sheets and the chamber pot.

My father took them from her hands. The linen got tossed on the porch, but the contents of the chamber pot stopped him in his tracks.

"Let me take care of it, Father," I said forlornly.

"No," he said, hesitating. "It's my.....it's my response-bility."

Anne emerged in a clean nightgown. "It smells good in here," she swayed, eyeing Sean clutching the pot.

Nawaji took her back to bed while I rushed to bring in food and water.

Sean returned to an empty kitchen and worried until laughter filled the air: Anne's laughter.

Nawaji was braiding her damp hair as I forked scrambled eggs into her mouth.

"Patrick," Anne said delicately between mouthfuls. "You may want to introduce Nawaji to some cotton knickers or silk bloomers."

"After you've drunk this all up," I replied, giving a glass of water with authority. "We all know how important water is to a thirsty body," my voice mimicked my father's.

Sean sat heavily in his chair, grateful to hear verve in Anne's voice. Reaching for a slice of bacon, he figured he'd deal with his son's sarcastic tongue later. It was then that the words casually slipped out through greasy lips, "Please forgive me, Lord, for the sins I have committed, and for the sins I will commit to keep my family safe."

****

It was very hard in the beginning for Nawaji, Stands firm. Her name should also mean….stands stubborn, angry, messy, and impatient. While I could ignore her foreign voice, her sign language was clear as a bell.

One evening, I came out from my bunkhouse and sauntered over to my father, who was sitting on the porch with a jocular grin.

"You know, maybe I won't learn too much of that Lakota too soon," I said, a red mark blatant on my face.

"You need protecting from that woman's touch?"

Chuckling, I turned to find Nawaji tossing one of our plates into the pasture.

"You don't need to understand the language to see what she's doing now," my father spoke glibly. "Why don't you try explaining that her feelings are just feelings and that she shouldn't go throwing around china plates?"

His laughing was short-lived by a clatter at the corral's rails.

"It looks like she's inventing a new sport," he intoned facetiously. "Why don't you try catching those dishes before they hit the fence otherwise you'll be eating out of your hands, which might be what she wants."

"Thanks, for the advice," I said, ambling back to my house.

"See you in the barn later on this evening! I'll bring the blankets," he offered kindly.

Scratching the back of my head, I spun around. "I'm thinking of making this house bigger."

"Why? You finding it too small for the two of you?" he asked, sipping his coffee.

"No, but I think it'll be too small for the three of us…..Grandpa"

Sean choked. "So soon!"

"It happens," I said impudently. "Besides, life can change in an instant. I don't want to miss out on being a father. Oh, by the way, do you think the Mounties would hire me to keep the peace in this land?"

"I don't see why not. You're pretty lean, though you'd have to be willing to shoot a gun," he nodded, brimming with surety that that would never happen. "Mounties won't want you strapping a quiver of arrows to that red coat."

"Quite true," I replied, "however I do have a great teacher at my disposal."

Surprise mottled my father's face. "Don't wait too long, son. Eyesight's failing me."

"Stay away from the imbibing and your eyesight will be just fine," I mumbled.

"Pardon!"

"I said 'all the traveling I'd do might make my marriage just fine'!"

"Don't expect me to babysit!"

Moving to my not so quiet house, I took carefree steps, remembering the words Momma always said. They run through my mind every time I enter the corral to break a horse, every time I have one of those asthma attacks that threaten to take my last breath, every time I hear father argue with Anne, and every time I see my Nawaji lashing out in frustration…….

Love is patient and kind;
Love is not jealous or boastful;
It is not arrogant or rude.
Love does not insist on its own way;
It is not irritable or resentful;
It does not rejoice at wrong, but rejoices in the right.
Love bears all things, hopes all things,
and endures all things….

Acknowledgements

Deepest thanks to my spouse for encouraging me to write just one of the many stories that plague my thoughts. It is with warmest gratitude to my mother, children, and cover designer/editor Theresa Leonard for encouraging me to send it out into the world. I've been inspired by talented writers Guy Vanderhaeghe and Jeannette Walls.

I wish to thank Ajax Public Library. I've trudged through the aisles gathering everything from DVDs titled 'Wild Horse Redemption' and 'Saint Patrick' to books about North American Aboriginals; their history and culture during mid to late 19th century.

In remembrance of the late Deanna Durbin for singing the Stephen Foster songs mentioned in my book. Her voice will never be forgotten. And to the poet William Shakespeare, whose words will never be forgotten.

In remembrance of the late William Henry Walden, who started his career as a North West Mounted Police officer in 1877, and spoke of his experiences during a CBC radio interview in 1964 at 106 years of age!

A thank you to Joy Anderson at StoneRidge Farm, and a woman named Margot at 'On the Forest Boarding' for teaching me how to ride and care for horses. Their guidance and patience have been invaluable.

My gratitude to Durham Region's Pickering Museum Village for allowing me to live in the past as a pioneer.

About the Author

A graduate of Ryerson University, the author was also born in Toronto, Ontario, to a Sicilian father and a Canadian mother with English, Irish, and Scottish heritage. This novel is written under the name of Alek Leslie. The author's maternal Great-Grandfather was born in Assiginack, Manitoulin Island, Ontario, in 1880, and was raised by an unforgettable Ojibwe woman while his parents, immigrants from Donegal, Ireland, ran a hotel. As the final published story to this trilogy, the journey is complete.